# A THIEF IN TIME

## Also By Cidney Swanson

### The Ripple Series

Rippler
Chameleon
Unfurl
Visible
Immutable
Knavery
Perilous

### The Saving Mars Series

Saving Mars
Defying Mars
Losing Mars
Mars Burning
Striking Mars
Mars Rising

### The Thief in Time Series

A Thief in Time
A Flight in Time

### Books Not in a Series

Siren Spell

# A THIEF IN TIME

## Cidney Swanson

ISBN 978-1-939543-46-2

For Monique

# 1

## · HALLEY ·

Halley's biggest problem was her bikini top, the elastic of which was shot to hell. It was Fiesta Week in Santa Barbara, California, and August heat had finally chased away the coastal fogs of June and July. In four days, Halley's best friend Jillian Applegate would be helping host the fabulous Applegate Post-Fiesta Pool Party where Halley, Jillian, and DaVinci, the third in the trio of best friends, might catch glimpses of Hollywood royalty.

More importantly for Halley, she might grab the ear of the great Ms. Ethyl Meier, multiple-Oscar-winning costume designer. Which meant the worn out bikini was now threatening to stand between Halley and a coveted internship with Ms. Meier. How could anyone expect Ms. Meier to take seriously a costume intern candidate wearing a bikini top with the elastic shot to hell? It was the worst possible time for Halley's bikini to give up the ghost. Wealthy glitterati at Jillian's party might assume Halley's top had been distressed to *look* worn, but Ms. Meier would recognize the truth.

The real problem was that a new top would set Halley back forty-five dollars—dollars she didn't have to spare. She knew DaVinci would loan her a bikini. She knew Jillian would *give* her one. Or three or four. But thanks to her mom's line of work, Halley's life was an endless stream of things that had belonged to somebody else, and for highly personal reasons, Halley had developed an antipathy to taking things from others.

She'd already asked her mom for the money. It hadn't gone well.

*"Forty-five dollars? Are you* trying *to give me a migraine?"*

Halley's mother was always getting migraines. Especially when Halley needed shoes or a haircut or tires or a bikini top that didn't have the elastic shot to hell.

Consequently, on this sunny Friday of Fiesta Week, Halley was up early helping her two best friends set up a sidewalk sales booth at the Santa Barbara Arts and Crafts Show and hoping like anything she'd sell a painting or two.

Back in April, DaVinci had begged and schemed and connived to obtain a student-staffed sales booth at the famous art show. Students of Santa Barbara High School's Visual Arts and Design Academy being well-respected (and DaVinci being DaVinci), they'd received permission and an allocated space on the sidewalk sandwiched between East Beach and Cabrillo Boulevard, where tourists and the occasional idle rich showed up with money to burn.

Although DaVinci had secured a booth for the Friday, Saturday, and Sunday of Fiesta Week, by June, the girls had scaled back to *Friday only* because DaVinci's tapestries were being shown at a gallery, hanging on Saturday and opening Sunday. So Halley really only had one day—one shot at making cash at the Arts and Crafts Show.

Jillian, a born organizer, had ordered signs reading FRIDAY ONLY and was hanging one now, under DaVinci's direction. DaVinci was the true artist of the three girls. The one who had insisted they *all* apply to attend the Visual Arts and Design Academy, or VADA. Halley and Jillian had gone along with it because, well, *DaVinci*. She was a primal force.

Halley wasn't a painter. Not really. She studied painting and drawing as a means to an end. Her passion was costume history and design, and to work in costuming, she needed to know how to draw. But she had pulled five large painted canvases from storage for the art show, pricing them from forty-five to a hundred fifty dollars, which meant she only needed one sale to cover the bikini, although *four* sales would provide enough for a haircut, shoes, and tires for her truck. A bead of sweat trickled down her neck as she secured the last of the paintings against the back of the booth.

She'd chosen the five paintings her senior project advisor had praised most. Her best friends had approved them, too; Jillian had called Halley's paintings "bold" and DaVinci had nodded and added comments about movement, line, and color.

"Done," Halley said aloud, silently adding: *Sell— please sell!*

"Sunscreen," said Jillian, passing a bottle to DaVinci. Jillian had been passing sunscreen and other essentials to Halley and DaVinci since third grade.

DaVinci, freckled and strawberry blonde, accepted the sunscreen.

Halley didn't use sunscreen much. According to her pale-skinned Danish mother, Halley's light brown skin protected her, and *did she know how expensive non-allergenic sunscreen was?*

Halley walked outside the booth to examine it from the perspective of the customers already strolling the sidewalk. As she often did when nervous, she grasped for a pale jade ring on a length of chain hidden under her shirt. The ring had been a gift from her father on her seventh birthday. Her mother had once thrown it away to punish Halley for some unremembered transgression, but Halley had stolen it back from the trash. Eventually her mother had noticed. *It won't bring you a father,* she'd said. From then on, Halley had kept it on a chain, close to her heart and out of her mother's eye, a talisman to grasp when she needed luck or courage.

Today, she needed both. Well, along with *sales*.

"So?" asked DaVinci, "Does the booth say '*Summer Harvest*' to you?" She had a blob of sunscreen on the bridge of her nose.

"You missed a spot," replied Halley. She tapped the bridge of her own nose before answering DaVinci's question. "The booth looks more '*fruit basket*' than '*harvest*.'"

"Close enough," said DaVinci.

"These *Irina Tran's* are a half size too tight," murmured Jillian.

Halley wasn't sure if "Irina Tran's" were Jillian's sporty new sandals or her shorts, but she was pretty

4

sure each had individually cost more than Halley's own lifetime clothing budget.

A flash of movement in the sky behind the booth caught Halley's attention. Squinting, she watched as a hungry pelican dove into the ocean west of Stearn's Wharf. Halley's stomach tightened. She'd missed breakfast again. Or rather, she'd turned her nose up at the contents of the apartment's refrigerator: wilted lettuce and a half-eaten bowl of salsa.

Her mother's latest house-sitting job came with full access to a pantry and freezer loaded with food. *"Don't expect me to buy groceries this week,"* her mother had said. *"You can come here to grab a bite to eat whenever, since I'm letting you have the truck all week."*

It was Halley's truck, a fact her mother regularly, *conveniently*, forgot. Halley had bought it herself. The paint job was crap, and the tires were bald, but it ran and the truck bed was huge. They'd crammed seven of DaVinci's tapestries, Halley's five canvases, and the entire booth set-up plus a handcart into the truck bed this morning. Jillian had hauled her exquisitely detailed fruit sculptures herself, catching a ride with her mother's driver, who didn't have to drive Jillian's mom, Mrs. Applegate, to work on Fridays because Mrs. Applegate didn't work Fridays.

"It's so hot already," said DaVinci, swiping sticky curls up into a messy bun.

"No breeze," said Jillian, checking a weather app.

"Earthquake weather," murmured Halley.

"Don't say that," snapped DaVinci. She knocked on the booth's wooden stool and spit over her left shoulder.

"Sorry," murmured Halley. She knew better than

to joke about earthquakes. DaVinci's ramshackle house sat high atop East Mountain Drive where the ocean views were unsurpassed, but the soil shook like Jell-o during earthquakes. Jillian's fine stone estate, on the other hand, would probably survive nuclear holocaust.

When Halley had been young, she hadn't understood why Jillian and DaVinci wanted to be her friends. Jillian always had lunch box treats to share, and DaVinci always had funny stories to share.

Halley, on the other hand, never had treats or stories to share as the three pushed one another on swings beneath the swaying eucalyptus of Cold Springs Elementary. In all her life, she'd only had one golden memory which she might have shared, but she preferred to keep it tucked safely away, as if it were something that might become lost if she brought it out.

There had been spinning teacups and a man who called her *daughter* and frosty glasses of root beer floats at a bar nestled secretively between the Haunted Mansion and the Pirates of the Caribbean. It was the only time she'd met her father. That singular memory had worked like an irritant grain of sand, forming the pearl of Halley's ambition—a plan designed to bring her into contact with her father again. This was an ambition she disclosed to no one. Certainly not to her mother, who was determined to keep Halley from her father, and not even to Jillian and DaVinci.

The three had remained friends through middle school even though Jillian's diamond-encrusted mother tried to interest her daughter in "better" society. They remained friends in high school when DaVinci insisted they follow her to VADA, where

DaVinci clearly belonged and Halley and Jillian clearly belonged ... *less*. Now that they had graduated, they'd promised to remain friends even after they went off to separate colleges this fall, and except during her most pessimistic moments, Halley thought they probably would.

"Swimming *chez moi* after we sell everything," Jillian said, waving to indicate the items in the booth. "Branson's restocking the gelato drawers."

"Gelato," sighed Halley, fanning herself with a sheet of paper.

"*Bran*son," sighed DaVinci, eyes closed.

"Married," said Jillian to DaVinci. "*Very* married."

"*Customer*," whispered Halley.

Casually, she strolled to the back corner of the booth, making room for two women who stepped in to admire Jillian's *Basket of Strawberries, No. 1.*

"They look so *real*," cooed one of the pair.

Halley wasn't the only one who could use a sale today. Jillian's marzipan-inspired sculptures were her attempt to satisfy her mother's suggestion she explore a career in fine art instead of fine cooking, Jillian's passion. Of course her mother meant fine art *curation*, not fine art making. Jillian's parents had already refused to take their daughter's interest in cooking seriously. "*You want to own the bakery franchise, not decorate the cakes, darling*," was Mrs. Applegate's admonishment.

DaVinci, in fact, was the only one of the three girls who would probably still call today a good day even without a sale. Her family were all impoverished artists of one stripe or another and would have been baffled if she came home with cash.

Jillian, about to make the first sale of the day,

continued chatting up her customers.

"I got the inspiration from this adorable candy shop in Paris," she explained. "In the *septième arrondissement*. I thought they were selling rows of nearly identical apricots, but when I looked closely, I realized it was candy sculpted and painted to look like fruit. That one's three hundred," she said, pointing to the smaller of two baskets. "The larger one is six hundred. My mom uses one that size instead of having to replace fresh flowers in the upstairs loggia."

Jillian was a natural salesperson from a long line of natural salespersons. Within five minutes, Jillian had swiped an American Express and made a cool six hundred. Halley looked at her own price tags. Even if she sold all of her pieces, she wouldn't make six hundred today. But if she did sell everything … She allowed herself a momentary daydream. She would buy the necessary swim top and probably stick the rest in the bank. Already, she'd set aside eighteen hundred and forty-four dollars to someday pursue the ambition she kept hidden from her friends.

As the first hour passed, a few customers asked Halley about her largest piece, three bold stripes of differing greens against a black background. What was it called? What was it supposed to represent?

"Asparagus in the Night," she told the first customer. "Green Beans Lying on a Granite Counter," she told the next. "Aliens," she told a third.

DaVinci coughed into her hands when Halley said *aliens*, and normally imperturbable Jillian raised an eyebrow. The potential customers just smiled and said maybe they'd come back later.

"You have to take your customers seriously if you

want the sale," Jillian murmured to Halley as soon as the latest one departed.

Halley felt her cheeks heating. "I take them seriously."

"But you don't really take your *art* seriously," said DaVinci.

The flush spread to Halley's throat.

"Which is fine," added DaVinci, apologetically. "God knows my family takes it seriously enough for the whole of Santa Barbara County."

Jillian laughed and Halley, her face cooling, managed a smile.

"Can I make a suggestion?" asked Jillian.

Halley shrugged.

"It's your prices. No one is going to take a thirty-six inch canvas seriously at forty-five dollars. May I?" She plucked a sharpie from her bag.

Halley shrugged again.

With great care, Jillian added another zero, changing the price of "Red Sunset" or "Orange on a Bench" or whatever the hell it was from forty-five dollars to four hundred fifty dollars.

"And another thing," said DaVinci to Halley. "You should pick titles and stick to them."

Halley stared at the new prices, feeling worried. Who was going to pay nearly five hundred for *that*? The worry quickly shifted to a feeling of defeat. She wasn't going to sell anything today. Maybe she should skip Jillian's pool party this year. Ethyl Meier might not even come. She should probably save up for tires instead of a stupid bikini.

Her phone vibed in her back pocket. Probably her mother, needing something as usual. Her mother had the remarkable habit of becoming more demanding whenever Halley said she would be busy.

"Two guesses?" she asked her friends, pulling her phone out of her pocket.

DaVinci rolled her eyes and Jillian bit her lip.

Halley examined the text message. "Mom wants the truck." Another two texts followed. Scanning them, Halley felt a small surge of hope. She looked up.

"Give me a minute, guys? I need to call her."

Halley stepped out the back of the booth, sliding between the "asparagus" and the "tomato." She bounded across the grass toward the sandy beach. Incredibly, her mother's text sounded like good news. Her mom had picked up a *paying* house-sitting job. These were few and far between, even though her mother always required her clients to specify in reviews, "She doesn't come cheap, but she's worth every penny!" or something similar. In exchange, her mom's oldest customers got her house-, dog-, and cat-sitting services for free, and the ones who *did* pay paid through the nose thanks to the craftily worded recommendations.

"Mom? I got your message. We're done at 7:00 tonight—"

"I need you to come get me right away."

"I told you I'd be busy today."

Silence. A heavy sigh.

Halley cleared her throat. "I can't come get you, Mom. I'm working."

"It's a last minute booking and it *pays*." Her mother's Danish accent had become pronounced, as it did whenever her mother was excited. "Two Chihuahuas and a Siamese and a pool house and a *sauna—*"

"I'm *working.*"

"No, *I* am working. You're out playing with your friends."

"Mom, that's completely unfair—"

"*Spis lige brød!*" snapped her mother. Halley didn't really know if the Danish idiom, literally, *eat just bread*, meant "you're taking a time out" or "you need to chill," but the words made her feel like a four year old every time.

"What am I supposed to tell my friends?"

"Make something up."

"*Mom!*"

"A single bag of money is stronger than two bags of truth." It was her mom's favorite proverb. Halley despised it.

Her mother continued. "As a member of this family, I expect you to pitch in, Halley. In *Danmark*, it wouldn't even be a question."

Anytime her mother didn't like Halley's attitude or behavior, she brought up Denmark, which was apparently peopled by perfect families. Halley, never having been, had no way of fact-checking.

Regardless of the perfection of Danish families, Halley knew she was stuck. Her mother wasn't going to give up when there was a *paid* job in question. Halley was going to have to leave to drive her mother to the new location.

But Halley wasn't giving in without getting something in return.

"I need a new swimsuit."

"What?"

"I need a new suit. A new top. For Jillian's party

11

next week. That's my price if you want me to drive you right now."

"I am not an ATM, young lady—"

"So call an Uber."

Her mother sighed loudly into the phone. "We need the money."

It was always "we" when her mother needed her help, but when it came to spending the money, it ceased being "we."

"Do we have a deal or not?" demanded Halley.

"Fine." Her mother continued, having shifted into bargaining mode. "There's more. Besides giving me a ride, I'm going to need you to take over my current assignment."

Halley inhaled sharply. "No way. I already told you I'm working."

"Just listen. I still have the job at Professor Khan's, but only through this evening. It's a live-in assignment, so someone needs to be there for the rest of today. The professor returns tonight at 6:15. You can pick up my check and hand off keys and everything. After that, you're free to play."

Halley's mouth fell open. Not at the audacity of the request, but rather at the new information her mother had revealed.

"Your current job at the professor's is for pay, too?" Halley's belly knotted with anger. When she'd asked her mother for money at the beginning of the week, her mother had specifically said the professor wasn't a paying customer. "You said the professor paid you in groceries only."

"It was. Groceries only. And a little tiny stipend—"

"Why are you like this? Do you think any of my friends have to beg their parents for a freaking swimsuit?"

Her mother was silent. Then Halley heard what was probably meant to be a sniffling sound, the precursor to tears which, when Halley had been younger, had worked wonders. Halley closed her eyes and counted to three.

"So here's the deal," said Halley. "I need a new suit. And my truck needs tires. If you want to accept the new job *and* have me cover for you at the professor's, that is what it's going to cost you."

"Front tires only."

Halley opened her mouth to object. Then closed it again. She should have known better. If she'd wanted all four tires, she should have started with a timing belt *and* four tires.

"Halley, four tires would be a waste of money. That truck is on its last legs."

Anytime the vehicle's integrity was referenced, it miraculously became Halley's again. Still, this turn of events solved Halley's two most pressing problems—the suit and tires.

"Fine," she said.

"I need you here within the hour."

"Yeah. Fine."

Halley hung up. Why couldn't her mother treat her as a daughter instead of a ... *business* associate? Why did Halley have to argue and bargain for every little thing she needed? Her stomach was in knots. Her problems were solved, so why did she feel so ... defeated?

Arms hugged tightly around her waist, Halley

faced the booth. Customers were chatting happily with Jillian and DaVinci. Halley paused. It wasn't like her friends even needed her. They would nod understandingly when she told them about her mother's latest demands. Jillian would hug her. DaVinci would text her a link to an online support group for children of parents with a narcissism disorder.

Her throat tightened.

Casting a backward glance to the ocean, Halley chewed the ends of her black hair. The conversation with her mother had already taken a toll, and Halley didn't want to go through it all over again. She could tell Jillian and DaVinci that her mother had come down with one of her migraines. It was better than the truth: that she didn't love her daughter enough to buy her a swimsuit without bartering for it.

Halley pulled her hair back. Straightened her shoulders. And headed for the booth.

## 2

### · HALLEY ·

As Halley slipped back inside the booth, Jillian was completing a second sale and DaVinci was trying to speak knowledgeably about Halley's asparagus painting. Glancing at the "asparagus," Halley was forced to concur with the customer, who was replying that it looked more like a trio of anorexic zucchini stood on end.

A moment later, both customers, the purchasing one and the zucchini-remarking one, moved on, leaving Halley alone with her friends.

"That last woman was definitely interested in your green on black piece," said DaVinci to Halley. "She might actually circle back."

In response, Halley tried on a tired smile. It didn't fit so she discarded it.

"Mom needs me," she said.

"Another migraine?" asked Jillian. Mrs. Applegate was subject to migraines and Jillian was consequently sympathetic.

"Something like that. I won't be coming back,"

replied Halley.

DaVinci frowned.

"What?" asked Halley.

"It's just, when my dad has to call in sick to school, they hire a substitute for him. Couldn't your mom get a group of sitters together who would cover for each other when one of them is sick?"

Halley's jaw tightened. Her mom *could* if her mom wasn't paranoidally possessive about her clients. Halley opened her mouth to explain, but then changed her mind. Jillian and DaVinci would just feel sorry for her, and she didn't want their pity.

Avoiding DaVinci's gaze, Halley said, "I'll pack up my paintings."

"No." Jillian shook her head. "No, no, no. They stay. Removing them will make the booth look empty. That large one in back is what draws everyone in for a closer look. In fact, I probably owe you a commission, Halley. My last sale was thanks to your anorexic zucchinis getting people in the booth."

Halley smothered a laugh.

"But the rules …" said DaVinci. "The sellers have to be the makers."

Halley turned to her paintings, noticing Jillian had added an extra zero to the rest of her prices. "I should take my stuff."

"The paintings stay." Jillian's eyes flashed, dark and threatening. "I can make a lot more trouble for the show monitors than they can make for us."

"You're just scary sometimes," murmured Halley.

Jillian shrugged. "What's the point of affluence and power if I can't use it for good?"

"*Really* scary," added Halley.

"Besides," said Jillian, "The monitors will be off having fun today. It's the Friday of Fiesta Week. And we're not going to be here Saturday or Sunday, so who cares?"

"I guess," conceded Halley.

"It's settled," said Jillian. "The paintings stay. And I'll get Branson to help us break down and pack up tonight. He owes me. I talked Mom into ordering him a Hobart."

"*Bran*son." DaVinci grabbed a flyer to fan herself.

Halley had no idea what a Hobart was, but she appreciated Jillian for thinking ahead and lining up solutions to problems Halley hadn't even thought of. Her mother hadn't bothered to think ahead or line up solutions. Feeling heat behind her eyes, Halley blinked rapidly. She'd sworn off crying over the things her mother didn't do for her.

DaVinci straightened the asparagus or zucchini or aliens painting. "So, before you take off—I'm going to need more to go on so I can talk to people when they ask about your work. What inspired this piece?"

Halley laughed. "You know what?" She picked up the Sharpie again and added two more zeroes to each of her paintings. "That should stop people from asking questions."

"A hundred fifty thousand?" said Jillian, eyeing the zucchini/asparagus painting. "Either it stops the questions or it gets you invited to show in a very exclusive gallery."

"Oh," said DaVinci. "Speaking of galleries, Dad can't help us hang my show tomorrow. I could get the twins…."

"God, no," said Jillian. "I love your sisters to

death, but the permanent Chihuly display wouldn't survive them. The three of us can handle it, right Halley?"

"Of course," she replied. "Okay. I gotta run. Thanks, you guys. I owe you."

"Don't be ridiculous," said Jillian. "We owe *you* for getting customers to stop and have a look. And wouldn't it be fun if we sold one of your pieces?"

"Yeah. And probably a sign the world was coming to an end." Halley hugged Jillian and then DaVinci and then turned to run the four blocks to her truck.

~ ~ ~

Halley drove west along Cabrillo Boulevard, heading back to Montecito. She would need to grab some things from the apartment if she was stuck house-sitting all day. Despite the manifold attractions of the full freezer and pantry at the professor's, eventually Halley would get bored of simply eating.

The small, second story apartment where Halley lived with her mother (when her mother wasn't working) was on the end of a complex that could boast of being Montecito's ugliest residence. Halley couldn't believe a developer hadn't bought it out from under her mother's landlord already, but the landlord said she was waiting for the right deal, not the latest offer.

Halley grabbed a book, her laptop, and her toothbrush and jammies, just in case. Her mother's clients as often as not extended their time away. If this turned out to be one of those clients, Halley was okay sleeping over, but she was *not* sticking around the place 24/7, no matter what her mother said. Halley had to help her friends hang DaVinci's show on Saturday. She was not letting them down twice.

After getting directions, Halley got back onto Coast Village Road and then turned up Hot Springs Road. Professor Khan's house wasn't too far from Jillian's estate. Eucalyptus grew thickly along the road and the oily, pungent scent of the leaves drifted in through Halley's open windows. A half dozen lefts and rights later, Halley turned into the driveway of Dr. Jules Khan's residence. Where she encountered a severe—and very *closed*—gate.

"Of course it's gated," she muttered to herself, already dialing her mother.

"Halley, where are you?"

"At the *locked entrance*, Mom."

"You should have gone to the back entrance like I told you."

Halley ignored the fact her mother had *not* told her about a back entrance and spoke a single emphatic word.

"*Mom.*"

Her mother hung up and the solid oak gate swung soundlessly open. Solid gates were popular in Montecito. That and high walled enclosures. Halley could still remember being small and pretending the estates were walled castles, back when she'd accompanied her mom to work.

Pulling the truck up to the first building she saw, Halley killed the engine and hopped outside. The property smelled of roses, and a quick glance around showed both climbing vines with tiny pink blooms and a more formally arranged rose garden, surrounded by low boxwood hedges. A heady scent wafted from the formal garden.

"Wow," she murmured. Even though she was a frequent guest at Jillian's, Halley never really got used to the extraordinary properties her mom watched. Halley could see the appeal of life as a house-sitter. She could even see why her mom house-sat for free for some clients, but Halley had vowed not to follow in her mother's footsteps. The fear she could resemble her mother in this or any other way was the unspoken terror of her life, as surely as the hope that she might resemble her father was its solace. One day, she vowed, she would learn the truth.

She walked toward what was probably a pool house or quarters for the help and heard water plashing nearby. As a pool came into view, she murmured, "Wow," again. The pool, outlined in patterned brick and boasting not one but *two* active waterfalls, looked like the setting for a 1930's gin party. She smiled, imagining how she would costume everyone, in bias-cut satin charmeuse and tuxedos. Her daydream was interrupted by her mother's laughter. Who was she with?

"Mom?"

Halley's voice was swallowed up by the dense mixture of live oak and palms and thick bamboo bordering the pool on three sides.

Her mother, Inga Mikkelsen, strolled out of the pool house/guesthouse/hired-help-quarters with a phone to her ear, smiling as if the person on the other end could see. "Yes, yes. I'll be there in less than fifteen minutes. Right. Thank you. Bye."

As soon as she hung up, her mother's smile fell. "What took you so long?" she demanded. Without waiting for an answer, her mother turned and walked back in the direction from which she'd come. "The tour will have to be quick. This is the guesthouse, where you can stay for the day."

Halley dutifully noted the locations of the guesthouse fuse box and glanced over the list of emergency contacts. After this, her mother grabbed keys to the main house to show Halley more fuse boxes and give a brief explanation of the alarm system on the professor's invaluable antiquities collection and the security features of his inviolable office and basement spaces. Halley duly swore to stay out of the basement, the office, and the main house unless an emergency demanded her presence. She promised not to touch the climate controlled cases of the professor's Gutenberg Bible, his Stradivarius violin, or his Leonardo da Vinci landscape painting. Halley wondered what the professor kept locked in the basement, if he had items like this on display.

"Professor Khan is punctual," said her mother. "I've even known him to be early. So you should be free to go off and play with your friends sometime shortly after 6:15. Do *not* let him tell you he'll mail my check. I want it in hand."

Halley nodded. She was already wishing she'd grabbed her ratty old swimsuit. The pool was gorgeous and the air was heavier up here, even hotter than at the beach.

"One more thing, Halley. I don't want you calling friends over for a pool party or doing anything else irresponsible. In fact, since you insist on being *paid*, I think it's only fair you should assume responsibility for any damages incurred."

21

Halley scowled. She wasn't being *paid*. Her mother had agreed to buy tires and a swimsuit.

"This client is a frequent one and we can't afford to upset him," added her mother. "Oh, and another thing. If anything in the guesthouse pantry catches your eye, it wouldn't be missed."

Halley, well-versed in translating her mother's utterances, knew this was code for: *Take all the food you can back home when you leave.* Her mother treated the open-pantry/open-fridge houses like her own personal grocery stores. It amazed Halley anyone hired her mother a second time, but they did. It was probably the glamour of the Danish accent.

An hour later, Halley had successfully delivered her mother to the House of the Chihuahuas and settled herself back at the professor's on a lounge chair in the shade, pushing her sleeves up and hiking her skirt as far as she dared. One of the few sensible pieces of advice Halley's mom had given her through the years was to never lounge in your underwear because pool maintenance or landscaping would invariably show up if you did.

The other was to avoid sheltering beside water heaters, major appliances, and tall, heavy furniture in the event of an earthquake. It was this second piece of advice Halley thought of when the ground began to shake.

3

· *HALLEY* ·

Much later, DaVinci would remind Halley of her ill-
timed remark about earthquake weather. Now, as the
ground shook violently, Halley's California-trained
responses kicked in. She looked up, making sure she
was clear of limbs, chimneys, or electrical lines which
might fall. But before she had time to do more than
that, the rumbling and shaking had come to an end.

Overhead, dry palm branches shivered for several
seconds after the ground had steadied, sounding like a
hundred whisperers asking one another *was it safe now?*
Halley counted to twenty, bracing herself just in case,
but the ground remained still. The digital clock beside
her re-set itself to 12:00, meaning the power had
briefly turned off. The pool water sloshed from side to
side, and she became vaguely aware of a siren wailing
in the distance. Fire and injury were common after
southern California gave itself a shake, and Santa
Barbara had had four in the past six months. This one
had felt worse than last month's 5.5.

Halley reached for her phone to text her mother

and her friends, almost immediately reminding herself the lines would be jammed with emergency personnel needing cell service. But then she began to worry if her friends on the beach were safe. If the epicenter of the quake had been out to sea, it could bring a tsunami.

Her phone's internet connection lagged, but before too long, she'd confirmed it had been an inland quake, initial estimates of 6.1, centered east in nearby Santa Ynez. Although sobering, it was good news on two counts. It meant the siren wailing in the distance wasn't a tsunami warning. It also meant Los Angeles and its environs would be practically untouched. It meant the object of her secret dream, nestled between the Haunted Mansion and the Pirates of the Caribbean, was safe. Halley turned her phone off and took a cursory look around the guesthouse.

Halley had rarely been "home" at her apartment during the more than a dozen earthquakes she'd weathered. Her mother's employment kept them living somewhere besides their apartment for at least half the year, and while Halley had lately been staying home by herself, she'd been with her mother for each of the last four quakes. Inga Mikkelsen inevitably developed post-earthquake stress migraines, so Halley had been in charge of recent post-earthquake checks on behalf of absent estate owners.

The pool water continued to slosh lazily from side to side, but there weren't any obvious cracks in the pool or surrounding areas. Dutifully, she crossed to the main house with the keys in hand, searching first for foundation cracks, then plumbing leaks, gas leaks, and other things quakes left in their wake.

The siren was still making noise. Oddly, it didn't

seem like it was approaching. Or receding. Halley frowned. Could it be an on-property alarm? She opened the front door of the main house. The siren noise was more obviously an alarm noise now, and it was much louder inside.

A quick search revealed the sound was coming from none other than the forbidden basement.

"Of course," she murmured. "The murder basement."

Sighing heavily, Halley marched downstairs to the basement. The basement door, which Halley had seen locked an hour ago during her mother's abbreviated tour, was now tilted ajar, but the alarm didn't seem to be tied to the door. The sound was coming from inside. She tried to peer inside, but the basement was dark except for a few flashing LEDs.

Halley settled her hands on her hips. She wasn't supposed to enter the basement, but what if the alarm indicated something important? It might be a flood alarm or smoke alarm. What would a responsible house-sitter do? She pulled out her phone and called her mother, but all she got was an *"all lines are busy; please try your call later"* message. Halley's fingers beat out a rhythm on her crossed arms. The alarm wailed its own frustration.

"Fine," she said, entering the off-limits room.

Overhead lights flickered on.

"Whoa...." She surveyed the room. It contained an odd mix of items, looking half like a garage for injured rockets and half like a museum of Egyptian artifacts, including, eerily, several sarcophagi. "Weird," she murmured.

The alarm noise was coming from across the

room where a sort of podium stood between two large sideways-coiled structures angled so as to face one another.

"Tesla coils," she said softly.

DaVinci had worked shapes like these into a metal sculpture for her father's birthday last year, calling it a "non-drivable Tesla." So what was the professor doing down here? Building engines for some "Tesla" knock-off?

Halley snapped a few quick pictures for DaVinci and then crossed the room to address the alarm and determine if it indicated something that would necessitate a call for further assistance. Not that she had phone service.

She continued across the room to where the sound seemed to originate from—a wide podium set between the Tesla coils, or whatever they were. The podium held two items. A scrapbook, which was obviously *not* the source of the noise, and an inset computer screen, currently dark.

"Tesla coils and scrapbooking?" she muttered to the empty room.

She glanced at the open scrapbook page and did a double-take. It was filled with pictures of people in historical costume. Beautiful costumes. Jacobean women's gowns supported with proper bum rolls and farthingale petticoats; starched white collars sewn into miniature pleats, the outer edges embroidered with black silk; pork-pie caps sewn with jewels and thread-of-gold. And the men's costumes were no less elegant.... Halley tore her gaze away. She wasn't here to admire costumes, and besides, the alarm was still blaring from the computer screen.

Not seeing a keyboard, she lifted her hand to touch the screen, which awoke flashing bright red words against a black background.

*CAUTION: Sequence Interrupted! Failsafe protocol initiated.*

*Reboot: Y/N?*

Her mother had pointed out the systems reboot for the encased artifacts upstairs: *In the event of a power interruption, it's imperative you reboot to protect the climate of the cases. Understand?*

Her finger hovered over the "Y" for *yes*. She should call her mother and make sure she was doing the right thing. Except ... *no service*. Besides, her mother had made clear *she*, Halley Mikkelsen, was responsible for this property. After a moment's hesitation, Halley punched the "Y" for "yes." It was what she would do for the system upstairs, so it had to be the right step in this case, too. Her heart pounded fiercely as she tapped "Y."

The alarm went silent and Halley let out the breath she'd been holding. The podium's computer screen began flashing through long lines of uninteresting code. Halley's eyes drifted to the scrapbook pictures once more. She flipped a few pages, seeing breathtaking costumes from every historical period in western history as well as some from Imperial China and shogun-era Japan—it was an unbelievable collection. Oddly, in many pictures, those who wore the elaborate costumes stood beside a man wearing a very dull costume—sometimes monk's robes, sometimes what looked more like graduation robes.

"The professor," she murmured. He was

snapping selfies next to ... actors? Re-enactors? She flipped through a few more pages while the podium screen hummed and blipped beside her. The detail in the costumes was unusual. These had to be professional actors. Did the professor work in the film industry? Maybe he could give her advice on getting work with Ethyl Meier.

In addition to the costumes, some of the set backgrounds in the photographs were exquisitely detailed. Halley had only taken one set design class, but if she was any judge, these were expensive sets. They had to be from movies. The man she was house-sitting for had a Hollywood connection. *A Hollywood connection!* Hope fluttered inside her. This might turn out to be the most important day of her life.

She felt a pang of familiar hurt. Her mother had never thought to mention the professor's interest in Hollywood. Her mother *knew* Halley hoped to work in the film industry, but she'd never once said anything. The pang didn't last long—Halley had layers of emotional scar tissue that dulled most responses to this sort of repeated injury. It was just one more example in a long line of examples of her mother's inability to care for any needs but her own. DaVinci, who insisted Halley's mother had a *narcissist* disorder, would just call this "additional proof." Halley didn't like to think about the disorder. There were studies that suggested it was passed on genetically.

Halley closed her eyes and took a calming breath. Reminded herself she came from *two* sets of genes. Then she opened her eyes and flipped back to the first page of the scrapbook, hoping for a description of what movie or movies these came from.

The first page was unlike the rest. It had only one picture of the monk-robed professor standing between the Tesla-coil-like devices. Standing, in fact, right where Halley now stood. The professor's feet were placed inside the outline of twin footprints. Glancing down at her feet, Halley saw the same outlined footprints, although the paint was faded now. She looked back at the picture. The professor's expression was serious, or even nervous. Not self-assured like in the other pictures. There was something written in very bad handwriting, but before she could decipher it, the screen beside the scrapbook flashed brightly, demanding Halley's attention.

Onscreen was a circle, a rapidly filling "pie" with the percentage of completion expressed in numbers below. It was nearly fixed, then. Good. She'd done the right thing. She knew she should leave and continue checking the rest of Dr. Khan's property, but her eyes drifted back to the scrapbook, to the hand-written scrawl under the photograph: *My first use of the singularity to travel backward through time.*

Halley's eyebrows rose. She frowned. And then she figured it out. The set she was standing on must have come from a movie about *time travel*. The professor had bought (or been given) the set piece. Maybe he was a science consultant to the industry— her mom had said he was a scientist.

She really should get back upstairs and check the rest of the property. But these costumes.... She flipped to the second page in the book. Just another minute.

On the second page, the professor was standing with someone in front of what looked like ... a printing press? Halley examined the photograph more carefully. There, under the professor's arm, was a book. She leaned in. It was a Gutenberg Bible. Was it the one she'd seen upstairs? The one he kept in the climate-controlled case? She looked at the caption.

*Johannes Gutenberg, Mainz, 1455.*

Halley flipped to the next page.

*Admiral Zheng He, Cathay, 1410.*

Here, the professor was holding a vase that looked like something Halley had seen downtown at the elegant Hong Kong Palace, her mother's favorite Chinese restaurant. She flipped to another page, finding another vaguely pirate-y costume. The caption read: *Master Aspley, London, 1609.*

She leaned forward and read the words on the manuscript in the professor's hands: *Shake-speares Sonnets, Neuer before Imprinted.* She'd seen that manuscript too. Upstairs. In the case next to the Gutenberg Bible.

Halley released a single guttural laugh. The professor was a total *poseur*, keeping movie props in climate controlled cases to impress people. Or maybe props made to this degree of historical accuracy required careful preservation. Or maybe the professor had an odd sense of humor and the cases were a private little joke.

The screen beside her turned black, catching her attention again. She sighed. She ought to get back upstairs. She closed the scrapbook. Then, frowning, she opened it again. She didn't know what page it had been opened to. Really, though, it didn't matter. She was going to have to confess to the professor she'd been down here to fix his alarm for his ... whatever it was. But just as she was about to step away from the podium, she saw the computer screen flicker to life again.

**The Curtain Theatre**
**Cheapside, London**
**AD 1598**

That was ... random.

It was her last thought before her muscles seized up as if she'd been Tasered.

# 4

## · EDMUND ·

Edmund Aldwych, grandson of Edward Aldwych, the first Earl of Shaftesbury, wasn't ready to take up the title of *earl*. It should have fallen to his father, but his father had left this world six months ago, never to inherit the earldom. Edmund's grandfather, as if eager to follow his son to the grave, was dead as well—two days gone—leaving twenty-one year old Edmund, second-born and oldest surviving male, the heir. Edmund was not ready to take up the title, but take it up he must.

When Edmund had been small, an ancient servant given to fortunetelling had prophesied Edmund would travel far and restore the family fortunes. Edmund, affectionately known as Ned, had grown up hearing the wise woman's words repeated and he believed them, first as a matter of course, and eventually as a matter of necessity. The wealth of the earldom had been much decimated by the honor of not one but *two* visits from Good Queen Bess during her famous "progresses" throughout the kingdom, at which time Edmund's grandfather had added cupolas, turrets, and chimneys in imitation of the Lord Burghley's great house. The cost had been enormous, and the family's fortune had not yet seen fit to restore itself.

Having decided "travel far" meant "travel to the New World," young Ned had longed for the day he would board a ship and see marvels. The prophesied riches, though necessary, were only of secondary interest to him: it was the siren call of adventure and discovery that wooed him and kept him burning costly candles late into the night, as he poured over the latest reports of explorers new-returned. Not the eldest son, Ned was free to pursue this course, having worked out by the age of nine that he would travel far and restore the family fortune while his older brother Robert would inherit the title and his younger brother Geoffrey would go a-soldiering. Ned was a great planner.

But when young Ned was twelve, his older brother Robert had died of a purulent fever, leaving Ned as his father's heir apparent. Ned's hopes of a voyage to the New World crushed, his education turned to husbandry of the estate, for which he had talent if not eagerness. Seemingly casting off his childhood ambitions with his childhood name, "Ned" became "Edmund," who now kept secret his dream of seeking the illusive Northwest Passage.

But then his father had died, and now his grandfather was dead. There would be no brave journeys across vast oceans. The funeral costs from the first loss were scarcely paid off, and now it was time to prepare a second feast. That honor would fall to Edmund's mother, as Edmund had no wife himself, much to his mother's disappointment. *The sooner he found a wife and got her with child, the better for all,* was his lady mother's constant refrain.

Staring at his grandfather's waxy figure lain in the bed wherein he'd died, Edmund felt as if the weight of the entire castle was pressing down upon him, determined to crush him by degrees. His surviving brother Geoffrey, already a profligate at merely eighteen years of age, sat moping in the corner of the room, playing some unfathomable game with a cord dangling from their grandfather's favorite tapestry: *The Lady and the Lion.*

"Cease that behavior," murmured Edmund.

Geoffrey ceased. For an entire minute. Then began again. Until such time as Edmund fathered a son, Geoffrey was the next heir to the earldom. The thought filled Edmund with dread for the livelihoods of all those under the protection of his household. Friendly enough to servants and family, Geoffrey nonetheless failed to exhibit any sense of concern for their welfare. Only once had Edmund's grandfather made the mistake of asking Geoffrey to pay the wages of a departing servant. Geoffrey was too much like their father, who had eaten and drunk his way to an untimely grave.

Eyeing the arc of the sun as it glanced off a high cupola outside, Geoffrey cleared his throat and asked Edmund the same question he'd already asked twice.

"Must I remain, Ned?"

Edmund's pulse stuttered, hearing his boyhood name. He must abandon "Ned," and all Ned's boyish dreams. He must become Edmund, Second Earl of Shaftesbury.

"Must I?" repeated his brother.

"Thou must remain," replied Edmund. "It is seemly."

"*Seemly*," repeated Geoffrey, harrumphing. "All must be *seemly* for his lordship the earl."

"By the rood, Geoffrey—" Edmund broke off, grimacing. He ought not to allow himself to be goaded. He snapped at his brother because he was tired. Two nights ago he'd stayed up all night with his grandfather during his final hours of life, and he'd taken little rest since. This, Edmund did not resent; he loved his grandfather. But worry over his inheritance and his lack of readiness had left Edmund very tired, indeed.

Still, he ought to guard his temper. Geoffrey loved goading his brother even more than he loved spending his brother's money. Edmund must begin his relationship with his brother on a new footing. A better footing. One that persuaded Geoffrey to become a model of behavior so gradually that even Geoffrey would not see it happening.

It certainly wasn't going to happen *without* Edmund's help.

Geoffrey was now winding the tapestry cord round and round his arm, threatening to tug down the tapestry from where it hung.

"Get thee gone," said Edmund at last. "I shall await the midwife. Only see thou upset not the guests. 'Tis a day for solemnizing."

"A day for *sermonizing*," muttered Geoffrey, rising.

"Geoffrey," began his brother.

Geoffrey turned around.

"Help our mother," said Edmund. "Her grief is doubled, now."

"Aye, very well," replied Geoffrey, vanishing

before Edmund could lay additional demands upon him.

Edmund rubbed his tired eyes, wondering what had delayed the midwife who would perform a final duty for Lord Shaftsbury, washing and shrouding his body. The linen lay neatly folded on the chair beside the bedstead. The linen winding cloth had cost more than Edmund had been wise to spend, but his mother had made such a fuss over the fineness of the linen for her husband's burial cloth, and Edmund felt he could hardly choose cloth that was mean or coarse for his grandfather after burying his father in fine linen.

As it was, the earl—the *former* earl—was to have a nocturnal funeral to cut back on expense. Edmund's mother put it about that the family, still mourning her husband, had no stomach for another great event. By burying the earl at night, they would cut the attendance to perhaps a quarter of what it might otherwise have been. The feast immediately after would be consequently less costly, although the family must still provide cakes and ale for the servants and gifts for close family and friends.

To remember his father, there had been heavy rings of gold, shaped into a pair of crossed bones for those dear to his father, echoing the rings procured when Robert had died. Edmund was not sure they could afford rings of gold for his grandfather's mourners, but as with the burial cloth, it would reflect badly on the family if they gave out remembrances of inferior quality.

Edmund looked down at the heavy ring upon his finger. It was not for his father, but for his eldest brother Robert, gone these six years. His father's ring,

Edmund had been forced to sell already to pay Geoffrey's debts. Perhaps he should sell the ring he wore for Robert as well, which might in turn pay for smaller rings of a lesser metal for the most honored mourners. Ready-made ones, perhaps, rather than the elaborate customized rings they'd ordered for their father and Robert. The goldsmith kept a ready supply of rings with skulls, if Edmund recalled aright.

Skulls would have pleased his lordship, thought Edmund, smiling. Heaven knew he had failed to please his grandfather in other ways. Edmund had neither sired an heir nor even married. He preferred reading and riding to life at court. Well, riding was necessary, was it not? How else was he to see to his grandfather's estate, to learn what he must learn in order to run it himself, as now he must do?

He sighed. His father ought not to have died. His grandfather ought not to have hurried after. Ought not, especially, to have left Edmund with the rearing of young Geoffrey. Profligate, degenerate, only-just-eighteen Geoffrey who spent every penny he had and many he had not on brothels and ale and good seats at whatever play or hanging or cockfight was to be had in nearby London. Perhaps a wife would tame Geoffrey where others had failed. But who would unite their daughter to the younger brother of an impoverished earl who avoided court life?

The improvements to the manor for her majesty's visits, the foodstuffs and wines, and the gifts to her majesty and her favorites had left the first earl of Shaftsbury with debts he could never in his lifetime repay.

These, too, would fall upon Edmund's shoulders.

Small wonder Edmund's father hurried off from such a life to take his chances in the next. Edmund might still read of voyages to the New World, devouring anything he could acquire upon the subject, but his dream was hopeless, now his grandfather was gone. Edmund must look after the estate and those who farmed it. Brother Geoffrey certainly would not.

The slow shuffle of a pair of slippers roused Edmund from his gloomy thoughts to his gloomy present. He greeted the midwife who'd delivered him, his siblings, and his father. He listened to her lamentations that it should come to this, my lord gone so soon after his son. Edmund found himself in the odd position of comforting the midwife regarding the cause of his own sorrows.

Having at last pointed out the linen shroud, Edmund left her to wash and wind his grandfather's body while he chased down his brother. Geoffrey had left the room a quarter of an hour ago, plenty of time in which to make mischief rather than helping his mother as Edmund had requested.

But when Edmund sought out his mother, he learned Geoffrey had, indeed, left on an errand at his mother's command.

"I sent him to town," said his mother. "We must have rings and gloves for the mourners."

Edmund felt a pinch of alarm. "Good my lady mother, didst thou supply him with ready payment?"

"Aye. I gave him the ruby and pearl pendant your grandfather gave me when I wed your father." She swiped at a tear. "I never cared for it overmuch."

Edmund frowned. All who knew his lady mother knew she had treasured the pendant. That she should have given it to Geoffrey ... Edmund had to chase down his brother at once. How could his mother be so blind to Geoffrey's habits?

"I must ride into town as well, my lady." Concealing his distress as best he could, he kissed his mother and departed.

In the stables, he had two horses prepared, taking the stable hand Jem along with him, uncertain what state Geoffrey might have drunk himself into by the time they recovered him. As he rode away from the manor, Edmund glanced mournfully at the elaborate cupolas and chimneys adorning his home. Chimneys might keep his family and servants warm come winter, but cupolas would feed no one.

On the small chance his brother *had* gone for rings, Edmund rode with Jem to Cheapside, but the gold and silversmiths of Goldsmith Row had none of them seen his brother. It was as Edmund had feared, then. His stomach soured on two accounts. Firstly, Edmund had more important things to do than to chase down his reprobate brother. Secondly and more urgently, the estate had no coin to spare, and Geoffrey could spend coins faster than a lover seeking his mistress's favor.

Edmund breathed out an angry sigh. Geoffrey likely *was* buying gifts for the latest strumpet to catch his eyes. Edmund knew no one who craved admiration more than his brother. Nor did he know anyone more ready than Geoffrey to believe admiration could be purchased instead of earned.

Resigning himself to the inevitability of loss, Edmund had a choice to make: Shoreditch or Southwark? Both teemed with brothels, gaming houses, and theaters. Edmund had overheard people in the lane discussing the baiting of a famous bear to commence at noon in Shoreditch. Geoffrey liked bear baiting. Edmund turned east and then headed north, passing up Bishopsgate along with his stable hand until they reached the vicinity of the Curtain—the theatre most likely to house the bear baiting. Upon arriving, however, they learned the match between dogs and bear had been postponed as the dogs had torn one another to pieces, allowing the poor bear yet another day to draw breath.

Edmund frowned. "Perdition take him," he muttered, looking about as if in hopes Geoffrey might suddenly appear. But his brother was most likely in a dark hole and not the open street. "Know you which brothel houses my brother favors?" Edmund asked of Jem.

Jem shrugged.

Edmund's fists clenched, yearning to knock someone's pate. Geoffrey deserved a lashing and Edmund was ready to apply it. Indicating Jem should remain with the horses, Edmund dismounted, turning into the rank lane in which the brothel stews were housed. As he rounded a corner, stepping with care to avoid noxious midden heaps, he felt a faint tug at his waist. Reaching down, he noted he'd been relieved of a small wallet of food.

Fists at the ready, Edmund turned and spied a child running with haste. In three heartbeats, he had the child in his grasp. The little thief was already devouring a chunk of brown bread. His breath drawn to rebuke the urchin, Edmund lifted the boy with two strong arms.

And saw *he* was a *she*. She was scrawny, with large dark eyes. Something about the terror in the thief's eyes as she looked at him took the reprimand from his mouth. She had the look of his sister Susan, buried just after her seventh birthday.

"Please, sir, I'm sorry, sir," whispered the child.

He could feel her trembling in his grasp.

Cursing softly, he set the girl down. "Dost thou know the punishment for thievery?"

"I was hungry," she murmured, an anxious glance at the food still held tightly in her filthy fist.

"Where is thy mother?"

"In the ground, sir."

"And thy father?"

Her eyes dropped. "The same."

"Hast thou no relations living?" asked Edmund, his voice more gentle than before.

"No, sir. I begged a farthing from a gentleman earlier, and I mistook you for him. I thought perhaps you would not mind, but I see you are not him." She hung her tiny head in shame. "It was wrong, but a boy stole my farthing and I was so hungry."

"Thou sawst a gentleman who had my look?" asked Edmund, his pulse quickening.

"Aye. The one as gave me the farthing. He wore black gloves trimmed in yellow."

*Geoffrey.* Edmund felt relief alongside mounting anger. The yellow-trimmed gloves had been their grandfather's.

Edmund withdrew a penny and placed it in the child's free hand. "Canst thou tell me whither this gentleman went?"

"Aye, sir," replied the child. "He would go to the

41

theatre, he said, though the bear fought not today. He was in hopes to game with the players."

Edmund rose from his crouched position and looked toward the theatres as if expecting to see Geoffrey down the lane. Instead of seeing Geoffrey, however, Edmund saw Jem approaching, without the horses.

"Jem," cried Edmund.

"The horses are safely held, my lord," Jem said hastily. "Young Geoffrey is gone to the theatre—"

"Aye," said Edmund. As an afterthought, he added, "If Geoffrey means to gamble, he must have coin yet remaining." The thought was steadying.

Jem was staring at the urchin beside Edmund. Edmund was sore tempted to send the child on her way, but how should an orphan fare in such a part of the city? The child was courteous, or at least knew enough to address a lord as *you* and not *thou*.

She'd finished the bread but looked no less hungry than before.

Edmund sighed. He would not leave the wretch to the fate that awaited her hereby. He addressed Jem. "A moment."

Then, squatting, Edmund spoke to the girl. "What is thy name, child?"

"I am called Nan."

"Canst thou brew or bake or mend?"

"I can mend, sir."

"And wouldst thou promise never more to thieve, were I to find thee a place of employment?"

Her round eyes grew larger still. "Aye, sir."

At this, Edmund stood and spoke to Jem. "Bring this child home. Take her to Marjorie and see she is fed, clothed, and given work."

"Aye, my lord," replied Jem. "Right away, my lord."

"Stay—where hast thou bestowed the horses?"

"At the Shorn Sheep, lord. The ostler is brother-in-law to my wife. He will see they are kept safe."

Edmund nodded, then turned to the girl. "Godb'ye, Nan. I shall come visit thee in a few days time to see thy needlework."

"An' it please you, sir," Nan said to Edmund, "You are best to go round the side of the playhouse. The door to the side doth not latch aright."

Edmund nodded, wondering if the theatre, when empty, was where the child had sheltered since losing her parents. He took off on foot, striding swiftly to make up for lost time and aiming for the two great theatres lying side by side in Curtain Road. In truth, he knew not which was the Theatre and which the Curtain. It had been many years since Edmund had been idle enough to waste two hours of daylight and the pennies it cost to hear a play. He determined to try the closer of the two houses.

When Edmund arrived, the little side door was unlocked as the child had said, so he walked inside, seeking out the backstage tiring room where he thought the players might be found at dice.

Unfortunately, the entire backstage area was empty. Edmund made his way onto the stage itself, jumping down to the straw-strewn floor and looking this way and that for any living soul. The place was empty. Cursing, Edmund turned to exit.

As he strode away, there came a great thumping noise and a sound like that of someone having the breath knocked clean from them. Was it Geoffrey, falling dead drunk from the raised stage? Edmund turned in fearful hope, but saw instead the fallen form of a youth dressed in the oddest shift and petticoat ever worn by a boy playing women's roles.

Edmund crossed back to the figure to make certain it was not Geoffrey. Overhead, a casement window hung open. Frowning, he overlooked the figure. It was a pretty youth, but it was not Geoffrey, and Edmund had no more time to waste on London's riff-raff. Edmund made to go but then he paused. He looked once more upward to the window casement. 'Twas a fall of two stories. The youth might be dead. Or dying. Cursing the ill timing of the youth's fall, Edmund bent to check.

He noted a rounded softness of breast. This was no boy, but a girl. A girl of rare beauty. He felt a sudden desire for pen, paper, and time, to copy her likeness. Her skin was of a color out of the common way, warm and brown. From Araby or Afric, perhaps? Her dark brows arched high over eyes closed. Was she concussed or dead?

Placing his ear and cheek over her mouth, he attended for any sign of breath.

# 5

## · *HALLEY* ·

The first thing Halley noticed after she'd been frozen in place between the Tesla coils was a warming sensation, gentle like when the Santa Ana winds blew in from the desert. The sort of warmth that put a smile on your face. But in seconds, Halley felt as if she'd stepped into an inferno.

And then, even more suddenly, all heat vanished. Halley didn't feel hot. She didn't feel cool. She felt ... *nothing*. The absence of sensation. She couldn't tell anymore if her limbs were frozen in place. There was nothing left to feel. The nothing stretched into several long seconds.

And then, without warning, her senses were flooded. Blinding light assaulted her eyes. Noise pummeled her ears, the sound thrumming through her breastbone. She could feel the air leaving her lungs. She was falling, falling, falling, and then she seemed to land with a *thud*, toppling backwards. The fall knocked the breath right out of her.

Several seconds passed before she could suck in a

breath. What had just happened? Was she … alive? Her heart raced. If she had a heartbeat, she had to be alive. But what had happened? Another quake? Had something hit her head? Had she passed out? Slowly, she blinked her eyes open. A man's face, in profile, filled her entire field of vision. He was hovering over her, checking to see if she was breathing. That was one exquisite profile. Chiseled. Perfect. She might be dreaming…. She blinked to see if the vision would disappear.

The face above hers shifted from a profile to a frontal view, and she found herself staring at a perfect brow. And into a pair of anxious eyes. Eyes a feline shade of amber, flecked with brown, encircled with a dark outline. They were the most beautiful eyes she'd ever seen. Above the most beautiful mouth. And cheekbones carved from … what was it? Alabaster? She had to be imagining this. A vision brought on by trauma to the head.

The face exhaled. Or rather, the *man* exhaled. Okay, so he was real. Definitely real. Still impossibly beautiful, but very, very real.

She blinked a couple of times. The exquisite face receded, and that changed what was in her field of vision. Where the basement ceiling ought to have been, she saw a clouded sky. Which was … disturbing. She didn't remember leaving the basement.

At least she didn't feel pain anymore. She wiggled fingers and toes. Everything seemed to be working fine. Had she imagined the pain? She must have been unconscious for awhile, because if she couldn't remember leaving the basement, that meant someone had dragged her out unconscious.

Suddenly the handsome face hovering over hers made sense: he must be a paramedic. Or a fireman. Halley shifted her head. The ground seem to shimmy, and she groaned, squeezing her eyes tightly shut.

"Drink, mistress," said the handsome fireman or paramedic or whatever he was.

*Mistress?*

Halley put her lips to some kind of leather water pouch and sipped.

She swallowed and then sputtered. That was *not* water. Unless her taste buds had gone crazy, it was some kind of sweet wine.

*The heck?*

The wine burned as it slid down her throat. She propped herself up on one elbow. For half a second, the Earth seemed to spin. She was in the dirt, looking at a wooden wall that formed one side of a tall, jutting deck attached to a building. The building was of an architectural style that didn't match the rest of the professor's estate.

"Tudor Revival," she murmured to herself, recalling the term from the freshman architecture class DaVinci insisted they all take. *Tudor Revival* had been big in Montecito in the 1920's. She took in all of this in a moment, before the wine had finished burning down her throat. The world was still spinning, so she closed her eyes again.

She still couldn't figure out why she would have been moved to … whatever part of the professor's estate this was. Who would move her? And why? Unless … had there been another earthquake? If the ceiling had collapsed, somehow …

"Did the basement tumble down on me?" she

murmured to the man beside her, opening her eyes just a crack. Wow, was he gorgeous. Maybe it was a requirement for working in the fire department. She closed her eyes again. She wished the world would stay still for a minute.

The fireman spoke. "The ... *casement*? Tumbled thou from the *casement*?"

"*Base*ment," she corrected, but then she wondered if maybe there was something wrong with her ears. She'd heard "thou." Maybe he'd said "down"? He had a strange accent. Or maybe the loud noise from earlier had damaged her hearing. She felt the dizziness receding. Cautiously, she opened her eyes. As abruptly as it had started, the dizziness was gone. She glanced up and then swung her gaze around in a hundred and eighty degree arc. Wherever she was, it wasn't just a Tudor Revival outbuilding. It looked like she was in some sort of Tudor-era theatre replica. She'd definitely been moved. She wondered who'd called emergency services on her behalf. If the building had collapsed, it might have set off alarms.

*How long had she been unconscious?*

Halley struggled to sit upright. Her head felt only a little fuzzy now. At this point, she noticed what the fireman was wearing: it *wasn't* fireman clothing.

"You're not a paramedic," she said. She glanced around at her surroundings and thought of the pictures of the professor standing with costumed actors. Maybe the professor's estate had its own theatre. Although, who had *their own theatre*?

"Montecito," she muttered with an eye roll. Montecito residents were generally fabulously wealthy, and "Montecito," uttered like that, stood as the generic excuse for any extravagance. But then her heart sank. If the professor was a theatre aficionado, maybe he didn't have Hollywood connections after all. The pictures could have been from productions at this theatre.

She looked back to the man beside her. "Are you rehearsing here? Are you an actor?"

The chiseled face grew haughty and cold. "Mistress, mistake me not for a player."

A player? *Player, playhouse, playwright* ... The words came back from some class or other. She frowned at the man. When she'd worked on costume crew last year, Halley had met actors who wouldn't step out of character when they had a costume on. She'd always thought it was a pretentious drama geek thing, but maybe it was just an actor thing.

She touched the rich fabric of his shoulder cape. "Nice costume." His hose and breeches (late Elizabethan or maybe early Jacobean) hugged powerful thighs, outlining his muscular calves. She cleared her throat.

"So, where are the paramedics or whatever?"

Almost as soon as the question was out of her mouth, she was distracted by shouting and what sounded like the crack of a whip. And horses neighing.

Horses? Neighing?

Her mother hadn't said anything about horses. Her mother specifically excluded horses from animals she would watch. There was no way her mother had just ... *forgotten* the professor's estate had horses. Forgetting it had a theatre, maybe, but not horses.

Halley heard voices shouting nearby, possibly ... rehearsing?

But this brought up another issue: why would people be rehearsing at the professor's estate while he was gone and the estate was supposedly unoccupied? She must have been taken off the estate. It was the only explanation. Her nose wrinkled as the pungent scent of horse piss and dung wafted past. At least Jillian's stables *never* smelled bad like this.

"Where are we?" asked Halley.

"The Theatre. Or the Curtain. I know them not one from the other."

Halley frowned. This actor was starting to annoy her. She just wanted a straight answer. She wanted to know where she was and how long she'd been unconscious. She wanted to call her friends. As she reached for her cell, a heavy wind gusted past, leaving her shivering in her tank top. The temperature made no sense whatsoever. It was a *hot* day. With no breeze. Or it had been. You didn't go from 85 and sunny to 50 and windy in the blink of an eye.

"How long was I ... unconscious?" she asked softly, reaching for her cell phone. Her screen was dead.

"I take not thy meaning," said the man. "Un ... *conscious?*"

"How long was I out of it? Passed out? Eyes closed?"

"Thy fall was but a moment ago," replied the handsome actor. "Thou didst awaken almost without delay. What makest thou here?"

Halley frowned but didn't answer. She had her own questions, thanks very much.

"Where am I? Seriously. All joking aside. And who moved me here?" she demanded.

"Thou art in Shoreditch, hard by London. At the playhouse. 'Tis the Curtain theatre, methinks."

At his words, her skin prickled.

She remembered standing between the Tesla coils, reading those words on the podium's computer screen: *Shoreditch. London. The Curtain Theatre.* But that was impossible. Ridiculous. All the devices in the basement would have to be ... would have to be ...

She closed her eyes. Of course the devices weren't real. Time machines weren't real. She was being ridiculous to consider it. There was some rational explanation for all this. There had to be. But from behind her closed eyes, she saw again the words on the podium screen just prior to whatever the hell had landed her here.

*The Curtain Theatre*
*Shoreditch*
*London*
*AD 1598*

"No way," she murmured. Her hand squeezed tightly around her phone. This wasn't possible. Panic rose inside her. Where was she?

She looked up at the cloudy sky again. Shivered again as another gust of wind blew past her. Slowly, she formed her next question. "Are you trying to tell me this is ... *London?*"

"Aye, mistress." The stranger stared at her, eyes narrowing. "Where else should it be?"

"And ... the year is ...?"

He stared at her oddly. "The year of our Lord 1598."

She clenched her eyes tightly shut.

"You are not well," said the stranger beside her.

No. She wasn't. Not at all well. Not anywhere in the same universe as well.

She clutched her cell phone. She opened her eyes and looked at her screen again. It was dead. Blank. No power. No bars. No anything.

"Impossible," she said again. Because it *was* impossible. Wasn't it? She thought again of the blinding light. The sensation of having been frozen— *tasered*—between the Tesla-coil-like structures.

*Shoreditch, London*
*AD 1598*

6

· *HALLEY* ·

"No way. No way. No *way.*"

Halley's heart beat like a hammer against her chest wall. It was impossible. It had to be. Except for the inexplicable fact that she was no longer in Montecito. She was ... *here.* And "here" was ... *London.* In 1598. The professor wasn't a cinemaphile or a theatre lover. He was ...

*A time traveler.*

His Gutenberg Bible, his Stradivarius—these weren't movie props. They were ...

*Impossible.*

Halley's stomach seemed to drop through the floor.

"I have to get back," she murmured to the man at her side.

"Prithee, who is thy master?" asked the handsome man.

"I've got to get back," Halley said again, standing up. Ignoring the beautiful questioner, she looked wildly around the theatre, as if hoping the Tesla-coil machinery had followed her here. "No," she murmured. "No, no, *no!*"

"Peace, wench," said the young man.

"I'm not a wench!" snapped Halley. Then her brow furrowed. Maybe she was. "Does 'wench' mean *girl?*"

"Aye. Wench. Girl. I'll not call thee trull." A slight smile played about the corner's of his mouth.

"Okay. I won't call you … 'trull' either."

The mirth vanished from the handsome face. His expression grew confused and then distant. He stood. "I will help thee to thy master if I can, but my business is pressing and calls me elsewhere. Unless, hast thou seen Geoffrey Aldwych herein?"

"Um, no. I haven't. I've only seen you."

He was clearly anxious to leave, but something held him back.

"Thy pretty pate took a goodly knock, it would seem," he said.

He was worried about her.

"Um," said Halley, "You're sure this is Shoreditch, London?"

"Aye. Thus much we have established."

Half a smile pulled at his mouth. Was he amused by her? Well, that was better than being afraid of her. It was better than hauling her off to be burnt at the stake, which they might plausibly do in *Shoreditch* in 1598 to girls who appeared out of thin air. She grasped her ring again, its carved, ridged surface comforting against her fingers.

"This is no place for girls, unless thou wouldst become a common trull," said the young man. "Thy weeds have been ta'en from thee, methinks."

"My ... *weeds*?"

He frowned again, creasing all the smooth planes of his face. "Thy garb. Thy costume. Thy apparel."

"Oh. My clothes. Right. Yes. You know, I think maybe I did lose a few layers." If Halley was in the sixteenth century, she was dressed *very* provocatively indeed. Practically in her underwear.

She pressed her lips together, feeling her throat tightening in a prelude to tears. She couldn't afford to lose it. This guy seemed friendly. And if she was stuck in 1598, she was going to need friends. No. She was a woman—she would need more than friends. She was going to need *protection*. A sword. A pistol. Something.

She thought quickly. No one was going to *give* her a weapon for the asking. The first thing she needed was money.

"Any chance you could get me some, uh, work for hire? I'm a hard worker. And an honest one. By the way, my name's Halley." She held out her hand to shake.

The young man frowned at her extended hand. Did they not shake hands in this society? Dammit! She had no clue what she was doing. Her throat tightened again. Her hand flagged.

The young man sighed. "It would seem this is hiring day. Canst thou bake or brew or mend?"

"Yes," said Halley, nodding rapidly. "Oh, for sure I can."

"What, all three?"

Halley shifted uncomfortably. "I can try."

A sad smile bloomed on the young man's face. "I know not how thou cam'st to be here, but thou art too comely to safely tarry hereby in a state of undress." He removed his outer cloak and placed it around her shoulders. "I am called Edmund Aldwych."

And then, just as he finished his introduction, Halley felt heat flaring through her torso and out to her extremities. *Now what?* The Earth seemed to drop from under her feet. Sensing herself falling, she instinctively grasped for Edmund.

Her muscles froze and once more, all was darkness.

# 7

## · *EDMUND* ·

Edmund had felt the earth shifting beneath his feet
and then, briefly, he'd burned as with fever. He
thought there had been some great noise, too, and
possibly a brief swoon. Upon finding himself fallen
into a strangely lit chamber, his first thought was that
the trembling ground had spilled Mistress Halley and
himself through some part of the raised stage wall. It
was certain *something* had given way. Edmund
wondered if they had, perhaps, fallen into what the
actors did call "hell," that region beneath the
playhouse stage. He'd heard of the mighty engines
housed below-stage that caused spectacles to be
displayed for the audience. He was, in fact, less
ignorant of theatre and playhouses than he wished
Mistress Halley to believe. He had heard *Henry VI* in
this very playhouse, and seen the witch Jeanne d'Arc
swallowed up into the bowels of hell, conveniently
located below-stage.

Looking about, Edmund observed diverse
contraptions—large engines, the likes of which he had

never before seen, crowded the space and seemed to confirm they had, indeed, fallen belowground into "hell." He and the girl had landed between two of the stage engines. Odd, unearthly lights flickered around them, seeming to pour down from overhead. Edmund was on the point of examining the source of the strange light when the girl in his arms stirred.

Mistress Halley inhaled as though awakening. This had been her second fall of the day; she would likely require the attentions of either a midwife or barber-surgeon.

"Mistress Halley, are you well?"

She didn't respond. Her expression said much, however. She was clearly startled by her surroundings. In this matter, at least, he could set her at ease.

"It would appear we have fall'n below-stage into what the players do call *hell.*"

The girl grunted and then said quietly, "No. This isn't hell. Definitely not hell."

Having said thus much, she stood, placed her hands on her hips, and staring at him, whispered, *uh-oh.* Her voice was low. Soothing. As soft as her fair cheek, her lovely hands....

Edmund stood. He couldn't afford additional distractions today. He began to brush straw from his breeches and jerkin.

"Stop, stop, stop!" said Halley. Pulling Edmund and herself off of the raised dais upon which they stood, she then began to pluck up the bits of straw, shoving each of them into her pocket.

"Is that all of them?" she murmured to herself.

Was she ... damaged of mind? She'd spoken sense above ground, but perhaps the second fall had taken a greater toll.

She faced him. "The pieces of ... *hay* or whatever will give us away. We can't leave any sign someone was here." She placed her hands on her hips. "Oh my God. What am I supposed to do with you?"

"Mistress Halley—"

"Just *Halley*." Her gaze darted wildly from the engines to a clerk's desk and thence to a sort of ... *pulpit* situated before them. Avoiding the dais, she approached the pulpit, gazing upon its surface.

"Mistress *Halley*. I shall see thee safely to mine estate, where your injuries may be tended, but I must beg you will first remain with me while I seek my brother."

"Um ... your brother's not here."

Edmund smiled. "Aye, Mistress—aye, *Halley*, thus much have I observed." Turning, Edmund looked for a way out. On the far side of the subterranean closet, he saw what might be stairs. "Let us depart," he said with relief. He held his hand out, to indicate the exit and then turned to face Mistress Halley.

Once again, he was struck by her appearance. Her face, though of a darkly shade, was flushed with color. She was altogether the loveliest creature Edmund had ever beheld. She gazed at him for a long moment, brows furrowed. Then she spoke.

"We're not going that way," she said decisively. "We've got to get you back where you belong. Yeah. I need to get you back." She nodded.

"Aye," said Edmund, with a soft laugh. But then he frowned. Should he first take Halley to the estate before seeking Geoffrey? It would be easier to travel London's streets without the half-dressed girl. If he were to be set upon by more drunken idlers than he could fend off alone ... His hand wandered to his sword hilt.

"Upon further reflection," he said, "I believe it would be best if I were to entrust thee into the care of my steward and *after* seek out my brother."

"Um, okay. Just hang tight for a minute while I get this thing rebooted."

Mistress Halley was now examining the small pulpit set between the strange engines. She began to repeatedly tap the surface of the pulpit. "What's wrong with you?" she said to the pulpit.

Edmund's frown deepened. He was uncertain what her utterance signified.

"Come," he said, growing impatient. "We must be gone."

"I know. I *know*. I'm working on it."

His responsibilities, already crowding round him, began now to press upon him. Edmund had no time to reason with a girl at once headstrong and ... dim-witted.

"The door, good mistress, lies to the other side of this room." He took two steps that direction.

"No!" She looked up from the pulpit with a frightened face. "You can't leave. Don't go that way. It's not safe."

An odd-colored light flickered from the pulpit. Edmund could not see the source of the light, but assumed it must be a colored-glass lantern. Pulling his attention from the light, he addressed their current plight.

"I see but one exit, mistress," he said.

It was only at this moment that it occurred to him

there was no trace of where they had broken their way through to this room. There was no gaping hole to the sky. No dirt upon this smooth slate flooring. No splintered wood from the stage wall. Had they perhaps fallen down by means of the stairs? How then did they end up on the other side of the room? He felt a sudden urgency to depart this uncanny place with its strange machines, its devilish lights.

Taking large strides, he crossed to the stairs, calling, "We go," in his most commanding tone.

"Don't go!" cried Halley. "If you leave, I'll never get you back where you belong."

He glanced back. She remained at the pulpit.

"Come wench. I can no longer bide here below-ground." He approached her. If need be, he could carry her. She surely weighed no more than eight stone.

He held out a gloved hand.

"Let us away," he said, not unkindly. He would, at any rate, keep his temper.

"I have to reboot the system," muttered the girl, still bent over the pulpit.

"Wench?" His tone was less patient, his hand still extended. It was high time he got back on Geoffrey's trail.

She ignored him, continuing to mutter to herself. Edmund was growing more certain she needed a midwife's care, and soon, too. He couldn't just ... *abandon* her. He exhaled heavily. He would have to take her, *will-ye* or *nill-ye*.

"No help for it," he muttered under his breath. Then, more loudly, he added, "I must go, and thou with me." Without further ceremony, he hoisted Halley as though she were a sack of grain and strode

61

towards the stairs.

"Put me down! Hey! Let me go!"

Edmund ignored her instruction. "Thou art not thyself. My own midwife shall physick thee. When thou art recovered, we'll speak of ... *goings*."

"I'm serious. You can't walk up those stairs."

The girl wriggled to get free, but Edmund's hold was secure. He'd carried struggling beasts before this time, and the girl had neither hooves nor horns with which to injure him. She did, evidently, know enough about a man's body to aim a kick where it might have crippled him had he not grasped her foot in time.

"By the rood, girl," said Edmund, testily. "I do thee no ill. I mean to *help* thee to medicine."

At this point, Edmund emerged from the smooth-daubed stair passage and into a place most strange. This was no theatre stage, nor tiring house, neither. Where was he?

What was this place?

His grip relaxed and the girl succeeded in wriggling from him.

"God and all his angels have mercy on my soul," murmured Edmund. "Methinks I am transported to ..." He knew not how to complete the sentence. Transported he had been, but where? And how? Was the girl some faerie changeling? Or something more sinister?

"Back downstairs," she said. "Now!"

Her voice was commanding, but she seemed to have no charms to force his limbs to obey. No devil, then, she.

"Mistress, whence hast thou taken me?"

"It would only confuse you if I tried to explain.

Trust me when I say—"

Abruptly, Mistress Halley broke off her speech and turned her gaze to the place from whence they had emerged. "Uh-oh," she said.

From the stairs, there arose a strange noise, as of many beasts groaning together.

"What devilry is this?" asked Edmund.

"Follow me!" commanded Halley as she dashed back downstairs.

# 8

## · HALLEY ·

Halley's relief at being returned to the professor's estate and her own century was completely overwhelmed by the unfortunate facts of her situation. She'd brought someone with her from a different century—and continent—without having a clue how it had happened. Or even if it was over yet. Was the machine, clearly in activation again, preparing to pull them forward or backward another time? Icy tendrils of fear snaked through Halley's stomach.

She tried to reassure herself: if she kept away from the Tesla coils, she should be safe. And if Edmund could be convinced to stand between them, he should go back. Presumably. She hoped. Her stomach twisted again.

"This way," she called. But as she looked over her shoulder, Edmund wasn't there.

Cursing, she leapt back up the stairs.

He was standing beside the case housing the Gutenberg Bible, gazing at it with furrowed brows.

"What place is this?" he demanded, shifting his

gaze to Halley.

"This is, um, somewhere you don't belong," she said. "But I'm going to help you get back. We have to go downstairs—"

She broke off as the whine of the machine began to make the windows vibrate.

Terrified she might lose her window of opportunity, she shouted to Edmund, "Do you want to get home or not? Get downstairs!"

After a moment's hesitation, he preceded her back down the stairs to the basement. The noise from the machine pulsed in Halley's ears, resonating in her chest, in her bones.

"If it worked before, it can work again," she muttered.

And then, just as she was about to cross the threshold into the basement, jagged blue light flared between the coils. She stopped dead in her tracks. Edmund threw his arms around her to keep her from falling. She hardly noticed, because between the twin coils, the robed figure of the professor had just appeared, his back to them. From one of his hands dangled a heavy gold necklace. Halley's heart sank. The device hadn't been charging up to send someone *back*—it was bringing the professor *forward*.

The machine screamed, unabating, while the robed man leaned heavily upon the podium, as if catching his breath or balance or both. While resting, he emptied a pocket of several more pieces of jewelry.

Her employer was a *thief*. A time traveling thief.

Under cover of the machine's dying whine, she shoved Edmund, whispering, "*Upstairs! Now!*"

Following instinct, she quietly closed the

basement door. Nothing good could come of a time traveling thief discovering he'd been seen in action.

Edmund hadn't moved. His face was very pale. He, too, must have observed the professor appearing out of nowhere, and it would have been a lot more disturbing to him than to her. Even if she didn't understand the professor's basement experiments, she understood a whole lot more than Edmund did.

"*Go, go, go!*" she whispered, indicating the stairs Edmund had so eagerly taken moments earlier. By the time they reached the top of the stairs, the noise from the basement was all but gone. Now what was she going to do?

Panic clawed at her belly.

She had to leave. She had to *take Edmund* and leave. Right now, before the professor suspected anything. She dashed toward the door leading outside. She could jump in her truck and be away before the professor had recovered from his travel sickness.

But then she hesitated. If she were to run off, wouldn't that look suspicious, too? If she had nothing to hide, she obviously wouldn't abandon her post. It would ruin her mother's reputation as a house-sitter, and then the professor would be asking himself what could have been so bad that Halley would risk wrecking her mom's career?

So what could she do to prevent the professor from suspecting anything had happened amiss? She'd already shut the basement door. That was a good first step. As for her next step ...

She had no idea what her next step was.

Another wave of panic washed through her. But panic was a luxury she couldn't afford. The professor might come up the stairs any second.

Clearly, she had to hide Edmund. That was her top priority.

She grabbed Edmund's hand.

"This way," she said to him. His attention had fixed on the strange, modern furnishings. "Come *on*," she said, tugging his hand and leading him to the front door. She could hide him in the guesthouse.

But as she neared the guesthouse, she realized it was the first place the professor would come looking for her. She swore under her breath, looking at Edmund's clothing. If she hid Edmund inside the guesthouse, how would she get him back out, wearing ... *that?*

The costume was a real problem. And then it hit her: this was a costuming problem! If there was one thing she could do, it was costumes.

First step: *What resources did she have?*

As she locked the door of the main house behind them, Halley glanced down at her skirt. It wasn't much of a resource. Not without scissors, a sewing machine, and an hour or two.

She had to tug Edmund's hand to get him moving away from the main house. He looked dazed. He was staring at strange flora and fauna. He must be going through what she'd just gone through. *What had she done?*

Whatever she'd done, she had to fix it.

"Solve the costuming problem first," she said out loud. Maybe she could grab clothes from the professor? No. Snooping around in the main house was too risky. An idea popped into her head. *Her P.J.'s.*

As soon as they were inside the guesthouse, she

grabbed her overnight bag. Beside it she saw the paper with the key code for the gated estate entrance. If she could come back later, when the professor was sleeping or away, she could send Edmund back home. She hoped.

Snatching the paper, she then pulled a very dazed Edmund outside, heading for her truck, grateful she'd parked it out of the line of sight of the main house. Edmund's hand, strong and rough-skinned, felt warm in hers. It felt solid. Reassuring. She could do this.

They emerged into the sun and Halley felt the full heat of the afternoon. How could she have just been in *London* under a cloudy sky? She shook her head. This wasn't the time for questions like that one.

Upon seeing Halley's truck, Edmund uttered his first words since watching the professor appear out of thin air.

"What … what manner of … *haying wagon* is this?"

"It's *my* manner of hay wagon," she said tersely. "It's called a truck. I need you to wait in the driver's seat like it's your truck. Er, sit *here*." She opened the door, indicating he should get inside. "Listen, you're not in London anymore. Think of this place as … well, it might help if you think of it as the land of … *Faerie*."

That caught his attention. "Mean you that we have been stolen thence? Or … *hence*, rather?"

She didn't really know her *thence*'s from her *hence*'s, but she nodded anyway. "The problem is that you don't belong here. In fact, you're in danger here. Lots of danger. Extra danger dressed like that. Please, get in my truck!"

Edmund balked, standing his ground with his arms crossed over his broad chest. "I am not afraid."

Halley rolled her eyes to the sky and then closed them tight, counting to three. Edmund didn't like being bossed around. Fine. When she opened her eyes, she pleaded.

"I'm begging you to get in my truck. I am going to be in so much trouble if that man in the basement notices you here."

Edmund's brow furrowed. He dropped his crossed arms and submitted to sitting inside the cab of her truck. He didn't look happy about it, though, as he adjusted the sword hanging at his side.

"Next, and this is really important," she said, "I need you to take off your doublet. And ... all the rest of it. Put this on instead."

She shoved her oversized pajama tee-shirt into his hands and tossed the baggy shorts she wore as pajama bottoms onto the bench seat. "Put those on, too. These clothes will help you look like you belong here."

Edmund stared at the garments and then returned his gaze to Halley. His jaw tightened. He looked like some sort of Norse god. A pissed-off Norse god.

"I will do neither," said Edmund. "Until thou explain'st thyself further."

Halley swore under her breath. "The man you saw appear out of nowhere?"

Edmund gave a quick nod of comprehension.

"He's like a powerful, um, magician. Got it?"

"Mean'st thou he practiceth sorcery?"

"In a manner of speaking. If you want to see your brother again, I need you to sit quietly in the truck wearing this shirt and these shorts until I'm done speaking with him." She glanced behind to see if the professor had appeared yet, but the grounds remained

69

empty.

"Mistress, I am armed." One of Edmund's hand strayed to the sword at his left hip.

"No! Definitely no swords. Swords would make things so much worse."

"Odsbodikins! I assure you I am able to defend both myself and thee—"

"I don't need protecting!" snapped Halley. Then she reconsidered. The only time he'd agreed to do what she said was when she explained she would be in danger if he refused. Maybe she could twist his overdeveloped sense of chivalry to her advantage.

More gently, she added, "Actually, if you want to protect me, you can do that by staying in my truck and waiting for me to finish up. If you draw the, uh, magician's attention, it would seriously endanger me."

Edmund seemed to be grinding his teeth together. At last he spoke.

"I shall remain herein so long as it seemeth advisable to me."

"Please—just stay. And change clothes."

After a brief disapproving glare, Edmund began removing his doublet.

Closing the pickup door, Halley considered her next course of action. She needed to look ... *unsuspicious*. Should she be hanging out at the pool with a magazine? Yes—that was good. That was unsuspicious. Did she have any magazines? Did the guesthouse have any?

But then she remembered the earthquake. She was the *de facto* house-sitter. She shouldn't be lounging poolside—she should be checking the property, as she had been doing prior to her unintentional visit to the

16th century.

She reached into her pocket and, hands still shaking, grabbed the notebook and pen meant to record her sales at the Art Show, which now seemed eons ago. It took her several tries to convince the pen to write. By the time she'd succeeded, her hand had at least stopped shaking. She glanced back to her truck. Edmund was now dressed as a member of the 21st century. More or less. Halley's eyes narrowed as she observed him. There was still something … *off* about Edmund, but at a casual glance he looked like a boy sitting in her truck, waiting for her. Like a boyfriend who had driven over to make sure she was okay after the earthquake.

"You *wish*," she muttered to herself. Turning, she commenced note-taking on the property, trying her best to look "unsuspicious."

A tall, narrow, planted urn had tipped over and cracked, spilling dark earth over a pale sanded pathway. Halley noted this on paper just as a palm branch clattered to the ground, joining a makeshift dead-palm-branch graveyard. There were downed eucalyptus limbs, too, awkwardly sprawled across the formal rose bushes. She noted these and continued moving through the grounds, never out of view of the main house, an eye continually darting back to her truck to make sure Edmund stayed put.

After ten minutes had passed, Halley began to wonder whether the professor was coming out of the house at all. Maybe he was off to another century to steal some crown jewels. Would she even notice the whine of the machine from here? Biting her lip, she continued taking notes.

After a few more minutes passed, however, the professor emerged into view, wearing not his "travel" costume, but ordinary clothing.

Halley's heart beat faster as she waited for the professor to notice her. She was just finishing a note about a broken climbing-rose trellis when his voice boomed across the garden.

"Well, well, well," said the professor, striding boldly towards her, hand outstretched. "You must be Inga's daughter Halley."

Halley, noting with relief that Edmund was out of the professor's line of sight, shifted her notepad to her left hand and shook. "That's me," she said.

"Dr. Jules Kahn," said the professor. "I got the message about Inga being called away to take care of her mother."

Halley's teeth clenched slightly. *Called away to care for her mother?* Halley's grandmother had never been to the United States, not to mention she had died in Denmark just before Halley's birth. Halley was so sick of her mother's little lies meant to excuse self-interested behavior.

"I hope your grandmother is feeling better?" At this point, the professor became distracted by the overturned urn. "Goodness. What happened here?"

"There was an earthquake. Maybe half an hour ago. Maybe longer, actually. I'm not sure. It was centered in Santa Ynez." With a possibly unwise curiosity, she added, "You didn't notice it?"

"I must've been driving," he said, smiling and unperturbed. "That would have been shortly after I landed and retrieved my vehicle."

His excuse was plausible on two counts. First,

from inside a moving vehicle, earthquakes weren't always distinguishable from simply hitting a bump or two, and second, his garage was located at a distance from the house by the back entrance. She wouldn't have been able to see or hear him approach.

Nodding as though she swallowed his lies, Halley indicated her notepad. "I've been taking notes on the property. It looks like only minor damage, from what I can tell."

"Mm-hmm." The professor nodded and then frowned. He glanced casually at the top page of notes.

Halley felt her stomach clenching. She wanted to clutch her ring, but she was afraid the nervous gesture would arouse the professor's suspicion, so instead she just stood there, trying to look ... *unsuspicious.*

After a moment he held out a hand for the notebook and casually perused it.

"Lucky for me that you were here," murmured the professor. "Your mother indicated there were some difficulties, and I thought you weren't coming."

Halley felt a flare of indignation. Not coming? Her mother hadn't told *her* that the house-sitting was optional, and *now* look what had happened. Halley swallowed bile.

The professor continued flipping through the pages, but Halley didn't think he was really reading the notebook. Or rather, she had an uneasy feeling he was reading *her*, that he was waiting for her to simply blurt everything out.

Before she could stop herself, she began talking again, a little too fast. "There was a hiccup in the electrical power—I was out at the pool when the quake hit and the pool clock re-set itself to twelve o'clock, but the power can't have been out for more than a few seconds. Basically, by the time the ground stopped shaking, the lights inside were on again. There were some alarms I had to fix. And I went to the breaker boxes and re-set all the switches, just to be sure." She paused. "It was really disorienting. The earthquake and the alarms and … the whole thing."

She stopped herself. She'd said enough. Maybe too much.

"Hmm," said the professor, looking up at last. "It's a funny old place. The generator probably kicked on, if the power went out. There's a Cold War era bomb shelter under the guest wing of the main house, if you can believe it. It's a miracle the generator still functions. It makes an ungodly racket."

Her heart thumped wildly. He was making excuses for the sounds in the basement—the screaming engines that had brought him back. He seemed to be awaiting her response.

"Yeah. I, uh, might have heard something like that."

"Lucky you were here," he said again. Then he added, "So … unexpectedly."

She glanced nervously to check on Edmund. The truck door was opened. She hadn't noticed when he'd opened it. Now she could only hope he didn't decide to shut it. The noise would definitely draw attention to him.

"Anyway," said Halley, "I don't hear anything unusual now."

The professor used the toe of his shoe to nudge a river rock that had rolled from its place in the garden.

"The whole experience must have been extremely

unnerving," he said at last. "Did you notice anything else you want to tell me about?"

Halley let the question hang in the hot, still air. After risking a brief glance back to the truck, she spoke again. "It all happened so fast. I wish I could be more helpful."

"On the contrary," said the professor. "You've handled the situation quite ... *professionally*. I'm sure your mother will be very proud."

Halley was sure it wouldn't cross her mother's mind.

With uncanny insight, the professor added, "When I see her in ten days I'll be sure to mention to your mother how pleased I was with your efforts today."

Halley managed a small smile. And then she tried to ask as casually as possible, "Is she house-sitting for you again?" As she awaited the response, her heart beat a rapid tattoo.

"Yes. Summers are supposed to be relaxing, but I seem to be putting out one fire after another. Just ten days till I'm off and running again." He gave her a smile that didn't quite reach his eyes.

Ten days ... *Ten days!*

In ten days she could get Edmund back where he belonged.

She nodded. "Okay. See you then—I mean ... uh, I won't see you then. I mostly stay at the apartment when Mom works." She was babbling. "So, um, goodbye."

He held out a hand and shook, rather more aggressively than Halley would have expected for so compact a man.

"Oh, and one more thing ..." The professor broke off.

Halley waited while he patted his coat pockets. Smiling, he withdrew a pen from his shirt pocket and scribbled something onto a corner of notebook paper before tearing it off and giving it to Halley.

"My personal number. Call me if you should remember anything else regarding the earthquake. You may find other memories returning later. An earthquake can provide quite a shock to the system." He smiled broadly, patting her nearest shoulder. The back of her neck prickled; his hand felt heavy and possibly dangerous.

"Yeah. It was a shock," she murmured. "Super shocking." She had just remembered to ask the professor for a check when she saw something even more shocking.

Edmund, having exited the truck some fifty feet behind the professor, was now approaching them with a knife in one hand.

## 9

### · *EDMUND* ·

Edmund had been alarmed to see Halley engaging in conversation with the magician. He had vowed to do his best to remain in the strange wagon, but the circumstances were trying his patience. He remained only because he wished to bring no misfortune upon her family, as she had said might happen should the magician notice him.

But when the sorcerer grasped Halley by the hand, Edmund reached for his sword. Halley resisted the grappling, swiftly pulling her hand free, unharmed and seemingly unafraid. Had it been no more than a taking of hands? But for what purpose? Those who greeted one another as friends ought to bow and kiss, as was customary. Edmund hesitated, his right hand on his sword, his left resting on the odd door handle he'd seen Halley use.

Halley seemed safe for the moment. And yet, she was but a girl in physical strength. Had she perhaps her own magic? It was clear she had been a visitor to the realm of Faerie often enough to know its rules and dangers. She had not been at all surprised to find herself in this place of hunched oaks and pole-trees, daub and brick and window-glass so clear as to appear invisible.

And as for the *wagon* in which he was seated? She had called it her own. It was a thing of great mystery wherein he saw nothing familiar but his own discarded garments. He frowned at the odd breeches the girl had asked him to wear, which he had not yet put on. If he were to need suddenly to leave the wagon, he ought, perhaps to don the breeches. The strange tunic, he had already put on. Well, if the girl believed it would be dangerous for him to be seen in his own apparel ...

His mind decided, he unlaced his upper stocks, sliding off his hose and boots as well. It was infernally hot in this realm. Grasping the strange breeches, he pulled them on over his *braies*, preferring his *own* undergarment alone should touch his skin, the channel by which miasmas and all manner of illness entered the body.

Once the change of weeds was effected, Edmund focused again upon the girl and the magician.

The language of the older man's body whispered much to Edmund's experienced eye. The man feared the girl, or feared some power she might have over him. Edmund watched the magician's hand clenching and unclenching behind his back and felt suddenly sure the magician meant some harm to the girl. He felt equally sure this was the sort of man to be frighted into a peace if outnumbered or out-weaponed, and by the rood, he should like to prove it.

The magician grasped the girl's hand again and then placed a restraining hand on her shoulder. It was too much. Edmund reached for his sword, then recalled Halley had forbidden him the use of the weapon. Could the magician perhaps charm Edmund's sword against him? Cursing, he cast about his discarded garments seeking a small folded blood-letting knife. She had not forbad *that*. Finding it, he unclasped the knife, and, holding it at the ready, he stepped from the wagon.

# 10

## · HALLEY ·

Halley stared in horror as Edmund, now barefoot and dressed in her "pajamas," moved purposefully toward her. As he walked, he tossed a knife, tip over handle. *Toss. Catch. Toss. Catch.* He never glanced at the knife, but he caught it by the handle every time. He looked threatening as all hell. She had to diffuse the situation, and fast.

"*Min Kæreste,*" she called to Edmund: *my sweetheart.* She ran to stop him from getting any closer. "He's Danish," she called over her shoulder to the professor. "Speaks no English."

She stood on tiptoe to plant a kiss on Edmund's cheek, murmuring, "Don't even *think* about using that knife. And whatever you do, *don't speak.*"

The professor, meanwhile, had bent over and picked up the river rock at his feet. It was a casual motion. It might have meant nothing.

"He did grapple with thee," Edmund murmured softly. His breath ruffled the hair beside her ear.

"He *what?*"

Halley steered him back towards her truck. To her great relief, he didn't fight her.

"He restrained thee," replied Edmund. "Twice by the hand and then by the shoulder."

Halley was bewildered for a moment but then rolled her eyes.

"Those were handshakes. *Handshakes*, you know—" She broke off. Maybe he didn't know. "I'll explain later. Things are fine. Everything's fine. Trust me. And get back in the truck. We're leaving in a minute."

She swung the passenger door open.

Edmund glowered.

The professor was now shifting his rock from one hand to the other, face unperturbed.

Edmund, eyes on the professor, leaned against the passenger seat, occupying himself with clasping and unclasping a hinge so that the knife folded in half and then snapped back open. The professor's mouth produced a rather artificial smile.

"Just *wait here*," Halley ordered Edmund. Turning, she strode back toward Khan.

"So, um, my boyfriend got a text and we have to run. If you could maybe mail Mom's check?"

The professor ceased passing the rock from hand to hand, but he held it tight in his grasp as he stared at Edmund. Faint hostility rippled in the heavy air. Was the professor suspicious of Edmund?

"Yes, of course," said the professor at last. "I'll mail it."

Halley took the notebook back and scribbled her address down. "Okay. That's where we live. Send the check there."

Examining the address, he murmured, "I'll have it out right away."

"Thanks."

Halley dashed back to her truck, entering on the driver's side. She didn't care how odd it looked that she was driving her "boyfriend's" truck. She just wanted to get out of there. Now. Before Edmund gave the professor any reason to suspect he didn't belong in this century.

Sticking the keys in the ignition, she murmured, "Try not to react. This is going to be a little noisy."

# 11

## · KHAN ·

Back in his basement, the professor stared at the navigation panel of his temporal singularity device, struck by the uneasy feeling that something was not right. His gaze rested upon a picture in his retrievals catalog. It was, in fact, a picture of his first retrieval— his Gutenberg Bible. Head tipped to the side, he tugged at his goatee. Had he left his retrievals catalog open to this page? He couldn't recall with certainty. The last time he could remember doing anything with the catalog was over a week ago, when he had been meaning to insert another ten or twelve pictures. They lay nearby, scattered across his desk. He was woefully behind in cataloging his retrievals.

"A day late and a dollar short," he muttered. It was spoken ironically. If anyone had less reason to run short of time or money, he would like to meet them.

He flipped the catalog to the empty pages at the back. It was perhaps foolish to produce so tangible a record of his handiwork, but it helped him to keep track of what he had already sold, and to whom. It was a thoroughness demanded by his scientific mind, this tracking of interactions with those who alchemized his treasures into dollars and yen, pounds and dirhams.

He frowned. Had he really left the catalog like that?

Again, suspicion stirred within him. Was it possible someone had been down here? The girl? Or the girl's mother? His heart suddenly hammering, he strode to his desk and opened a program on his computer designed to record the activity of the temporal device.

The tracking program showed that a complete system re-boot had occurred forty-six minutes earlier, following a brief power outage. A re-boot? That was interesting.... And fortunate. Without the singularity device, his return journey would have been potentially disastrous.

An unpleasant thrill trailed along the professor's spine.

The machine's original inventor, Dr. Littlewood, had likely made copious notes pertaining to emergency protocols, but Khan had not been able to recover these notes. He'd barely been able to steal the designs for Littlewood's failsafe program. For obvious reasons, Khan had never tested the failsafe. Well, until today—*unintentionally*. He hadn't even been clear what the failsafe would do in an actual emergency. Would it forcibly re-instate travel in progress or re-initiate travel from the last setting?

He had his answer here in today's records: the failsafe had done *both*, covering all contingencies. How very like Dr. Littlewood to cover all contingencies. Khan smiled, recalling Littlewood's hyper-caution. It was a miracle the man had ever tested his own invention.

Khan sighed. Sometimes he wished he had Littlewood as a partner. But a partner introduced all sorts of messy complications, and the professor hated messy complications.

He patted the podium affectionately. Computers might be complicated, but they were never messy. In any case, the fact that the program had successfully re-booted indicated that either (*a*) the failsafe had worked or (*b*) the failsafe had been unnecessary to begin with. And regardless of which was true, there was *still* no evidence that anyone had tampered with his equipment.

Other than the retrievals catalog being opened to the wrong page.

The professor drummed his long fingers on his desk.

He was being paranoid. He must have shifted the pages himself. He knew he could be absent-minded at times, although he preferred to label it "distractible." "Absent-minded professor" gave the wrong impression.

Not that labels should bother someone like him. He was the greatest explorer since Magellan. More intrepid than Scott. More important than Neil Armstrong. And someday, naturally *after* he shuffled off this mortal coil, the world would know he had blazed the trail of temporal exploration.

"*Après moi, le deluge,*" the professor murmured, quoting a king whose miniature portrait had been his first sale. After the professor was dead and gone and mankind harnessed the temporal singularity, all hell could break loose, for all he cared. And it probably would.

Meanwhile, however, he must guard his work from outside ... *attention*. Just to be safe, he searched the past six days' security records, looking for evidence of a physical break-in to his sacred basement. He saw nothing unexpected until he reached the current day's records. Forty-nine minutes ago, the basement door seal had been breached. He checked the US Geological Survey records, discovering the Santa Ynez-based quake had, in fact, occurred forty-nine minutes and twenty-one seconds earlier. This meant the breach, and presumably the brief power outage, had happened three minutes prior to the computer program's re-boot. Three minutes wasn't an unreasonable amount of time for such a complex system to come back to full functionality.

But the door ... the *door*.

He cursed himself for not fixing the door a month ago when he'd noticed the latch mechanism was faulty. His neglect might prove to be costly. And messy.

The professor stared into space, thinking the situation through logically. The door seal had been breached in concert with the earthquake. It seemed highly unlikely the girl had decided to snoop and succeeded in unlocking the door at the precise moment an earthquake had struck. The odds against such would be astronomical. So the earthquake, and not the girl, must have been responsible for the door-seal breach.

But had she, upon noticing the door was already opened, snuck inside and examined his retrievals catalog? The door was sealed *now*, which meant someone must have closed it. It was suspicious the girl hadn't mentioned having closed the basement door. He flipped through her notes on the property. Ah— no, he was mistaken. There it was, her confession: *17) Basement door lock apparently disabled due to earthquake or brief power loss? I closed it again, which locked it.*

So she *had* been down the stairs. That much looked certain.

The only question that remained, then, was this: *had she entered the basement?*

# 12

## · HALLEY ·

Back when Halley turned ten, her mother had taken a month-long job at an estate with a pair of six-month-old Greyhounds. The pups had been intelligent, affectionate, and ... *reserved*, at least in Halley's opinion. Alert and curious about everything, they'd also been quiet, observing strange sights, sounds, and smells rather than barking at them.

Having Edmund in her truck right now was like having one of those Greyhounds along for the ride. From the initial roar of the truck engine to the opening of the automatic gate, everything plainly startled Edmund, but he made no sounds to indicate shock. He just held himself in ready alertness, exactly like those pups.

Was it only this morning that making a favorable impression on Ethyl Meier had been the gravest of Halley's concerns? Now she had to figure out how to entertain—or maybe just *con*tain—a sword- and knife-wielding member of a different era for the next ten days. At which point she would have to figure out how to break into a Cold War era bomb shelter and return him where he belonged.

What was she going to do with Edmund for ten days? *Ten days.*

Halley took a curve too fast. She wasn't paying attention. She wasn't even sure where she was heading, let alone what to do with Edmund. With regard to her heading, however, her hand was shortly forced. Around the next curve, a palm was draped inelegantly across the road, presumably a victim of the quake.

"Fantastic," she muttered.

Halley could think of three or four alternate routes to circumvent the palm tree blockage, but really, what she needed was to stop and *think*. So, instead of turning around, Halley pulled the truck to the side of the road and killed the engine. Edmund startled but again, he made no sound.

"So here's the thing," Halley said, facing her inadvertent tag-along. "I need to coach you a little on life here, because it's going to take awhile to get you back where you belong."

"This, then, is the road to London?" asked Edmund. He leaned forward as if to size up the tree blocking the road. "Had I the use of an axe...."

"The tree in the road is not the problem."

"If this be the road to London—"

"It's not. This road does *not* go to London."

Edmund frowned. "Mistress—er, Halley, I must return forthwith. Wherefore travel we this road if it be not the road to London?"

Groaning, Halley collapsed her head onto the steering wheel. She tried to calm her rising sense of panic. What was she doing? What was she supposed to do? She had a man from the sixteenth century in her truck!

"I needed to get you away from there," Halley said, head still collapsed forward.

"Halley, what place is this?"

Halley ground her forehead into the steering wheel and muttered, "Give me a minute."

She had to make a choice. She could tell Edmund the truth. Or she could continue the ruse of "Faerie Land", which Edmund seemed ready to accept. Apparently her Shakespeare class teacher had been right about educated Elizabethans accepting the existence of fairies as readily as they accepted the existence of cats and dogs. But Edmund was going to be with her for ten days. *Ten days*. Really, there was no choice. He was going to need to know the truth.

As she raised her head, her phone buzzed in her pocket. Edmund looked at her pocket with curiosity.

"Text message," she said. "It's, um, a way to dispatch messages. Minus the horse and rider. Like, a messenger that travels through the air. Invisibly."

Edmund looked puzzled by her explanation, but at least he wasn't holding up a silver cross to ward off her witch-y ways. He was just taking it all in, like those Greyhounds.

Her phone buzzed again.

"Your ... *messenger* persists," said Edmund.

Cursing softly, Halley withdrew her phone from her pocket. It was DaVinci.

*U ok from the earthquake? Super freaky! And you totally called it! Anyway, the show monitors are letting vendors leave if they want.*

*We. Want.*

*Branson can't get us bc the Applegate's driveway is blocked with a tree down.*

*Can you come get us? I want to make sure my family is okay. I haven't been able to reach them. Jillian tried calling a cab, but we can't get through to them either, and we have all this crap to haul. Pleeeeeease?*

Halley's jaw clenched. She had to help. Of course she had to help. She took a deep breath and turned to Edmund.

"My best friends need my help. But before you meet them, there are a few things you should know."

# 13

## · EDMUND ·

During the past half-hour, Edmund had concluded that his fair companion was most probably an enchantress. Fearless, she was; her beauty, otherworldly. And careless of displaying her limbs as well: he'd caught tantalizing glimpses of her calves and thighs. Her skin was everywhere the same warm fawn color of his best gloves. Beside her, he felt daub-colored, winter pale though it was high summer.

She was surely fey. She commanded a beast hidden within the cavern of her wagon—her *truck*—compelling it to go and to halt, he knew not how. And if he understood her aright, she received messages through the air, though he heard no speech—only a buzzing sound, as of bees. Surely she was an enchantress of this, the land of Faerie.

No sooner had he reached this conclusion than the words of the wise woman bent over his cradle came back to him.

*One day shalt thou travel far,*
*Thy family's fortunes to restore.*

His eyes grew wide. This must be the "traveling far" spoken of by the wise woman. His heart began to race. He was so accustomed to the prophetic words, they had lost their impact, like a word spoke over and over till it seemed void of meaning. But to live to see the words come true? He felt laughter welling inside. But just as quickly as glee possessed him, he felt his bones chilling. If he was truly a captive in the land of Faerie, how was he to return to his own land? His chest tightening, he fixed his eyes on his captor.

He must resist her enchantments. He must keep his head clear so as to return safely home. The fate of his family—nay, that of the estate and all its dependents—lay in the balance. The sword at his side comforted him, but if he was in the power of an enchantress, would it protect him? He uttered a silent prayer for aid.

Mistress Halley, meanwhile, was gazing at the source of the buzzing noise—a flat, narrow device the size of a playing card. Repeatedly, she stroked the magical, glowing item. This seemed to calm her. Then, clearing her throat, she placed the device into a concealed pocket and raised her enchanting eyes to meet his.

"There are a few things you should know." She dropped her gaze once more. Her eyes were shaded by thick lashes, her brows finely arched and black as deep water. Had he the use of pen and ink ...

"There are a few things I need to explain," she added.

"Indeed, lady." By his reckoning, there were more than a few.

"First of all, you're not actually in the, er, *Faerie*

*Kingdom,*" she said. Her cheeks and lips seemed to redden with the confession.

If this was not Faerie, what manner of land was it? Edmund's brows pulled together. Either she spoke with deceit now or she had done so earlier. Which was it?

"I'm sorry I lied," she said, forestalling his questions. "I mean, I didn't want to lie to you. I *don't* want to lie to you. It was more like I just said the first thing I thought of. Well, the first thing that would help you understand you weren't in Kansas anymore. I mean, well, *London.*" She exhaled heavily, as one annoyed might do. "Listen, a lot of my world will seem ... *magical* to you. But it's not magic. This is just the normal world."

Edmund's frown deepened. "This is *not* the common world, mistress. No more than thou art a common maiden."

"It's normal for me, I mean. And for everyone else living now." Her red lips pursed as if in frustration.

Swallowing hard, Edmund removed his gaze from those lips. He felt her charms work upon him as surely as the midwife's cures worked upon sickness. Perhaps he was in a dream and would awaken as soon as ever the roost cock did crow.

"Let me start over," she said. "What's the most complicated machine you know of?"

Warily, he answered her. "I have ne'er heard tell of a ... *complicatette* machine. Mean you the sort of engines they do use in playhouses to lower and raise the gods to the heavens?"

"Um, yes. Sort of. Forget I said complicated. Just tell me about the machines where you live. Do you have a mill-wheel?"

"Aye. We use it to mill grain by power of the stream which turneth the millstones."

"Perfect!" Halley clapped her hands together. Edmund observed how unmarred her hands were, neither chapped nor chafed by rough use. The hands of a lady with many servants.

"Okay, so you understand how the power of water is harnessed."

"I have never before thought to speak of it as 'harnessed.'"

"But you get what I mean, right? You understand how the mill uses water for power?"

"Aye."

"So, where you live, you harness power from horses and from water? Right?"

"Aye, and from oxen."

"Right. Oxen. Well, where I live, we harness *different* things for power."

"Mistress, mean'st thou … *magic*?"

"No. I don't mean magic. What we do might *look* like magic to you, but it's not."

Edmund nodded. Surely an enchantress would boast of her power and not deny it.

"Basically," continued Halley, "We harness different things besides horses or water to provide power to get jobs done. Primarily we use something we call *electricity*. It's like the lightning that flashes in the sky. We harness it, and we use it to power all kinds of things. My phone, for instance." Halley withdrew the narrow box from her pocket. "Having servants to deliver messages is expensive," she said.

Edmund nodded. Thus much he understood.

Servants were an expensive responsibility.

"It's the same with horses and oxen," said Halley. "They're too expensive for ordinary people. Using electricity is cheap, so we have made a bazillion kinds of machines that do things for us using electricity."

Edmund felt the stirrings of comprehension. "Doth thy … *truck* harness such power?"

"Sort of," said Halley. "The truck runs on gasoline, not electricity."

At this point, Halley threw her head back against the seat and observed the ceiling. A heavy sigh escaped her throat, which was now stretched and exposed. Edmund felt again the yearning to draw her so that the world might know of her perfections.

So softly as to be almost imperceptible, Halley murmured, "Explaining my world to you is going to be impossible."

Edmund smiled. "Lady, the impossible is merely that we have not yet known to be possible."

She smiled back. It was a melancholic sort of smile. "I guess."

Edmund was unsure the precise moments wherein Halley had gone from *wench* to *mistress* and thence to *lady*, but the appellation suited her.

"May I ask, lady," began Edmund, "How I might return me to London?"

No sooner had he asked, than the great lady did frown, cover her face, and utter forth an astonishing series of strong oaths.

# 14

## · *HALLEY* ·

One rainy day in sixth grade, DaVinci had entertained Jillian and Halley by reading aloud the dictionary definitions of all the naughty words the girls knew. They had been shocked, and a little disappointed, to find how old the worst words were. (The Romans in particular had a lot to answer for.) Which meant that Edmund, seated beside her in the truck, probably knew every last one of those swear words.

Halley was on the point of apologizing when Edmund began to laugh. This, in turn, made Halley laugh, which made Edmund laugh harder, and soon neither of them could stop laughing. When laughing, Edmund went from handsome to gorgeous. After a minute or two, Halley struggled to catch her breath. A shiver ran through her.

She wanted to sit and stare at Edmund all day.

She wanted to take his picture.

She wanted to keep him.

She looked away.

"Lady," said Edmund, his laughter abating with

hers, "In truth, I feared this was not the road to London. Might I offer a suggestion? Within the magician's subterranean chamber I believe we might discover the way to return to London from hence."

Halley raised both eyebrows. He was a quick study. "Um, yeah. That's pretty much my plan, but how did you figure that out?"

Her phone buzzed. She ignored it.

"It was unto that place we were first transported," Edmund replied, matter-of-factly. "And in that same place did we observe the magician appear. Is it not rational to conclude some engine of *electricette* doth work to call and send those who can wield its power?"

Edmund was ... *smart*. She wasn't sure why this surprised her. Should it not surprise her? Really, why shouldn't people from another century have been smart?

"You're right," she replied, nodding slowly. "*Electricity* powers the, uh, 'engine.' Possibly with a side of quantum physics."

"Very well. When the sky hath blackened with night, I shall determine how heavily guarded the chamber may be."

"No. I don't think that would be safe. I don't trust the professor. It's too dangerous to go there while he's home. However, ten days from now, he'll be gone. We'll have a chance to send you back then."

Her phone buzzed again. "Oh good grief," she muttered, reading the message.

*Halley? You okay? Can you come get us?*

Quickly, she responded.

*Gimme half an hour. Some trees are down here, too.*

"More messages from thy friends?"

"Yes. I have to drive down to the beach and help them pack up a booth. They're at an Art Show. It's sort of like a Renaissance Faire. Do you have those? Never mind. Of course you don't have Ren-Faires. You're *from* the freaking renaissance."

"We have fairs, lady."

"Oh. Okay. So I have to pick up my friends and all the stuff they were trying to sell at a faire."

"Traveled your friends from far distant lands as well?"

"Um, no. They live here."

Edmund nodded.

"Which brings me to my next point. There's something else I have to tell you. You and I weren't just transported out of England."

"Indeed?"

Halley took a deep breath. "We were transported to a different time."

"I understand you not."

"What year were you born?"

"In the year of our Lord fifteen hundred and seventy-seven."

Halley did some quick math, rounding off a little. "I was born four hundred twenty years after you. We're in *my* time now, not yours. So, yeah. Edmund Aldwych, welcome to the twenty-first century."

## 15

## · *EDMUND* ·

Edmund heard not one word in three for several minutes after that. A wholly different *time*? It was impossible. Reason demanded its impossibility. Time was no river, that mankind might wade upstream and down at will. Was Halley mad, then? Or ... was he?

He placed a hand over his heart. His pulse was temperate. Nor did he feel the fever of a maddened brain. He was perfectly well. Halley, too, spoke as one possessed of her wits. And as for dreaming, no dream of his had ever such a likeness to life.

If what she spoke were true, however, it would explain much. His tutor had once remarked that had they lived four hundred years in the past, they would have known neither pistols nor portable clocks, have tasted neither cinnamon nor pepper. The world of the future would, therefore, contain things a man might find wondrous—and baffling. Halley's explanation had the scent of truth.

But, four hundred years? That would mean ...

It meant everyone he knew was dead.

His breath caught in his throat. His family and household weren't worried about him, or wondering where he was. They were all ... *dead*. Long dead.

"You okay?" asked Halley.

Not understanding her, he made no response.

She added, "*Okay* means, feeling better than unwell, even if you aren't feeling ... *well*."

"I am *oak-ay*," Edmund said dully.

Four hundred years? It was no marvel he could not understand all the lady said.

"How is it I am yet alive?" he asked. "Ought I not to have become dry bones as I journeyed forward to thy time?"

Halley shrugged. "I don't know how it works. Or why."

"That is cold comfort, lady."

"But it brings me to another point," said Halley. "My friends can't know you're ... not from here. Time travel isn't normal. Even in the twenty-first century. No one I know will believe it's possible. I know I wouldn't. So, anyway, it would be simplest if you pretended you belonged in this century. We could say you're an actor, studying for a part."

The suggestion was as profoundly insulting this time as it had been the first time she'd called him a performer, inside the London theatre. He drew himself up stiffly.

"I am no actor."

"Truly, no offense intended. I've heard actors got a bad rap back in your time, but nowadays, actors are like rock stars."

Edmund raised an eyebrow.

"I mean, actors are like ... like *royalty*. Movie

actors, especially. And if you pretend to be one, it'll explain all the weird language. All the thee's and thou's."

This was a concern that had troubled him. "I have noted thou dost employ neither."

"No. No one here does. You're just going to have to trust me that my friends will excuse a lot of strange speech and odd behavior if I tell them you're preparing for an acting role. Otherwise, the language thing is going to make you sound crazy. Not to mention it's confusing."

Edmund paused before answering. Her request was not unreasonable. After a moment he smiled.

"We seem indeed to be sundered by our common speech."

"Sundered?"

"It denoteth separation or division."

Halley laughed. "You can say that again."

Edmund paused and then complied. "It denoteth separation or division."

Halley laughed with greater enthusiasm. Her laughter was such stuff as summer days were made on.

"I didn't mean literally, *say that again*," explained Halley. "It's a saying: *You can say that again* means, *I agree strongly*."

"Ah," said Edmund. "I do comprehend thee."

"Okay. I'm going to drive us to my friends. Just remember: you're an actor."

"Art thou certain this excuse will suffice to explain my ... *differences?*"

Halley laughed. "Actors are a *special* class unto themselves."

"Thou *art* certain, then."

"Is the pope Catholic?"

"I am no papist, madam," he said, caution coloring his voice. He was not given to popery, but like most Englishmen, his grandfather had been once. Was it an executable offense here as well?

"Sorry," said Halley. "*Is the pope Catholic* is just a saying. It means 'duh.' Um, I mean ... You know what? Never mind."

After Halley commanded the truck to advance, Edmund was silent for several minutes, thinking of all she had spoken. Ten days. He was a captive in this wondrous land, for ten days. Every curve in the road revealed new marvels: wagons the size of cottages, hung about with giant claws and shovels and endeavoring to move fallen trees; persons traveling upon conveyances with but two spoked wheels; great halls closely set beside another. How, Edmund wondered, should the lords of such halls graze their sheep, their cattle, their horses, upon lands of such small portion?

Edmund had questions, questions, *questions*. But as they rounded a curve of road, revealing a new prospect, all his questions fell away.

"The sea," he murmured, caressing the word as though confessing the name of a lover.

"The Pacific Ocean," said Halley.

"The *Pacificum*," whispered Edmund, enchanted. "Is this an island of those waters?"

"No. California's still firmly attached to the United States. Oh. You've never heard of the United States. I guess you'd call this America?"

Edmund raised an eyebrow.

"Hmm," said Halley. "Maybe that name didn't

exist for you either. Oh. I remember. This is what you call the 'New World'."

The New World? It was every man's dream, every boy's ambition. Suddenly, Edmund couldn't remember how to breathe.

## 16

### · *HALLEY* ·

Halley wasn't sure if she should be worried about it, but Edmund hadn't said a thing since she'd spoken the words *New World*. He was staring at everything as though he wanted to memorize each detail. He stared at the power lines overhead. He stared at oncoming vehicles. He stared at the bikini-and-board-short clad volleyball players at East Beach.

As Halley pulled the truck into a prized parallel parking spot on Cabrillo Boulevard, she decided a little explanation was in order regarding ... *fashion*.

"People dress like that now," she said, indicating the girls in bikinis. "At the beach, anyway. Don't stare, okay?"

Edmund removed his gaze from the girls, murmuring he had read of the strange costuming habit of the noble savages that ruled the New World.

Halley cringed. "Do *not* call people 'noble savages.'"

"Are they not noble? What am I to call them?"

"People. We're all just ... *people*."

"Just people."

"Edmund? I'm going to be honest. The less talking you do, the better."

He inclined his head in a bow.

"Oh, boy. And no bowing. No bowing, no talking, no knifes, and *definitely*—" Halley leaned down to make sure Edmund's sword was covered by his discarded clothing—"Definitely no swords."

She shook her head at the impossible turn her morning had taken. And then she grabbed a ratty beach blanket from under the bench seat and bundled it on top of Edmund's clothes and sword. Just in case.

"Okay," she said. "We're getting out here. It's just a short walk."

Edmund tried to move from his seat, but his seatbelt held him in place.

"Oh. Sorry. Let me help you." Halley showed him how to unbuckle. "I guess you already figured out how to open the door," she murmured, shaking her head as she remembered. "I swear, when you stepped out of my truck back at the estate, I thought you were going to stab someone."

"Had it been required, I should have."

"Okay, so seriously? No stabbing. I don't know about sixteenth century London, but if you stab someone in *my* time, you go to prison. And I won't be able to get you out. You'd be stuck here in my time. *Forever.*"

"I understand thee. I shall keep my blade concealed."

Halley, examining Edmund in her pajamas, sighed. "I guess that will do. People wear stranger things on East Beach. Good thing I didn't pack a nightie."

"A 'nightie,' mistress?"

"A dress. And try not to call me 'mistress.' I don't know what that means where you come from, but here it means, uh, a woman you sleep with who isn't your wife."

"I meant no such disrespect, mistress—that is … What am I to call thee?"

Halley rolled her eyes. "Never mind. Just call me whatever."

As they walked down the sidewalk, they passed vendor after vendor in varying stages of packing up for the day. A few were staying, optimistic or desperate enough to stick it out rather than miss a potential sale. One vendor had creatively hung a sign advertising: "*Art Quake Sale! Today Only!*"

When they were a couple of yards away from the booth, Halley stopped and held Edmund back with one hand on his upper abs. Which she noted were steely. *Actually* steely.

"Listen," she said, trying *not* to think about his steely abs. "I think you better wait here a sec while I talk to my friends."

She felt him balk at the suggestion and for a moment she thought he was traipsing down the path of, "*I shall do what seemeth advisable to me*," again, but he merely pressed his lips together and nodded curtly.

Halley still wasn't sure how she was going to explain Edmund, but before she had a chance to do more than touch the ring under her shirt, DaVinci flew towards her, giving her a hug which was equal parts tackle and embrace.

"We're so glad you're safe!" cried DaVinci. "There was a landslide on East Mountain—my family's fine, by the way—and a tree crashed down on Jillian's driveway, and our booth neighbors from Los Olivos are totally stranded because of landslides on 101 *and* San Marcos Pass! It's crazy out there!" DaVinci hugged her again. "I'm *so* glad nothing happened to you."

*Nothing?* Halley had to choke back manic laughter.

But in all seriousness, the closures of two highways leading out of Santa Barbara couldn't have been more fortuitous, for Halley's purposes. She could use the landslides to explain Edmund's presence.

"Thanks so much for coming to get us," said Jillian, hugging Halley as soon as DaVinci let her go. "Dad's out on the John Deere, trying to move the tree off our drive."

DaVinci rolled her eyes. "More like, he's trying to justify the expense of owning a John Deere in the first place."

Jillian flushed pink.

Halley, who knew something about being embarrassed over a parent, gave Jillian an extra hug, murmuring, "Good for your dad."

"*Halley!*" called DaVinci. For some unfathomable reason, DaVinci was whispering. "*Why is that superb specimen ogling you like a total stalker?*" She jerked her head to indicate Edmund.

Taking a deep breath, Halley gestured to Edmund to come closer.

"So, guys, this is Edmund. He's, um, stranded. He's an actor from Santa Ynez who helped me earlier when I was ... out and about. I fell and he, um, caught me. And then I found out he's sort of stranded—" She broke off, shrugging.

DaVinci was already circling him with a look in her eye that said, *"Hello-can-I-sculpt-you-please-say-yes?"* Halley could hear her muttering *trapezius* and *latissimus dorsi*.

Jillian, who was extremely well-mannered even in the face of handsome strangers wearing what were obviously Halley's pajamas, held out her hand. "I'm Jillian."

*"Take her hand,"* murmured Halley to Edmund.

Having taken Jillian's hand, Edmund executed a bow over it.

"Oh, and there we go with the bowing," Halley said, pointedly addressing Edmund. She turned to her friends. "He's preparing for a role. It's a Shakespearean role."

"Cool," said DaVinci, patently checking out his *gluteus maximus*. "Those are traffic-stopping," she muttered to herself.

"What company are you with?" Jillian asked politely.

"He goes to Allan Hancock," said Halley, improvising. She hoped the small community college had a theatre department. "But he can't really answer questions about school because he's in this, uh, week long challenge to act like an Elizabethan gentleman. With zero breaks. Whatsoever."

"Santa Ynez, huh?" DaVinci whistled. "You're going to be stuck here awhile with those landslides. Do you have any experience posing for life drawing? I'd love to sketch you."

"He's not taking his clothes off for you," murmured Halley.

DaVinci shrugged. "The clothes can stay on." She

109

peered more closely at "the clothes." And then she emitted a snorting laugh. "Oh. *Oh my gosh*. The clothes. Halley, are those your pj's?"

"He was wearing a valuable costume when he was … stranded. And he has to protect the costume. So, yeah. I gave him what I had with me." It was unnerving how easily she could lie to her friends. She was behaving like her mother. She brushed the thought aside.

"You poor thing," Jillian said, smiling sadly at Edmund. Her phone pinged and she shaded the screen to read the message. "Oh, super! Look at my dad."

She held up a picture of her father looking very pleased with himself, standing in front of a John Deere while wearing a pinpoint shirt and tie.

DaVinci, rolling her eyes, grabbed a stack of nested boxes from under a small draped table and started wrapping and boxing Jillian's sculptures.

"There was a fallen tree limb across our driveway," Jillian explained to Edmund. "And my dad moved it off all by himself! How about we all head over to my house once we're packed up, okay? Edmund, I'm sure I can find *real* clothes for you. We can lounge by the pool and eat gelato to recover from our Arts and Quakes debacle."

DaVinci looked up from the boxes and inhaled sharply. "Debacle? Ha! Tell Halley, Jillian! Tell her, tell her, *tell her!*"

"Oh, right! Oh my gosh, Halley!" Jillian had clasped her hands and was holding them excitedly under her chin. "We waited so we could tell you the good news in person."

DaVinci squealed. "We totally 'ate all the red vines,' or whatever your Danish saying is!"

"It's *op på lakrids*. 'Up on the licorice,'" said Halley. It was a Danish phrase indicating one had been busy or energetic.

"I was close," said DaVinci.

Jillian, shushing DaVinci with a raised eyebrow, explained. "I sold one of your pieces, Halley. I sold *Casual Tomatoes* to a studio lawyer from L.A."

Halley looked at her blankly. Casual tomatoes ... *casual tomatoes?*

"Are we up on our licorice or what?" squealed DaVinci.

"You *sold* my painting—the one with the two red blobs?" asked Halley.

"Blobs?" DaVinci shook her head at Halley. "*Blobs?*"

"I sold it," confirmed Jillian.

Halley's heart thundered in her chest. "For how much?"

Jillian beamed. "Full price, naturally."

"I don't ... I can't ..." Halley paused to breathe. Her heart was a curling wave crashing on sand. "What was the painting marked at?"

"Fifteen thousand," squealed DaVinci. "Well, minus whatever American Express takes."

"Fifteen thousand?" Her heart thundered.

"The most mom's ever spent on a painting is twenty-one thousand," added Jillian, grinning. "I could hardly believe it, but I guess that lawyer really wanted to impress his date!"

"My lady?" said Edmund. He grabbed a small stool from the back of the booth and placed it beside

Halley. "Be seated."

"Yes, sit, sit, sit!" cried DaVinci. "*We* can pack. *You* should kick off your shoes and plan a trip to Europe!"

Jillian rearranged a fruit sculpture in its box. "Or I could help you with investing," she suggested.

"*Sit*, Halley," murmured Edmund.

Halley sat. Her pulse was racing. She wasn't going to Europe. And she wasn't going to invest her earnings. Not in the way Jillian meant. She thought of the tiny paradise snuggled between the Haunted Mansion and the Pirates of the Caribbean. The scent of root beer wafted through her mind. This was her chance. Her future. She could picture it all: working as a costume assistant (and eventually, a designer) in LA, meeting clients at Club 33 for lunch, and someday— *someday*—another meeting with her father. A connection. A spark. A new understanding of who she was and who she could be, free at last from the suffocation of living only as her mother's daughter.

# 17

## · HALLEY ·

Halley, Edmund, Jillian, and DaVinci squished into the cab of Halley's truck and drove to the Applegate's estate, called *Applewood* despite the lack of apple trees or apple tree lumber anywhere on the estate's seventeen acres. On the drive, Jillian settled it that Halley and Edmund would stay the night as her guests: *you'll be no bother at all—the West Wing is empty.*

Shortly after they arrived, Halley's mother sent six or seven texts. It had finally occurred to her to enquire if Halley was okay—*There might have been an earthquake while I was napping, maybe?* Halley considered several responses, but in the end she simply texted her mom she was fine.

DaVinci couldn't stay long at Jillian's. Her family had weathered the quake but not without incident. The 1970's addition over their garage had given up its pretense of structural viability, and after a quick swim and quicker ogle at Branson, DaVinci left for home, borrowing one of the Applegate's Smart cars. (They had two. Mrs. Applegate was serious about doing her part to save the environment.)

Edmund, Halley noted, did a stellar job of not staring at Jillian or herself in their bikinis. Halley had to borrow one of Jillian's with an inordinate number of fabric strips meant to somehow criss-cross her ribcage. *"It's Swedish,"* Jillian had said, shrugging and adjusting three or four straps.

At first Edmund had been unable to settle. In spite of Halley's explanations, he seemed incapable of understanding the appeal of lounging by a pool. After he'd spent half an hour pacing around the pool, the pool house, and the lawn next to the pool, Jillian ran off to check on the horses, and when she returned, Edmund enquired as to the possibility of riding one of them.

"You ride?" asked Jillian.

Halley sat up in alarm, suddenly afraid Edmund would decide to gallop up and down Montecito's back roads, but Edmund happily agreed to stick to a bridal path that circled the estate. Halley saw him trotting past three or four times, wearing boots and jodhpurs Jillian's groom must've loaned him. Edmund looked good on horseback, looked good wearing boots and jodhpurs. It didn't hurt that Halley's sleep-tee stretched tightly across his torso as he trotted past. If DaVinci had been there, equestrian sketches would have been demanded, and even Jillian commented on how well he rode.

When Edmund returned, Jillian announced dinner. "I hope you're both okay if we keep it simple tonight. Branson's just doing pizza."

*"Just pizza"* turned out to be wood-fired oven *Pizzette Quattro Stagione* (pizzas garnished with artichoke,

prosciutto, Mediterranean olives, fresh mozzarella, fresh tomatoes, mushrooms, and cubed pancetta) served with a light summer wine of Applegate Estate provenance.

As they sat to enjoy the sumptuous feast, a breeze picked up, cooling the patio. Halley shivered in her damp suit. Jillian, who'd been raised on a steady diet of *"Consider your guests, dear,"* ran off, returning with a bright armful of wraps. "Mom brought these back from Bali."

Halley slipped one on, the fabric smooth and slippery against her skin. She noticed Edmund became more talkative once they were all swathed in fabric. Had he been embarrassed earlier? Now, Edmund spoke in lengthy praise of Jillian's horses, property, and pizza.

Halley cringed with each antiquated expression that fell from Edmund's mouth, but Jillian just laughed, praising Edmund for his thorough character research.

By the time the three finished stuffing themselves, it had grown late, and Jillian apologized, saying she needed to check on the horses again.

"Bucephalus hates earthquakes," said Jillian. "The groom is sleeping in the stables tonight and I just want to look in real quick...."

She offered to first walk them over to the West Wing, but Halley assured her she could find "her" room.

Jillian smiled and explained to Edmund. "Even the staff refer to the *Sense and Sensibility* suite as 'Halley's room'. I thought we'd put you, Edmund, in the *As You Like It* suite. To help you stay in character," she added.

Halley grinned, turning to Edmund. "Each of the six suites in the West Wing are themed to a work of literature, and *As You Like It* is *Elizabethan.*"

Jillian started to go, but then turned back, looking torn. "Maybe I should help you two get settled first," she said.

"We'll be fine," said Halley. "Take care of the horses. I promise to show Edmund where the spare towels are."

"And pajamas," said Jillian.

"And pajamas," said Halley, because *of course* the Applegates had spare pajamas in each of the guest suites.

"I asked Branson to set out some clothes for Edmund, but I haven't checked—"

"Go see the horses," said Halley. "Really. We'll be fine."

Jillian, after winking at Halley, nodded, and strode away to the stables.

Halley murmured to Edmund. "It's probably causing her physical pain to not show you where the Evian water is kept."

Edmund raised an eyebrow.

"Evian is—never mind," said Halley. "Come on. Let's show you your room."

The Applegates never ate dinner before 7:30, and Halley had been up since 5:30 in the morning, not to mention having traveled across entire historical time zones. She yawned as she showed Edmund the towels, pajamas, clothes (three outfits Branson had somehow found), and bottled Evian water. Halley even located a spare toothbrush for Edmund. He was first amused by and then frightened by the toilet, not expecting the loud flushing noise. He didn't seem too sure on the use of the toothbrush, either, but Halley thought it politer not to ask questions about Elizabethan oral hygiene.

Halley's own mother had one simple rule of hospitality: *don't offer it*. Fortunately, Halley had picked up her manners from Jillian. "I'm across the hall if you need anything," she said.

Edmund bowed deeply, wishing Halley a tight rest, whatever that was.

She stumbled into "her" room, out of her Balinese wrap and Swedish bikini, somehow managing to pull her tank top and panties on before falling into a heavy sleep.

Her clock read 2:09 AM when she awoke to a familiar sound. Unless she'd imagined it, someone had just shut the door of her truck. She sat up, her heart pounding.

# 18

## · EDMUND ·

Worry kept Edmund from sleep long past midnight. To consider everyone he knew as long dead filled him with dread. But if it was dreadful to consider them thus, it was also … impossible. He could not imagine them as reduced to worm-meal. They were alive to him still, lost in an alternate location. And so he worried.

He worried about his mother, who would be frantic when her eldest son didn't return from the great city. He worried about his brother, not knowing what Geoffrey had done with his mother's pendant (or rather, the money from selling the pendant), or what Geoffrey might do, tasting the possibility of power in his brother's absence.

Most of all though, Edmund worried about his return home. Halley had spoken of an opportunity in ten days—now nine—when her mother would guard the magician's domicile, but this felt like an eternity. And what if the magician had lain spells on his engines, such that no other person could engage them?

Edmund knew the man to be dangerous. He had observed carefully the magician's body: his clenched hands, the way he weighed the rock as a man weighs a weapon he thinks to use. Edmund had not survived to adulthood so near London without developing an uncanny sense of when a knife might be drawn or a sword unsheathed.

In addition to all his other concerns, Edmund worried because he wasn't sleeping and hadn't slept well for the past three nights and knew he *needed* sleep.

After tossing in bed for over two hours, he rose and crossed to the balcony doors of his chamber. They opened with ease, and he marveled at the clarity of the glass panels, marveling even more when he realized the doors were constructed of single pieces of glass made to *look* as though they were divided into panes. He stepped into the night. The air was warm and redolent with scents he could not name. The scent of horses, far off, was the only thing he could identify with certainty; even the grass and trees smelled different.

He turned his gaze overhead to a lonely sprinkling of stars, leaned against the balcony railing, and slowly exhaled. Whatever peace or ease of mind he had been hoping to find, it wasn't to be found out here.

Had he been at home, he would have taken exercise walking the long hall between his rooms and the kitchens. The hall in this, the West Wing, was not so lengthy as that of his home, but perhaps the exercise would weary him enough that he could sleep.

He opened the door slowly, warily, to keep it from creaking, but it made no sound. In this world, things which ought to be silent (a chamber pot) were not, while things which ought to creak and squeak (the bedstead, the door) made no sound. Even the floorboards as he stepped into the hall were silent. He began a slow, measured walk.

*What was his mother thinking? What was his brother doing?*

Was it even possible to ask, if they were long-dead? Confusion churned in his stomach. He paused to steady himself, but as he did so, a chill ran along his shoulders. His proper sphere of concern was not what his mother thought, nor what his brother did. He ought, rather to concern himself with his own course of action: *what was he doing?* And more importantly: *what ought he to be doing?*

Phrased thus in bluntness, the answer became plain. He ought not to be wandering the halls of another's manor—he ought to be seeking a return to his own estate. His wonder at this new world and his infatuate regard for Mistress Halley had turned him from what ought to be his first concern. He was Edmund Aldwych, shortly to be installed under oath as Earl of Shaftsbury, and he was bound by honor and duty to seek as swift a return as could be accomplished.

For a count of ten, he tried to see a different way forward, but there was none. His duty was clear: he must break into the magician's chamber or die trying. And he must do it now, not nine days hence.

For a brief moment, he paused before Halley's door. If he woke her to take his leave, she would try to persuade him to stay, to wait another nine days until the magician was away. His chin sank to his chest. He knew the power she held over him. There could be no God b'ye. Swiftly, he turned from her room and made his way to her truck to retrieve his sword. If he met with the magician again, he would not this time meet him unarmed.

The air outside had grown chill and moist, and once Edmund had strapped on his sword belt and sword, he secured the door to Halley's truck, lest the damp should enter therein. This done, he began his march upon the estate of Jules Khan, praying his recollection of the way did not fail him in the darkness of night.

# 19

## · *KHAN* ·

Khan had descended into his laboratory at 2:17 in the morning, finally admitting to himself he wasn't going to sleep. He theorized it was one of the side effects of passing through the temporal rift. He'd written a paper on the topic, examining the effects of the ultra-contracted voyages through space-time, noting that while things such as muscle tone and bone density were virtually unaffected, the shock to the nervous system was registered in the release of catecholamines, especially adrenaline, which was observed to produce insomnia, nervousness, and lowered immunity toward illness.

Dr. Khan had, of necessity, become a diligent hand-washer.

The fact that there was no "American Space-Time Journal" meant the paper could not be published in his own lifetime, which was a pity. It was at moments like this he wished the singularity device could be used to send travelers *forward* in time, but if it was possible, he had not uncovered the secret. Such a shame. He would have liked to attend a future conference, perhaps to hear a lecture from the *Jules A. Khan Fellow* from MIT or USC....

Tonight however, he was employing himself in updating the retrievals catalog. Flipping through some of his earliest recoveries, he recalled his dismay at being unable to sell an original Van Gogh to a wealthy collector. It hadn't passed muster. The item's provenance had been called in question because it had failed to test as "old enough" to be genuine. He'd been unable to sell either the Gutenberg Bible or the copy of Shakespeare's Sonnets or any painting over forty years old. He'd quickly switched to items made of porcelain or gold or silver after that, developing a brisk trade in amber and rubies, chalcedony and jasper. The paintings, tapestries, and rare books he kept for himself, enjoying them in all their original glory.

Several times, he'd come close to destroying the records of his retrievals and sales. He worried future scholars would judge him for having used his knowledge for financial gain. In fact, this was what had kept him from buying up stock in the past and selling it when it peaked—there would have been a paper trail suggesting he'd done, well, just that. He wanted to keep his reputation untarnished.

He really ought to destroy these records....

Running a hand through his thinning hair, he looked up from the catalog. It was almost three in the morning. It wasn't only insomnia that was keeping him awake tonight, he admitted to himself. He was still troubled by the possibility—however miniscule—that the girl Halley had ventured into his lab and seen his equipment. It was unlikely.

Unlikely, but not impossible.

The girl's mother was harmless enough. He'd conducted a thorough background check on her, revealing among other things that her bank account balance was consistently in the mid-three digits to the low-four digits, that she had smoked marijuana only once and avoided all other narcotics entirely, and that she'd had no lasting relationships. Chatty enough when plied with caraway-scented Akvavit liqueur, Inga had admitted to having had her daughter out of a fear of being alone only to discover she liked being alone just fine, thanks all the same. The professor was convinced she had a narcissistic personality disorder.

As for the girl Halley, Khan had never done more than a cursory amount of research into her habits, interests, and vices. He hadn't expected her to be here today; her mother had been rather vague as to whether her daughter would be available. Khan would have made different plans had he known Halley Mikkelsen would actually show up.

And then there was the girl's boyfriend. Who was he? The professor didn't know the first thing about the young man, other than the fact that he was alarmingly comfortable with knives. In appearance, he was much like any other Southern California beach rat: blond, barefoot, and wearing shorts and a tee shirt. Still, Khan imagined he would sleep better knowing the young man wasn't a physics protégé or fluent in industrial espionage. He reached for his cell phone and had nearly dialed *Mikkelsen, Inga* before noticing the time.

"Hmmph," he grunted, setting his phone down.

There would be plenty of time to ask Inga about

her daughter's boyfriend *tomorrow*. He had, after all, all the time in the world.

## 20

### · *HALLEY* ·

If there was one sound Halley was familiar with, it was the sound of her truck door slamming shut. When Halley was home, the sound warned her that her mother was taking her truck without asking permission and that she had thirty seconds to race downstairs if she wanted to prevent it.

But Halley was at Jillian's tonight. There was no way her mom was outside. Was there? Shaking off her grogginess, Halley grabbed the Balinese wrap, throwing it on possibly backwards and certainly inside-out. She raced outside, but no one was anywhere near her truck. Had she dreamed the sound? She had just decided she must have dreamed it when she saw the Applegate's motion detector lights flick on down at the end of the drive, just past the gentle curve that hid the entry gates from view. Now that she thought about it, the lights all the way down the drive were already on.

Someone had been inside her truck and was now leaving the estate. Suddenly her brain made the connection.

"*Edmund!*" she murmured.

Barefoot, Halley raced down the drive, passing a neat stack of logs and brush from the fallen tree Jillian's dad had cleared out yesterday. Her feet complained about the rough asphalt. She should have thought to grab flip flops, but it was too late for that now. Where was Edmund going? What was he thinking, taking off in the middle of the night? She was afraid she already knew the answer.

As she rounded the curve and the gates came into view, she had a momentary glimpse of a man with a sword strapped to his hip escaping over the top of the entrance gate. She ran faster, pausing only to key in the code for manually releasing the gate. She got it wrong three times before finally punching the numbers in correctly.

"Edmund!" she called.

There was no answer.

# 21

· *EDMUND* ·

Edmund surmounted the estate enclosure with ease, wondering that Jillian's father did not make it more difficult for villains to come or go as easily as he had himself. He turned left and downhill, recalling well this first part of the mile or so separating the Applegate's manor from that of the professor. Halley had pointed Khan's manor out to her friends on their crowded drive back from the beach yesterday. Once he had passed from the pale of the gate lights, all was most dark, the moon having already set.

He kept to the side of the road and had just offered prayer for his safe return home when he heard two things in swift succession. Firstly, he heard Mistress Halley crying out his name. Secondly, he heard the approach of some great engine, foolishly driving in the dark of night. The noise of the engine made it possible Halley would not hear any response from him even had he wanted to respond, which he did not. He thought of the sailor Odysseus, withstanding the call of the sirens only by having bound himself to his ship. Having neither a mast and ropes nor waxen ear-stops, Edmund increased his stride.

The roar of the engine from behind him increased as well and unless his eyes betrayed him, some sort of light preceded it. Turning, Edmund was nearly blinded by twin beams bright as the sun and pointed straight at him. Without even thinking, he drew his sword and held it to defend himself against the coming brightness. He could not fathom the purpose of the blinding light unless it was some type of attack adapted for nighttime encounters. The engine sound grew louder and Edmund confirmed that the glaring light and the engined wagon approached in unison, bearing down upon him as dogs upon game.

He did the only thing he could think of to defend himself. He raised his sword and charged forward, meaning to attract attention should the wagon be friendly and to offer resistance if it were not.

~ ~ ~

Halley listened for a response from Edmund, not sure which way he'd turned. On the worrying chance he was heading for Professor Khan's basement, she turned left, calling his name a second time. An oncoming car drowned out her cry.

"Fantastic," she murmured. Would Edmund know to get to the side of the road? He must have had *some* experience getting out of the way of hay wagons and carriages. He wasn't an idiot. Halley stepped off the asphalt road and into the wide drainage ditch past the shoulder. This surface was even less forgiving than the road, and she cursed as she stubbed her toe on a rock.

Stepping back onto the road as soon as the car was past her, she opened her mouth to shout again, but then she saw him. Lit by the car's headlights, Edmund was standing in the road, his sword raised above his head, screaming something about England and Saint George.

Halley dashed forward, landed her heel on something sharp, and fell, shouting in pain.

~ ~ ~

Edmund hurled a last invective at the speeding wagon, which had veered sharply away from him upon seeing his raised sword. He kept his sword at the ready lest the engined cart should return for another pass at him. It did not, however, its eerie red aft-lights disappearing around a corner along with the engine noise. He was just sheathing his sword when he heard Halley once again, but this time she was not calling his name. She was moaning most piteously, interspersing her moans with oaths.

Edmund did not hesitate beyond the space of time it took his heart to beat twice. Halley was in pain and in need of assistance. He ran back, drawn to her as iron to a lodestone.

## 22

## · *EDMUND* ·

"I'm fine," snapped Halley. "It was just a stupid piece of gravel." She rubbed at her heel, wincing.

Edmund noted she did not even attempt to mask her anger at him.

"Allow me to aid thee—"

"I said I'm *fine*."

But when she tried to walk, Edmund saw plainly that her hurt, though slight, was enough to prevent her returning to Mistress Jillian's manor under conveyance of her own feet.

He held his arms out, indicating his willingness to carry her. "Thou canst not walk," he added.

"And whose fault is that?" Halley glared at him.

Edmund said nothing.

Halley tried once again to take slow steps forward and then uttered forth a sort of growling noise.

"I can't walk."

She mumbled her words, as though the admission were more painful than the injury to her heel.

"Seriously, Edmund, what were you thinking,

running off like that? You could have at least said something to me first." She sighed heavily and then, with an expression that spoke defeat, she held her arms wide. "Fine. Carry me."

Edmund lifted her as easily as if she were a fatted ewe.

"You could have gotten lost. You could have gotten yourself cited or jailed for waving that sword around. You could have caused a car accident." Up till this point she had addressed him directly, but now she turned her face away so that he could no longer read her expression.

"You could have been killed," she muttered, crossing her arms tightly over her chest. He felt the tension in her narrow frame as she spoke the final accusation.

"Aye, lady." He made the admission unwillingly, but she was in the right. He'd been foolish. As foolish, in fact, as a child of five who runs away following some indignity visited upon his backside. More foolish. As a lad of five he had known more of his world than he knew now of this world.

"I crave pardon," he said.

"Hmmph," grunted Halley. And then, "Were you planning to break into the professor's house?"

He hesitated but found he had no stomach to lie to her. "Aye, lady," he replied.

"Oh, Edmund," she said with a heavy sigh.

From thence, she fell silent until they reached the great gate.

"Walk over to the far right. There's a keypad."

She tapped a series of ciphers and lo, the gate parted open.

"Jules Khan might not look dangerous," she said once the gates had closed behind them, "But I think he could get dangerous really fast if he found someone messing around in his secret basement."

"I doubt it not," said Edmund. "My escape was foolishly conceived, from beginning to end."

Mistress Halley grunted in what he assumed was affirmation.

Besides the danger posed by the magician, Edmund felt now the greatness of his folly in thinking he could unravel the mystery of Khan's great engine. He understood not the engines of this age. How, apart from Halley's aid, should he have commanded the one that sent men forth unto differing centuries? How if he had sent himself to another age entirely?

"It was foolishly done," Edmund repeated. "Although," he added, "'Tis like I should never have found my way."

And then, in despite of her being plainly out of humor with him, Edmund heard her laugh. It was but a single laugh, grudgingly emitted, and yet it set his heart racing, drunk on the wine of her renewed favor.

"I can see the headlines now: *Idiot Wanders Montecito Waving Sword at Motorists.*" She shook her head at him, a sad smile on her face. "Put me down here on the grass. I want to see how bad my heel is now."

Halley tested her weight on her injured foot. She could walk, if a little haltingly. Slowly, they crept up the drive and back toward their chambers.

In his twenty-one years, Edmund had met no one like Halley. He'd seen women as fair as she, but it was more than her beauty that attracted him. What was it? Her manner? Her laughter? Her courage? Edmund had not counted courage among the attributes he might seek in a helpmate—not any more than he'd thought of taking a wife for her wit or humor. The few maidens to whom he had been introduced were silent to the point of sullenness, but Halley spoke freely with him, whether chiding or teasing or merely conversing.

As she walked before him, he imagined sharing a life—and a bed—with her. If her laughter made him drunk, the thought of her in his bed set his very soul afire. This was what he wanted: *Halley*. A lifetime of watching her sun-drenched smile light his hall. Of gathering her laughter when the rains fell. Of catching her whispers when night fell....

"I am totally freezing," murmured Halley as they reached their lodgings. "How can it be totally freezing when it was such a hot day?"

"Shall I kindle thee a fire?" Edmund asked, holding open the door that opened into the West Wing.

"Mmm ... *yes, please!*"

Her tone had warmed once more as though her anger at him were forgotten.

Edmund had meant to light the fire in her chamber, but she preceded him into the lodgings and entered his own chamber.

"Your room has the nice rug," said Halley, planting herself in front of the hearth on a thick woolen fleece.

To one side of the fleece, wood and kindling had been tidily stacked. Drawing closer, Edmund saw that the kindling had been glued together. He suspected the glue was highly flammable.

"Mom and I smoked the heck out of someone's

house, the one time we tried to build a fire," said Halley as he joined her at the hearth. "Are you sure you know how?"

A slight look of affront crossed Edmund's face. "I cannot build a fire without smoke, but I can so effect it that the smoke escapeth through the chimney."

A smirk tugged one side of Halley's mouth. "Please, do-eth it now-eth."

"Thou mockest me."

"I do."

Edmund found himself laughing, her laughter mingling with his. Was "mockery" another womanly virtue he ought to add to his list? He settled before the hearth to lay the fire. After he'd placed the combustible items in the correct layers, he looked about for the flint and fire-steel.

"Knowest thou where the flint is to be found?"

"Flint?" asked Halley.

"And steel. To light the fire."

"Oh. Right. We don't use flint in my world. We use matches."

"Matches?"

"Although," said Halley, "This place is fancy; I bet they have a remote."

She reached past Edmund and plucked up a shiny object shaped like a doorstop. This, she pointed at the hearth. At once, great blue flames burst forth, catching the assembled objects on fire.

Edmund drew back, crying *God-a-mercy*. The ability to kindle flame from air was surely the most basic mark of witchcraft. "Art thou not indeed a sorceress, lady?" If she were, he was lost, for he found that he cared not.

"Seriously?" Halley's tone was flavored with sarcasm.

"Thou didst call forth blue fire without any aid."

"I started the fire with *this* aid," said Halley, holding out the doorstop-shaped object. "It's a gas fire starter. It's just another of our fancy ways to get things done with electricity. Or, well, electricity *and* gas, in this case." She passed the object into his hand. "For a supposedly historical room, it's totally cheating."

Edmund took the object, turning it over in his hands. At last, he nodded. This was no different than the buzzing messenger she kept always about her person. It was merely a small engine. A machine.

"Lady," he said, passing it back to her keeping, "I should rather call the contrivance *wondrous*." He felt a tug inside—a sort of desperation to remain in this age of wonders. To remain with her.

Halley shrugged. "I guess it is." Then she held her hands out, catching the warmth of the fire. "Mmm. Now, *that* is what I call wondrous."

Edmund gazed at her slender fingers as they caught the flickering light of the fire. They were elegant. Like her wrists. Her arms. Her shoulders. Neck. He turned away, not trusting himself to gaze upon her mouth without longing.

He was lost, indeed.

## 23

### · *HALLEY* ·

Halley sank her fingers into the soft fleece rug set before the fire. She was in so much trouble. This was definitely the most romantic setting she'd ever been in, and here she was with a veritable *god* from the sixteenth century.

A *god*, who, she reminded herself, had just tried to run off in the middle of the night, endangering both of them. She sighed heavily.

For several minutes, neither of them said anything. The wood in the fire had caught in a bright blaze, so she reached for the remote and fussed with the blue flames until they went out. A brief but unpleasant whiff of natural gas took the edge off the romantic mood.

"Edmund, " she said at last, "We have to talk about your ... running away thing. I need to know you're not going to try something like that again."

Edmund's brow furrowed.

"Please. Or at least ... help me to understand. What made you think you had to?" Halley asked.

Edmund's gaze grew troubled. Halley thought he was debating keeping his thoughts on the subject to himself, but then he sighed and spoke.

"My grandfather," he began, "Is newly passed from this life. Or ... *was*, rather. I was meant today to attend to the arrangements for his funeral."

Halley gasped. His grandfather had just died? "I'm so sorry," she murmured. "Why didn't you say something?"

Edmund shrugged.

Halley bit her lip, and then said again, "I feel terrible."

"He was a great man. He seemed at times more a father than my own sire. I shall miss him greatly, but he made a good end, and it was not unexpected. I count our household fortunate that he lasted so long as he did." Edmund plucked at the wool strands of the rug. "With his passing, his title falls to me."

Halley frowned. "You have a *title*? Like, you're a royal or something?" How had *this* not come up already? She felt suddenly horrible for having put almost no effort into understanding who Edmund was. So far, she'd seen him as, alternately, eye-candy or a problem to solve.

Edmund, however, didn't seem troubled. On the contrary, his smile had returned, as though her question amused him.

"I am not royal, lady. I am but an earl's grandson, and a poor one, too, who stands to inherit the debts of his forebears."

"Still, an earl? That sounds impressive. Can I ask, um, what exactly an earl ... *does*?"

"That which he must, I suppose, lady."

Halley shifted on the rug so that she was facing him. She wrapped her arms tightly around her knees and pulled them close, resting her chin on top. "Such as …?"

"I am charged with the welfare of mine estate and all persons pertaining thereto."

Now it was Halley's turn to look confused. "An estate has … welfare to look after?"

"The estate is a great farm, lady. Are there no farms in this age?"

"Sure. We have farms. So, you're, like, a farmer-earl."

Edmund laughed. "Aye."

"What does 'persons pertaining thereto' mean, exactly? Do you have loyal subjects or something?"

Edmund grew solemn. "Her majesty the queen alone hath subjects. All those who dwell on my estate do serve her alone, and most loyally."

"Okay. Sorry. I didn't mean to question your, um, loyalty status. But you have … *staff*, right? Worker bees? Servants? Weren't you going to hire me as a baker?"

"Aye."

"What would that even *mean*?" she asked. "Would I have been, like, indentured?"

"Nay, lady. To become an indentured apprentice, thou wouldst have contracted with a master baker, paying him well to teach thee the trade. Servants, rather, are paid in coin, by the quarter, and in lean years when there is no coin, in foodstuffs or wool, or wood, as they have need and my grandfather has means." Edmund frowned. "That is, as I have means, now I am to inherit his duties."

"So if I needed a new dress and you paid me in …

139

*wool*, would I be able to trade that wool for clothes?"

Edmund bristled. "No member of my household has ever stood in want of clothing. I should have furnished thee with garments, both sturdy and in keeping with the dignity of my household. It should have been writ into thy contract of service."

Halley's eyebrows rose. She knew from costume history that clothing in Elizabethan times was expensive, taking a higher percentage of the overall cost of living than it did now. And yet Edmund had been ready to shoulder that cost the moment he had offered her a job.

"Does not Jillian's father provide Branson with *habillements*?" asked Edmund.

"Habil-*whats*?"

"His livery. His garb. His clothing."

"Oh." Halley stifled a laugh. "No. Definitely not. So you provide clothing for your servants? Plus you pay them?"

"Aye, and feed and house them. Who would serve without such compensation? Surely Branson does not, nor my lady's gentleman of the horse, neither."

"Um, they get a salary so they can pick their own clothes and food and place of residence."

Edmund was silent for a minute. "I have heard of suchlike arrangements in the City, but they are shameful. If a servant dwells not with his master, who shall care for that servant when he becomes ill? Or how shall aged servants be cared for when they can no longer till or carry? To throw them from the family in such a way is surely the most careless of cruelties."

"Maybe," said Halley. She was struck even more forcibly by how much Edmund had been committing to when he offered to employ her. He'd been ready to feed, clothe, house, and pay her, *plus* provide her with retirement benefits including medical care. At a time when *none* of those things were cheap—when "discretionary income" didn't exist as a concept for ordinary people. Halley didn't know a single person who would be willing to make such an offer to her. Her mom wouldn't so much as buy necessary clothing for her.

Looking up, she saw Edmund had collapsed his head into his hands. The fire had died back and Halley couldn't read his shadowed expression.

"What is it?"

Edmund was silent for several seconds before responding. His voice, when he spoke again, was flat, almost defeated.

"If I return not, the estate falls to my brother, who hath no care for our household, nor tenants, nor servants. He is like to turn tyrant and send forth the aged when they can no longer serve, or to dismiss the sick rather than call for the apothecary's services."

Halley's brow furrowed. "I'm sure we'll get you back. It'll be okay. We just have to wait until my mom's next house-sitting job. Ten days. Nine, now, I guess."

Edmund exhaled heavily.

"And besides," said Halley, "If your servants are used to being well cared for, wouldn't the rest pack up and leave if your brother started mistreating them?"

"Aye." Edmund's brow contracted. "Mayhap."

"That's what I would do. Find a better employer."

"Doubtless some would, at the expiration of their contract, but I would not see them forced to flee their

141

home, lady. My estate is their home, and they are my responsibility. Unless they choose to depart, I am bound to care for them for better or for worse, in lean years and fat years. I would not have them cast forth through my brother's cruelty."

"We'll get you back."

She leaned forward and placed a hand on his back, comforting. Edmund looked over at her and held her gaze, his own face still lined with anguish.

"It'll be fine," she murmured. "We'll send you back to the same day, so it will be like you never left."

"Aye, lady."

She thought this would work. She hoped it would work. She didn't really know if it would work. She kept her doubts on the subject to herself.

"I think it's wonderful," she said, "The way you care about your employees." She was quiet a moment, and then added, "I've never had anything or anyone to care for. Not even a fish. Mom doesn't own a house. We rent a crappy little apartment."

"You own a kind heart. And a brave one, at that."

Halley flushed.

"I just wish I had something to call my own, you know?" And then, like a warm breeze across her skin, the thought of her fifteen thousand dollar sale returned. She was rich. She was very rich. She could get what she wanted. Exactly what she wanted: something to call her own—something no one could take from her or sell out from under her.

Edmund regarded her with a puzzled expression. "What is't, lady?"

Halley hesitated. Her secret dream had always been, well, *secret*. Perhaps it was the lateness of the hour or the tenderness of Edmund's eyes—such beautiful eyes—but Halley felt her normal reserve on the subject receding ever so slightly. Besides, before she knew it, Edmund would be gone forever. He was as safe a recipient for her secrets as she could ever find.

"You said your grandfather was like a dad to you," she began, haltingly. "So I'm guessing your own father ... left a few things to be desired."

Edmund laughed softly. "'Tis a most generous way to speak of him."

"I don't really know my father at all," she said. "I only met him once." She hesitated, but then decided to just plunge in. "He took me to Disneyland. Disneyland is like ... well ..." She frowned. How would she begin to explain Disneyland to someone from another century? She thought of the sign at the front of the park.

"What is the happiest place on Earth, for you?" she asked.

"The merriest, ask you?"

"Aye." Halley used Edmund's word without noticing it.

"I suppose it was our great hall, when I was young. Grandfather kept then four minstrels and a juggler. Our winters were merry with entertainment whilst they remained with us, and Yule was the merriest time of all."

"Yule is Christmas, right?"

Edmund nodded.

It was a perfect analogy.

"Well," said Halley, "I think the people who made Disneyland wanted to make visitors feel that way—the way Christmas morning is supposed to feel. That was how I felt the day my dad took me to Disneyland."

"Are there entertainments at ... *D'Isigny* land?"

"Oh, yeah. Lots. Parades and shows—er, jugglers and minstrels. And rides. Huh. I don't know what to compare a ride to. A fast gallop on a horse, maybe? But the best part wasn't the rides or shows."

She paused and Edmund leaned in. "What was it thou didst prize above all else?"

She bit her lower lip. This was the most hidden of her secrets, enshrined within the *sanctum sanctorum* of her memories. She could just say it had been a great day, and leave it at that, but she felt her wishes and hopes pressing for release, pressing to be spoken aloud, to be shared. And here was Edmund, beautiful Edmund, asking her, his striking eyes boring into hers.

Before she could reconsider, she began to tell him everything.

"Dad took me to an exclusive restaurant called Club 33. Normally, you can't get in, even if you have a ticket to visit the park. You have to be a member, or taken by a friend who is a member, but we were alone, so my dad must be a member. Anyway, he took me inside and asked what I wanted to eat, and I said I wanted a root beer float."

Edmund looked at her blankly.

"Do you know what ice cream is?"

"*Cream* I know."

"Think of cream that's been sweetened and then frozen. It's the best. Actually, we were supposed to have some today, but I guess we forgot. Branson calls it gelato. Anyway, to make a root beer float, you put ice cream in your root beer—you probably don't have root beer, either—"

"We brew small beer at home."

"Small beer? Is it ... sweet and fizzy?"

"Sweet it can be, if made so. It doth bubble."

"Root beer is very bubbly and very sweet. And when you add vanilla ice cream, it's ... *heaven*."

Halley closed her eyes, remembering the way the fizz from the root beer tickled her nose and lips. She remembered how her father clinked glasses with her and didn't scold her when hers slopped onto the bar. The barman had laughed, saying it happened every day and not to worry. It was the happiest memory she had.

She looked up, meeting Edmund's eyes. The firelight sparked, dancing in his amber-flecked irises. She took a slow breath and then told Edmund the rest of it. Her plan.

"I'm taking the money I made from that painting I sold yesterday and using it to pay for a membership at the club. I applied a year ago when I didn't have anywhere close to enough money. Actually, at the time I didn't know how much it cost or I might not have applied.

"Anyway, last month I saw an LA Times article saying that Disney was trying to encourage applicants aged 18 to 30 to apply for membership. So now I have the money *and* I should have a better shot because of my age. I'm moving to LA as soon as I can, and if the club accepts me, I can visit every day, if I want to."

She kept back the most important part: that this was her best chance of meeting her father again. It was a crazy hope, but it was all she had: on one of those visits, someday, she would see him again and learn what had kept him from her life. Her throat grew tight. Swallowing, she reached for the ring at her neck. Her father would be there. Someday. Eventually. He wouldn't have paid that kind of money for a membership he didn't use, would he?

When she met Edmund's gaze, he was staring at her, his dark eyes like liquid pools.

She felt her cheeks burning. "I haven't ever told anyone about ... all this," she murmured.

"I am the more honored, lady."

"It might never happen. My becoming a member. I've got the money, but they don't have to accept me for membership."

"And why should they not accept thee?" asked Edmund.

Halley chest tightened as she considered Edmund's question. She slid her jade ring along her necklace. Why was she so afraid Club 33 would reject her application? It was true they'd already had it a year, but that wasn't unusual. She'd heard of people waiting several years before getting their letter of acceptance. But what if they said no? Her chest began to ache.

"I guess," she murmured softly, "When you want something so badly, it's hard to believe you could ever have it."

Edmund was silent for a long minute. At last, he said, "Aye, lady. I understand thee well."

Edmund's apologetic smile quickly faded.

"What is it?" Halley's voice was a mere whisper.

Edmund shook his head.

Halley sat up straighter, staring at him. A tiny furrow nestled between her brows.

Edmund, reaching over, smoothed the furrow with the flesh of his thumb.

Tension, doubt, fear melted away at the warmth

of his touch. After he withdrew his hand, she felt it still, a phantom. Her eyes rested half open.

"What is it?" she asked again.

Softly, he said, "It is nothing, lady. It is a mere foolishness."

His expression stopped her breath. She saw yearning. Desire. Hope, and its opposite. And then, with the look of someone telling himself all the reasons not to, he reached for her face and drew her closer.

# 24

## · HALLEY ·

Halley couldn't breathe. Couldn't think. Couldn't do anything. Edmund was going to kiss her. She saw his mouth, parted softly, lips trembling. His hand trembled too, where it cradled her face. He was going to kiss her. Their foreheads touched softly. His skin was warm. Her lungs forced her to exhale. She could feel the weight of his head pressed to hers. Close; so close. Neither of them moved. And then, noses brushed, hair slid forward, a sigh, and their lips met.

For several moments, that was all: lip touching lip, shallow breaths, closed eyes. And then she leaned into the kiss, her hand clasping Edmund's neck, her fingers threading lightly through his hair.

She was kissing him. He was kissing her back. Warmth suffused her face, torso, arms, belly. And then a spark, popping loudly in the fireplace, startled them apart. Quickly, Edmund brushed an ember off her Balinese wrap.

She took Edmund's hand in hers, as if to prove he was real, that she wasn't lost in a dream. Oh, she was lost. But Edmund was real and solid, his eyes fixed on her.

Again, she moved to kiss that exquisite mouth, but this time Edmund drew back.

"I crave pardon, lady." He shook his head infinitesimally. "I meant no insult. It is the lateness of the hour. I have not slept these several days—"

"Hush," she said. She placed her fingers against his lips. Heard his heavy exhalation. Watched as his eyes closed and then opened again, hungry with desire. "Hush," she said again, and then, before the sound had left her lips, he was kissing her, pulling her close so that they both crashed onto the fleece, his body cushioning hers. His hand was on her waist, fingers warm and wanting alongside her spine and then her belly. Something sounded, a sharp rap against wood, but Halley ignored it, thinking Edmund's foot or elbow must have knocked against the enormous bed behind them.

Then it sounded again. Three raps. Purposeful. Signifying ... *something*. Halley pulled herself from Edmund's sure grasp, lifted her head. *Rap, rap, rap.*

"Someone's knocking," she whispered.

Edmund grunted and pulled her back for another kiss, grabbing a handful of her fabric wrap and shifting it against her skin.

"Wait," she said. "It's your door!"

This got his attention. Edmund's eyes opened. He looked at the fistful of fabric in his hand. He closed his eyes and drew a slow breath. Then, with great care, Edmund sat up, shifting gently so that Halley slid onto the rug. It felt cool after the warmth of Edmund's body. She adjusted her wrap. Tried to smooth her hair.

Edmund stood and crossed to the door, opening it a crack.

Halley heard earnest whispering from the doorway—a few quick exchanges, and then Edmund returned to her side. He did not sit, however, and seemed to be forcing himself to look at the fire and not at her.

"It was Branson," he explained. "It seems he arrived early today to commence the baking of bread, and, seeing smoke here at such an hour, he wished to ascertain it signified no uncontained fire."

Halley tied the fabric belting more snugly. "What time is it?" she asked.

"'Tis half past four, if I read the clock aright," said Edmund.

"Oh. Wow." Halley stood, smoothing her wrap. "I guess we should, um, get some sleep. We're supposed to help DaVinci hang her show at 8:00."

"Sleep thou here," said Edmund, indicating the four-poster bed. "The hall outside is most cold, and thy room will be also. I will couch myself hereby," he said, indicating the chaise lounge.

Halley murmured, "It would be warmer if ... you know ... if we shared."

Edmund's cheeks flushed darkly.

"It would be warmer, lady," he said, smiling softly, "But I fear we should not sleep."

Halley shrugged, climbed in the canopied bed, and curled into a tight ball. The sheets were cold, the pillow hard. Edmund's words repeated in her head: *I fear we should not sleep....* Yeah. If she was honest with herself, she feared too. In nine more days, Edmund was leaving her life, slipping back four hundred years.

In two weeks, he would be ... *dead*. Halley shivered, swiped at a tear, and pulled the blanket over her head.

~ ~ ~

It took Edmund a long time to drift to sleep, and when he did, it was with the image of Halley's face nearing his, her ruby lips more intoxicating than the sweetest wine. But then his dreams took a dark turn, and he saw Halley in the grip of the magician while he looked on, powerless to aid her.

He woke in a sweat to the sound of someone crying Halley's name in alarm.

# 25

## · *KHAN* ·

Dr. Jules Khan waited until 6:31 in the morning to call Inga Mikkelsen and inquire as to her daughter Halley's boyfriend. Naturally, he wasn't so transparent as to make it obvious he wished to know more about the boyfriend.

"Good morning, good morning," he said jovially. "It's Professor Khan. I wanted to get back to you and thank you for making sure there was someone on-property yesterday."

Inga's voice was scratchy, as though she'd just risen. Which she probably had. Khan continued with pleasantries to give her a chance to wake up, asking after her mother, how they had both weathered the earthquake, and so on. Eventually he returned to the topic of Halley.

"I was very impressed with her professionalism," he said. "She took extensive notes on the property, annotating damage, checking for leaks, and so on. She managed to deal with a few immediate issues before I even got home."

"She did?" asked Halley's mother. "It's good to know she's listening." Halley's mother sounded surprised rather than smug.

"Of course, she had help," said the professor. "That boyfriend—I didn't catch his name?" His intonation made it clear he was asking a question, and his heart struck heavily against his ribs as he awaited the answer. A name. A story. An educational institution. Something.

"Did you say ... *boyfriend*?" asked Inga.

"Yes. The boy from Denmark."

There was silence on the line, followed by what Khan assumed was grunting laughter.

"Halley doesn't have a boyfriend. She won't put in the effort to make herself presentable most days, much less attractive. The number of times I've seen her leave the house—"

Khan cut her off. "Sorry—I've got another call coming in. Can I place you on a brief hold?" There was no other call, but he needed a moment of silence in which to think and plan. The mother didn't know Halley was dating. Surely it was no surprise that a teenage girl kept secrets from her mother. Still, he needed a name. If the boy was Danish, the mother should have *some* idea as to his identity. How many Danish young men was Halley likely to know that her mother didn't *also* know? He clicked back to Inga.

"So sorry about that. Where was I? Ah, yes. The Danish boy."

"A boy from Denmark? *Dansk*? What boy? What was his name?"

"I don't think I caught his name ..."

Inga was muttering, in Danish, under her breath.

153

He tried redirection.

"Maybe I should send them a little something to say thank you. A Starbucks gift card, do you think? You must have some idea who the boy is. Perhaps it wasn't a boyfriend—a cousin maybe?"

"I don't know who she was entertaining, and I promise you it won't happen again. Halley knows better than that."

"No, no, no. I'm sure she didn't mean to cause trouble. I think she said he only came by to make sure she was okay following the earthquake. Quite understandable."

Inga made noises indicating mollification.

"Why don't you just thank him for me in person when you meet him?" suggested the professor. "Or, even better, after you've met him, send me a quick text with his name and I can add it to a thank you note."

Was he pushing too hard? He didn't think so. The mother was so busy being angry that her daughter had concealed a boyfriend that Khan's excessive interest in the boyfriend went unnoticed. A moment later they said their goodbyes.

Khan breathed out heavily. He had learned nothing. He didn't even have a name. Who was this boy? Did he pose a threat to Khan's carefully kept secrecy? The professor slammed his palm on the surface of his desk. He had to rule out even the slightest possibility of discovery. Maybe he was being paranoid. If someone wanted to spy on him, why would they send a teenager? The girl and boy were almost certainly harmless.

The professor, however, required *certainty*, not *almost certainly*. He had to rule out even the slightest possibility of discovery.

Perhaps ... *perhaps* he could catch Halley and the boy at her apartment. There, he might find some documentation indicating the boy's identity. He uttered a single laugh, mumbling, *"Documentation,"* in self-censure. Much simpler to *ask* for the boy's name, ask what he was doing in the United States; if he were a student, what was he studying?

Within moments, the professor had a plan. A delivery in person, at her apartment, of flowers and a card ... An offer to place the flowers in water ... Yes, he was good at worming his way into people's good graces when he wanted to. And he very much wanted to.

Before half an hour had passed, the professor was knocking on the apartment door, flowers, pastries, and a thank you card in hand. Was it too much? He debated while he awaited an answer at the door, rearranging his frown into a friendly expression, but there was no answer. He tried again. Still nothing. Cursing, he tried the door handle. It was locked. He stepped backward, off the welcome mat, and lifted it, uncovering a key.

He grunted in disapproval. Some people were just *asking* for trouble.

Silently, he let himself in, calling softly in case anyone was inside but *asleep*. The apartment proved to be empty and the professor set about searching for something to identify Halley's boyfriend, but there was nothing to be found. No wallet ... no passport ... no evidence at all that the boy was a part of Halley's life.

Khan swore softly. Another dead end. Well, they couldn't stay away from their apartment forever.

Maybe they'd gone for coffee. He waited outside for another half hour, sitting in his car. At last he could wait no longer. He had an appointment to divest himself of some very valuable sixteenth century jewelry.

"Another time, then," he said. Then he started his Tesla and sped away, rearranging gravel across the quiet parking lot.

# 26

## · HALLEY ·

Halley heard someone calling her name. Not her mom. Her mother never rose this early. Peeling one eyelid open, Halley contemplated the grey cast to the morning's light. Fog.

"Halley?"

It was Jillian calling for her. Right. She was at Jillian's. She opened her eyes. She was at Jillian's, but she was *not* in the Jane Austen room. She was in Edmund's room. In Edmund's bed. Halley lifted her head. Why did Jillian sound panicked?

Because she was not in her room.

Halley jumped out of bed, thudding heavily on the dark walnut flooring.

Edmund lay tangled in a throw blanket on the chaise. It sounded like he was having a bad dream.

Halley crossed to him and jostled his shoulder. "Wake up," she croaked, her throat scratchy from last night's wood smoke. Last night ...

Last night had been ...

She didn't want to think about what last night had

been.

She didn't want to think about anything *but* what last night had been....

Crossing to the door, she opened it.

"In here," she called.

Jillian spun to face Halley. She looked surprised to find Halley emerging from Edmund's suite. Being a well-bred Applegate, she tried to hide her shock, but then she released a tiny laugh and then a bigger one.

Halley felt herself blushing from head to toe.

"So, um, it's time for breakfast," said Jillian. "I can have Branson bring up trays—"

"No need," replied Halley. "Just give me a minute to put some clothes on."

Jillian nodded. "I left a few things on your bed. I mean, the bed in the other room."

Still blushing, Halley crossed to her own room, where she found a (no doubt very expensive) pair of leggings and bulky cotton sweater that she suspected was a one-of-a-kind hand knit item. She slid her feet into her own flip-flops, leaving Jillian's complicated-looking strappy sandals behind.

She thought she heard Edmund's voice trailing across the hall from behind his closed door. It sounded like he was swearing. Or maybe praying with great fervor.

Halley was just reaching to open the door and leave her room when she heard Jillian's voice.

"Oh, Edmund, wow ..." Jillian's voice trailed off as Halley emerged into the hall to find Edmund *dressed*. Sort of.

Edmund, a dark expression on his brow, was wearing the clothes Branson had left stacked for him in the bathroom. His trousers were on … backwards. They'd been carefully tucked into a pair of socks. And his shoes? Halley wasn't entirely sure Edmund had put the correct shoe on the correct foot. His shirt was worn out and buttoned to the collar. Around his waist, he had attempted to tie a scarf meant to drape around his neck.

"Oh, my," murmured Halley. She turned to Jillian. "He's taking the 'stay in character' thing pretty seriously, I guess."

Jillian, with practiced restraint, suggested Branson might provide dressing assistance if Edmund required it.

"I understand not the closure of the breeches," he murmured, at which point Halley realized he was clutching the zipper fly shut over his backside.

"There's no need to send Branson," she said to Jillian. "I'll … fix things."

Jillian nodded, maintaining the fiction Edmund didn't look completely ridiculous. "Right. So I'll tell Branson you'll all be down in a minute?"

Halley nodded and then turned to Edmund. "Come on. Back in your room."

With a very straight face, she explained the *zipper* by demonstrating its use on a separate pair of jeans. She then showed Edmund how to drape a scarf, explained shirts were often worn with a button or two left undone, and sorted Edmund's left and right shoes—after learning Elizabethan shoes were agnostic as to left or right.

Once Edmund apologized for his ignorance and thanked her for her kind instruction, Halley had only to wait for him in the hall, trying *not* to imagine what he looked like out of his new clothes.

Breakfast was another of Branson's "simple affairs" which were anything *but*. On a sideboard in the breakfast room, Halley, Edmund, and Jillian were presented with Hungarian cultured cream to go with assorted blackberries, blueberries, and raspberries, alongside hard-boiled eggs, prosciutto, bresaola, capicola, lox, capers, schmear, bagels, and the variety of miniature fruit-and-nut loaves Branson had arrived so early in the morning to prepare.

"Coffee?" murmured Halley, ignoring the sideboard.

Jillian jumped up and stationed herself beside a Jura espresso maker. "What can I make for you?"

"Espresso."

"I'll make it a double," said Jillian.

"I love you," replied Halley. She sank into a chair and stared at the assortment on Edmund's plate: lots of fish, lots of fancy Italian dried meats, and a handful of blackberries.

"No coffee?" she asked Edmund.

Jillian responded. "There was none in the age of Queen Elizabeth I. No tea, no hot chocolate, and no coffee."

"Really?" asked Halley, while Edmund looked blankly at Jillian.

"Really. You're supposed to drink beer for breakfast, right?" asked Jillian

"I should be much in your debt, mistress," Edmund said with a slight bow.

Jillian handed Halley her espresso and strolled to the doorway, calling over her shoulder that she would see what Branson recommended.

Edmund broke the strained silence.

"I trust you slept well, lady?"

Halley felt her cheeks flushing as she pretended to consider her espresso. She'd slept well. Quite well. She'd dreamed of kissing Edmund under the drooping branches of a weeping willow. And then under a canopy of stars. And then under the canopy of his bed.

"I slept fine," she said, returning his smile with one of her own.

"Yet you eat nothing?" he asked.

"Caffeine comes first." She lifted her tiny cup.

Edmund looked puzzled. "You stand in want of ... the dark liquid?"

"Yes." She took a shallow sip. It was hot. And dark. And richly dotted with oil from the freshly ground beans and completely delicious. Her brain sparked back to life somewhere between her second and third sips.

"Why are you calling me 'you' and not 'thou'?" she asked. Had she done something wrong? Was he regretting certain ... *behaviors* last night?

Just as the morning fog dissipated outside, a tiny smile passed over Edmund's face. Light poured through the great arched window of the breakfast room and lit his face, all angles and edges. His lips stood out redder than before, and Halley remembered the feel of them against hers.

"I wish to speak in a manner befitting your world," Edmund said in reply.

Before Halley could comment, Jillian sailed into the breakfast room with two large glasses of amber-colored liquid.

"I have a Rudgate Ruby Mild and a Magner's

Hard Cider," she said triumphantly.

Edmund graciously accepted both, and the three set to breakfast, Edmund remarking upon the excellence of Jillian's cider.

"You will please to give your brewer my praise," he said.

Jillian laughed. "It's official," she whispered to Halley. "He's bewitching."

Halley said nothing and focused on the lavender-hazelnut-brown sugar loaf Jillian had insisted she try. It was moist, sweet, and fragrant, but Halley's mind was too busy to give it the attention it deserved.

She was busy *not* thinking of how the back of Edmund's neck had felt under her palm last night, busy *not* remembering the scent of lavender that had clung faintly to his face and hands as he'd touched her. She had to let him go—the scent of him, the idea of him, the nearness and *here*-ness of him. Halley had no need of yet another impossible desire.

She set the loaf aside, hardly touched, silently swearing off anything lavender-scented.

Ten minutes later, the three were seated in Halley's truck, on their way to hang DaVinci's first gallery show at Montecito's exclusive Plaza del Mar.

## 27

## · KHAN ·

Before slipping behind the wheel of his Tesla, the professor checked his pocket one final time. Yes, the three gold chains and one heavy carcanet, or collar, were safely in his pocket, lovingly swathed in organic cotton roving he'd ordered online from a hippie farmer in New Mexico.

He double-checked the message from his buyer, an art and antiques dealer, to make certain of the date and time. Khan had stayed in the parking lot of the Mikkelsen's apartment complex until the last possible moment, having considered asking his buyer, Martin Nieman, to reschedule a little later. Nieman had, after all, jumped at the opportunity to acquire pieces of sixteenth century European provenance. But the early Saturday appointment would mean both the antiques shop and attached art gallery would be closed. The dealer preferred to undertake his acquisitions without interruptions by the curious. The professor preferred this, too.

In fact, most of the professor's assignations were

conducted under more rigorous conditions than this, but he wished to raise cash quickly and the close proximity of the tiny Montecito antiques dealer-*cum*-gallery owner made Khan willing to cut corners. Besides, he knew Nieman. Nieman was good at keeping his mouth shut, which Khan appreciated in a buyer. Even in person, the man seemed determined to speak as little as possible. Although, this was perhaps to maintain the fiction of his English accent. Khan assumed the dealer's fraudulent accent was meant to reassure both "old money" and the *nouveau riche* that here, at least, was a dealer who knew what he was about. Khan didn't care if the accent was real or fake—the cash payments were real, and Khan needed cash to continue funding his research. He was so close to a breakthrough—he could almost taste it. Thank God he wasn't stuck relying on research grants for the sums he required.

As Khan slowed for a "California Stop" at the next stop sign, he passed another Tesla. They'd become commonplace in Montecito. It made him want to shop for something more exotic. As he pulled forward, he wondered if there was a weight limit as to what could brought back through the temporal rift. On the other hand, how would he drive a '37 Bugatti Roadster out of the basement?

He continued along the eucalyptus lined streets, winding his way down Montecito's charming back roads and finally turning into the tiny parking lot of the area's most exclusive strip mall. Of course no one would dream of calling the collection of shops by so crass a name as a "strip mall." It was called a "center" or "plaza" or some such nonsense.

When he pulled in, the parking lot was not empty. The back of Khan's neck prickled. A wine shop stood a few yards from the gallery and antiques shop, but it wouldn't open for another two hours. Montecito did not rise early on the weekends. Leaving his own car running, the professor assessed the potential danger of additional persons in the vicinity. The sporty Mercedes on the far side of the parking lot boasted vanity plates that read "NIEMAN1." Khan curled his lip in disgust, ignoring the fact he'd once inquired as to the availability of "OUTATIME." (The DMV regretted to inform him it was unavailable.)

He turned his attention to the beat-up pickup truck parked directly in front of the gallery. A janitor, perhaps? And then, with a shock, the professor realized he'd seen the truck before. It was Halley Mikkelsen's truck. What good fortune. What incredibly good fortune.

But then, the professor had always been a strong believer in the proposal that Fortune favored the bold.

He didn't bother locking the car as he exited.

## 28

### · *EDMUND* ·

"Some help, here?" asked DaVinci.

Edmund, who had just finished holding a ladder steady for Mistress Halley, turned to assist Mistress DaVinci, who was standing at the opposite end of the gallery owned by some acquaintance of Jillian's lady mother. Together with Mistress Jillian, DaVinci was attempting to mount a wide and doubtless very heavy tapestry upon a set of hooks. Neither lady was of a height sufficient to reach the hooks.

"Allow me, Mistress DaVinci," said Edmund. He made slight bows to DaVinci and Jillian.

"Ooh-la-la," replied DaVinci. Grinning, she allowed him to take the heavy piece from her.

The hooks were at such a great height as to make it a challenge even for Edmund, but he had just succeeded in securing one side of the tapestry when he heard Halley greeting some person newly arrived.

"Wow—what a surprise," she was saying. "Sorry—give me a quick sec."

Edmund turned in time to see her turning slightly

away from none other than the magician. She was rapidly brushing the surface of her message-delivering device. Edmund felt the overwhelming need to rush to Halley's side, complicated by the fact he doubted she would thank him for it. Also complicated by the fact he was stuck supporting Mistress DaVinci's tapestry.

"Halley Mikkelsen," said the magician. "A surprise indeed! What brings you to the gallery—ah, I see. Tapestries. My goodness. Impressive."

As Edmund hastened to finish with the tapestry, he heard buzzing sounds emanating from both DaVinci and Jillian's message devices. He secured the tapestry and turned for Halley, but Jillian grabbed him by the arm, restraining him. He saw a puzzled look on Mistress Jillian's face, echoed by a like expression upon Mistress DaVinci's as both regarded him.

Drawing him near, Jillian whispered in Edmund's ear. *"Halley says to remember you don't speak English."* She held up her phone, with a message which included that information.

He nodded his assent and then strode to Halley's side.

*"Min Kæreste,"* Halley murmured, taking his hand in hers.

Edmund tried to indicate by a squeeze to her hand that he had received her message. He spoke no words. As he gazed at the magician, he saw again a certain something he could not like. A communication writ in the dark squint of the magician's eye—in the nervous way he curled his fingers against his palms. The magician had the look of one who hid secrets. Of one who knew how to be dangerous.

"And how nice to see your friend as well,"

167

murmured the magician to Halley.

Edmund widened his stance and anchored his free hand to his hip while focusing his attention on the magician. The posture was one he'd imbibed from his grandfather, a man who knew how to render himself as large and imposing as possible.

"I didn't catch his name before…."

"Edmund," murmured Halley. "Edmund Aldwy—Aldwys*sen*."

The mage turned to Edmund. "*God morgen.*" He enunciated carefully, striking his syllables hard.

While Edmund stared at the man with a darkening brow, Halley replied to the magician.

"The Danish pronounce it *goh-morn*," she said to the magician.

"Do they indeed?" asked the magician.

"*Goh-morn*," said Edmund, repeating Halley's pronunciation, with a nod.

Tense silence followed, until a loud clatter drew everyone's attention to DaVinci.

"Can I please borrow your ladder?" DaVinci called to Halley. She bent to retrieve her fallen tapestry.

Edmund instantly resumed his watch upon the mage, but as Jillian approached to grab the ladder, Halley addressed Edmund.

"*Hjælpe hende*," Halley said, pointing to Jillian. "Help her."

After considering the request for a count of three, Edmund gave a curt nod and strode away with the ladder. Halley was introducing Jillian to the mage, which activity even Edmund could admit was perfectly safe. As he returned back to Halley and Jillian, he overheard the mage asking questions about *him*.

"He understands some English," Halley was saying, "But he doesn't like to speak it in public. He's embarrassed about making mistakes."

"I should probably get back to work," Jillian murmured, excusing herself.

"Of course, of course," replied the magician. "I've got an appointment, too, actually. Until we meet again," he said, smiling at Halley and Edmund.

The magician turned to go but then spun back around and reached for Halley's forearm.

Edmund's right hand flew across his waist to his left side for his sword—a sword that was not there. He had only time to curse his luck when, just as quickly, the magician released Halley, having passed her what looked like a letter. The man turned to leave once more, calling over his shoulder, "Just a small token of gratitude."

"Thanks," Halley called back.

The heavy door closed behind the magician and Edmund felt as though he could breathe freely once more.

Almost as soon as the door to the gallery had latched shut, Jillian turned to Edmund and Halley. "Why are you two both pretending he's Danish?" she asked.

DaVinci, hands on her hips, evidently had the same question.

Before Halley could answer, Edmund replied. "That man is a treacherous conjurer."

"Dr. Jules Khan?" asked Jillian.

"Is a treacherous *what*?" demanded DaVinci.

"Who are you, really?" asked Jillian.

Edmund turned to Halley, a questioning

expression on his face.

"Oh, no," said Halley, sighing.

"Oh, no, *what?*" asked DaVinci. "What's going on here?"

Halley reached for the ring she kept strung about her fair neck. She withdrew the ring, grasping it tightly. After a moment, she spoke. "You're not going to believe me."

"Try us," said Jillian, her arms folding across her chest.

## 29

### · *HALLEY* ·

In freshman year English, Halley had made the mistake of explicating a very personal poem of her own composition; it was a mistake she never repeated. Later in the same class, Halley encountered Emily Dickenson's advice: *Tell all the Truth, but tell it slant.* Halley had focused on the second part of the line. While she was essentially honest, there were some truths she told "slant": with a certain bent or emphasis or adaptation that offered protection to her soft underbelly. There was safety in sharing only carefully apportioned pieces of the truth, especially with her mother, but sometimes even with her friends.

But now, standing in the art gallery, DaVinci's show half-hung and DaVinci's eyebrow raised in expectation, Halley knew a *slant* version of the truth about Edmund was not going to satisfy her friends. She should have known better. DaVinci, like Jillian (who was failing miserably at keeping her face well-manneredly neutral), wanted the truth, the whole truth, and nothing but the truth. And then there was

Edmund, who still believed—because she had told him to—that the professor was a magician. Exposed underbellies be damned, Halley was going to have to explain things honestly.

She searched for a way to begin—for something that didn't sound completely insane. But really, there weren't any reasonable-sounding ways to begin. Like removing a Band-Aid, this was best done swiftly and irrevocably.

To Edmund she said, "The professor isn't really a magician. He does what he does with electricity and physics, not sorcery. I'm sorry I didn't, er, clarify that earlier."

To DaVinci and Jillian, she said, "Edmund's visiting from the 16th century."

Her friends regarded her with expressions mingling confusion and disbelief. Halley continued anyway, focusing on DaVinci and Jillian and hoping Edmund would understand why she had called the professor a magician.

"The house I was watching for Mom yesterday had a time machine and I accidentally dragged Edmund back from London in the 1590's."

"From 1598," said Edmund.

DaVinci's deep belly-laugh reverberated in the echo-y gallery. "Right. God, Halley, you should write this stuff down. Be a screen writer, not a costume designer."

Jillian turned to face Edmund. "But in all seriousness," she said, her tone perfectly polite, "You're an actor, right?"

"Madam, I am no player."

DaVinci snorted with laughter. "'*Madam*, I am no

*player.*' What is that accent, anyway? Pirate?"

Jillian glared at DaVinci.

"I am no pirate, neither, my ladies," said Edmund. "Time's own hostage am I, captured and not captor."

DaVinci snorted again.

Twisting the ring at her neck, Halley pushed on. "I'm not making this up. I'm serious. Professor Khan is some crazy time-traveling thief. I saw him appear out of thin air, clutching a fistful of old jewelry. Pieces that would be priceless today. And he's got an original Gutenberg Bible and Shakespeare's sonnets and all kinds of stuff he stole and brought back."

"Halley," began Jillian, employing her calmest manner, "Seriously, what's going on?"

Halley sank onto a bench and cradled her head in her hands. "You think I'm crazy. It sounds crazy." Her voice was quiet as she spoke. "All I know is that there were these huge Tesla coils, and one minute I was standing between them, and then the next minute I was inside the Curtain Theatre in London. In fifteen-freaking-ninety-eight."

Tentatively, Jillian perched beside Halley on the gallery bench. "Halley, you know we love you. And we want to be here for you." She glanced up at DaVinci.

"Totally," agreed DaVinci.

"But what you're asking us to believe doesn't seem very … plausible," said Jillian. "Don't you think it's possible there's a more rational explanation?"

"Like what?" demanded Halley. Heat seared the backs of her eyes. She'd been an idiot to think they would just … *believe* her.

"As far as you can, um, remember," said DaVinci, "All of this happened after the earthquake, right?"

173

Halley nodded, rubbing the back of her hands quickly over her eyes.

"It's just ..." began Jillian. "Maybe you might be a little ... concussed?"

"A *lot* concussed," added DaVinci. "Come on. We should get you seen—"

"Edmund!" snapped Halley. "Back me up here." She shook her head in exasperation. "That means, tell my friends I'm telling the truth."

"Lady," replied Edmund, "I have been endeavoring to persuade myself of it. Thou didst tell me at first I had entered the Faerie Kingdom, only to admit that was a deception. Now you tell me I was deceived in believing that man a magician—"

"I was trying to keep you safe," snapped Halley. "I didn't have enough time to explain everything to you. You saw for yourself how long it took me to make clear what *really* happened. I said what I had to say to keep you safe, and then, with the professor, I just ... I forgot I'd called him a magician, okay?"

"Whoa, whoa, whoa," said DaVinci. "Hal, you're kinda scaring me here. I really think we need to get you to ER—"

Turning, Halley shouted, "I'm not going to ER! There's nothing wrong with my head. And even if there were, how do you explain *him*?" She pointed to Edmund. "Did we both have the same concussion or hallucination or whatever?"

"Don't shout at me," said DaVinci, crossing her arms. "I'm trying to help. And I'm not the one claiming I visited the Renaissance using a time machine."

"That much is true," said Edmund, his own voice

rising. "The lady came unto my time by means of some ... wondrous device. And by means of the same did we return. The lady seemed to fall and I reached for her, and from thence we traveled to your world."

"You didn't reach for me; I grabbed *you*," Halley said apologetically.

"Nay, I held my arms out to *you*," insisted Edmund.

"Fine. Hands were held out. Bodies were reached for," said DaVinci. "Can we please at least talk about the possibility of seeing a doctor?"

"No," said Jillian, standing and placing a hand gently on DaVinci's shoulder. "At least, not yet. Halley's right about one thing. Edmund seems genuinely convinced he's not from ... here."

"Well maybe Halley's right that they both had the *same* concussion," said DaVinci. "Because there's no way they were both in a time machine that just happens to be in someone's *basement* in Montecito."

"There's got to be a logical explanation," replied Jillian. "What's that Sherlock Holmes quote?" She turned on her cell, typing in a search phrase. "Here: *Once you eliminate the impossible, whatever remains, no matter how improbable, must be the truth.*"

"Uh, yeah," replied DaVinci. "Once you, you know, eliminate the *impossible.*" She pulled out her own cell phone and then carefully spoke into it. "*Is time travel possible?*"

A stilted voice responded with, "*Here's what I found on the web for 'Is time travel possible?'*"

DaVinci stared at her screen. And stared some more. And finally grunted, "Huh. Okay." She showed the screen to Jillian. "Not what I was expecting."

"They say it's possible, don't they?" asked Halley, her voice emptied of her earlier anger.

"Well, yes, in theory. But it could be just a bunch of quacks," said DaVinci.

"If by 'bunch of quacks' you mean NASA physicists and MIT graduates," murmured Jillian, now examining her own cell.

"Okay, okay," said DaVinci. "Let's go at this another way. Edmund, you say you are from 1598. How old were you when Elizabeth the First took the throne?"

Halley, understanding DaVinci meant to turn this into Twenty Questions, looked up hopefully.

"Good mistress," replied Edmund, "Her majesty was already upon the throne at my birth."

"Hang on, hang on," said DaVinci. Halley saw her swiping open a calculator. "How old are you?"

"One and twenty," replied Edmund.

DaVinci tapped numbers into the calculator on her phone.

"Fine. Whatever. That one doesn't count. It was too easy. How about ... um ... How about tell me what George Washington is famous for?"

"I have not had the privilege of the gentleman's acquaintance," Edmund replied.

"DaVinci," murmured Jillian. "Don't you think you're being a little—"

"No, let her," said Halley. "Go ahead and try something really hard. Tell us how much a pint of ale would cost in 1598? No—wait. The questions should come from DaVinci so no one thinks I gave Edmund the answers ahead of time." She glared at DaVinci.

"How about a horse instead?" asked Jillian. "What

would a horse cost in 1598?"

"It would depend upon the horse, lady," began Edmund, "But a goodly steed can be hired for the day at a shilling, or bought outright for six crowns."

"Hang on," said DaVinci, scrolling on her phone screen. "This has it in pennies. How many pennies in six crowns?"

"Why, three hundred and sixty," replied Edmund, as if addressing someone of dubious intelligence.

"Huh. He's right," said DaVinci.

Halley, swallowing a laugh, turned to Edmund. "Don't worry, DaVinci can add and multiply. It's just that we don't use shillings and crowns or whatever. We use dollars and cents."

Edmund bowed to DaVinci. "I pray you will forgive any unintended discourtesy, lady."

"How much would you tip a servant?" DaVinci asked, eyes fixed on her screen.

"Three or four pennies, and the service they rendered was valuable," replied Edmund.

"Okay. So, how much would a, um, *tankard* of ale cost?"

"Only a fool or a drunkard would pay more than a halfpenny."

"Loaf of bread?"

"Tuppence."

"A chicken?"

Edmund laughed. "I know not. Ask in my kitchens, if you would know the answer. But at an inn of repute, for a cooked bird I might give a penny."

"He's getting all these right," murmured DaVinci. "How about a pound of cinnamon?"

"DaVinci," said Jillian.

"Cinnamon was *crazy* expensive," murmured DaVinci, still scrolling on her phone.

"I think you've made your point," murmured Jillian to DaVinci.

"Anything you can ask, he can answer," said Halley. "I guarantee it. We're telling you the truth. Edmund came here from 1598."

"It seems theoretically possible," ventured Jillian, still reading something on her phone.

"If by possible you mean crazy, then yes," said DaVinci.

Halley gave her a sad half-smile. "Yes. It's crazy."

DaVinci shook her head slowly. "The cow is on the Nissan this time for sure, my friend."

Halley groaned. "*Isen*, not Nissan." Turning to Edmund, she explained. "It's a Danish saying: *Ko på isen*. Literally, the 'cow's on the ice.' It means—"

Jillian emitted a small gasp.

"What?" asked Halley and DaVinci at the same time.

"There was an international symposium on space-time in 2001 at UC Santa Barbara," said Jillian. She looked up from her phone. "Any guesses as to who organized it and presented a paper there, *on time travel?*"

"Professor Jules Khan," said Halley, her voice flat as the sea in a dead calm.

# 30

## · *KHAN* ·

It was a tiny thing that disturbed the professor. It tickled away in the back of his brain during his financial transactions with Martin Nieman, purveyor of antique and estate jewelry. It troubled him as he sat in the parking lot outside the gallery, contemplating the sale of: *three golden chains with pendants, sixteenth century, manufactured by N. Hilliard,* and tried to decide how he would sell a fourth valuable necklace Nieman had regrettably declined to purchase.

Dr. Jules Khan was familiar with this odd ticklings, these just-out-of-reach inklings. They had led to his greatest breakthroughs in scientific discovery. As a post-doc with a freshly minted PhD, he had pursued these ticklings doggedly, attempting to corner and intimidate them. Eventually, he had learned this was a dead end, methodologically speaking. He learned that only when he exercised restraint, would the ideas bloom, unfold, and reveal themselves. The trick was to keep one's eyes averted. And then, *voila!* A breakthrough. A revelation. An *answer.*

So he averted his attention. Focused upon the fine-ness of the morning—another perfect day in Paradise. Considered what he would take for breakfast. A coffee from the Nordstrom Café Bistro, perhaps? Mused upon a pet hypothesis he was anxious to test. And then, as he turned a corner emerging into blinding sunlight, it came to him.

The young man. Edmund *Aldwyssen*.

There had been a moment when the professor been certain Edmund meant to harm him. Dr. Jules Khan hadn't survived dozens of forays into history without scenting the subtle shift that preceded a revealed firearm, a drawn sword, a pair of raised fists.

But the boy hadn't raised his fists like a boy ready to duke it out. He hadn't reached for a firearm concealed in a shoulder holster like an undercover agent. No, the young man had done neither of these things. Instead, he had shifted his right hand to his left hip like someone reaching for a sword. Like someone who'd been pulled into this century from an earlier one, by means of the singularity device.

Khan swore. This, then, was the subtle clue that had been itching and tickling the professor's brain—and it gave the boy away, the action of reaching his right hand across to his left hip, seeking a sword that should have been there.

Or had he misread the clue? Maybe Edmund had been reaching to scratch an itch. Maybe he had poison oak. Maybe he'd been swiping at a fly.

It was still possible the laboratory remained inviolate and unprofaned. Wasn't it?

In his mind's eye, the professor visualized his subterranean chamber. His sacred space. His hidden source of limitless wealth and knowledge. He was in trouble. In peril.

He slammed on his brakes as a frisson of fear ran its way up his spine. He had been so careful for so long. Would the girl have blabbed everything she'd seen and done all over social media? Exposure was unthinkable. Whipping out his cell phone, Jules Khan searched a few key phrases. Fortunately, he found nothing to increase his fears. Of course, there was nothing to abate them, either. If the girl hadn't told anyone yet, that was no guarantee she would keep silent indefinitely. Khan had a sudden vision of days, months, *years* spent holding his breath, hoping, praying, pleading, bribing.

He couldn't live like that. He *wouldn't* live like that.

Hoping Halley and her sixteenth century "boyfriend" were still at the gallery, Khan made a completely unprotected U-turn and then sped forward, uttering a very old, rather foul, and tiresomely common word.

# 31

## · HALLEY ·

"Eliminate the impossible," said Halley, "And whatever remains, no matter how crazy, is the truth." She looked over to Jillian, who had seated herself on one of the gallery's viewing benches. "Did I say it right?"

"Essentially," murmured Jillian.

"Guys?" said DaVinci, scrolling through her phone. "Check this out. If you Google Dr. Jules Khan plus time travel, the only hit is that one paper in 2001. I've gone back five pages, and that's it. One paper. What's with that?"

"It would make sense if he had actually succeeded and wanted to keep it secret," mused Jillian.

"That's my assumption," said Halley. She collapsed onto the bench beside Jillian. "This is a huge secret. Like, the biggest secret ever."

"Oh," said DaVinci, eyes widening. "*That's* why you said Edmund was Danish, so the professor wouldn't hear Edmund's Elizabethan mouth shooting off and figure out you had brought someone back—

uh, *forward*—in time."

"Yes," Halley said. "It was the only thing I could think of."

"Good thinking, really," said DaVinci. "So, um, I take it we are all ... believing Halley's, uh, explanation?"

Jillian nodded. Halley felt her eyes brimming. She hadn't been prepared for how good it would feel to include her friends in this secret.

"Sorry," she murmured, swiping at her eyes. "I'm being stupid."

Jillian hugged an arm around Halley's shoulders. "It's fine."

"It's just," said DaVinci, "Am I the only one who thinks it's an awfully big coincidence that Dr. Khan just happened to show up here where Halley and Edmund are? What is he doing showing up here? At a closed art gallery? On a Saturday morning?"

"That's why I texted you guys the warning," said Halley, miserably. "I don't think he just happened to show up here. I'm afraid he's *following* us."

Jillian frowned. "There's actually a very rational explanation for Khan being here. You said he came back from the time machine clutching jewelry, right?"

Halley nodded, as did Edmund.

"Well," said Jillian, "My mom's colleague—the one who owns the gallery and gave DaVinci this opportunity—her husband has an office in the back, and he buys estate jewelry and antiques."

Edmund spoke. "The professor carried several rings and a carcanet of great worth when he appeared before us from nowhere."

"He sells the things he steals," said Halley.

"Traveling in time to steal expensive jewelry for a living?" said DaVinci. "Why didn't I think of that?"

"That's my guess, anyway," clarified Halley. "He's retired, but he's, like, not even forty. And his home is worth four million easy, according to my mom."

"Um, hello, my parents teach," said DaVinci. "No way did he make that teaching at UCSB. But selling old art and jewelry like that, he'd be richer than a Swiss banker."

"He might *buy* what he brings back, rather than stealing it," suggested Jillian.

"In either case," said Edmund, "He would have good cause to keep the machine a secret."

"Well, if he's here at the gallery, he's probably selling jewelry," said Jillian to Halley. "Which would mean you have nothing to worry about. There's a perfectly good reason for him to be here, and it has nothing to do with you."

DaVinci rolled her eyes. "You always see the best in people."

"It doesn't mean she's wrong about why Khan's here," said Halley, trying to convince herself. "Although, he did ask about Edmund...."

Jillian shook her head. "He was just doing what anyone would do to be polite. Which leads me to another point. Er, Edmund, you come across a little ... intense."

"I beg pardon, lady, but I understand you not," he replied.

"She means you're all, 'Me Tarzan—me protect Jane!'" said DaVinci.

Edmund looked more confused than ever.

"Let's just finish up here," said Halley, rising.

Even knowing Khan hadn't come there for her, she was still eager to get away as soon as possible. As they hung the final tapestries and adjusted the lighting, Halley explained her plan to return Edmund to his rightful time when her mother next house-sat for Khan.

"The machine is in the main house basement—" explained Halley.

"Where *everyone* keeps their time machine," murmured DaVinci.

"So you're going to have figure out how to break into the basement," said Jillian, tapping one finger thoughtfully to her chin. "Branson might have some ideas...."

"Branson?" asked Halley.

"*Bran*-son," sighed DaVinci, pretending to fan herself.

"He's full of extremely practical tips," said Jillian. "Not that I'll tell him why or anything."

"I'm only helping if it's during daylight hours," said DaVinci. "I read this sci-fi story once about a time traveler who became a ghost every night at midnight." She gave an exaggerated shiver.

Jillian murmured, "*DaVinci.*"

Edmund looked amused.

"No offense, dude," added DaVinci. "And I still totally need to sketch you."

Halley groaned. "I can't ask either of you to help—"

"Of course we're helping," snapped Jillian. "What kind of friends would we be if we abandoned you in your hour of need?"

Halley, reminded of how she'd left them at the

booth yesterday, felt her face heating.

Edmund responded to Jillian. "I cannot ask either of you to place yourself in the path of harm, but I must return or perish in the attempt."

Halley felt her stomach tightening. Within seconds, her phone began buzzing with incoming texts.

It was her mother.

"Fantastic," she murmured.

## 32

### · *HALLEY* ·

Halley's mother wanted to know about her paycheck. Had Halley picked it up? Why hadn't she brought it over? Where was it now?

Halley sighed and shot back a quick response. Then she looked up to her friends.

"Mom's angry I didn't pick up her check last night when I promised to," she said. She couldn't quite keep the defeated sound from her voice. "I have to swing by the apartment just in case the check was miraculously mailed yesterday evening and delivered to our address this morning."

This time it was DaVinci who crossed over to hug Halley. "Just remember," she murmured, "You are an amazing daughter. It's your mom who has issues, and those issues have nothing to do with what you do or don't do."

"I know," said Halley. "It's not me. I know."

"You don't," said DaVinci, shaking her head at Halley. "But I hope someday you will."

"Okay," said Jillian. "Time for me to pick

Branson's brain on picking locks."

DaVinci snorted, released Halley, and said she had to get home, too.

"I'll pick you both up tomorrow at ten," Jillian said to Halley and Edmund. "Meanwhile, you should show Edmund how Santa Barbarians have fun." She winked at Halley, who flushed and turned to leave.

Edmund peppered her with questions once they were alone in the truck, and by the time Halley finished explaining about "checks" and the "postal service" (which Edmund found fascinating), they had reached the parking lot of her small apartment. She opened her mail box and pulled out several days' worth of junk mail, scanning for anything hand-written. Not finding it, she climbed back in the truck and handed the stack of mail to Edmund so she could text her mother.

*Nothing yet. I'll check again Monday.*

As soon as she finished typing the very ordinary word *Monday*, she realized that a week from Monday, Edmund would be gone. The thought carved a hollow space in her belly. She reached for her jade ring. She didn't want Edmund to leave. She wanted him to stay, punctuating her life with his laughter and his sense of wonder at ordinary things like the postal service. She wanted the shiver that came with accidental contact, the back of her hand brushing his forearm, their knees jouncing together on Montecito's pot-holed back roads. She wanted to hold his hand watching pelicans dive into the silver sea. She wanted to lean in until foreheads touched and the world shrank down to their two breaths.

Exhaling, she released her grip on her ring. She

was being a fool. Edmund had to go.

She put her keys back in the ignition and told herself to pull it together. Two days ago, she'd never even heard of Edmund, second Earl of Unobtainable. She pulled the truck out of the parking lot.

Except … Edmund *wasn't* unobtainable. Not at the moment. Which was maddening and wonderful.

His mood seemed to have shifted as well. He looked gloomy, his brow furrowing. Halley's eyes traced the slight growth of beard that had appeared overnight. She looked back to the road, and an achy part of her wondered what it would feel like to kiss him now.

"Are you worrying?" she asked softly, glancing back at him.

"Is it thus apparent?" His mouth turned up at the corners, and Halley noted how his face had small white creases that the summer sun of four hundred years ago had failed to reach.

"It's time for some serious distraction," she said. "I know just the thing. First stop, a modern grocery store. I'm introducing you to 'ice cream.'"

Pulling into the Vons parking lot, she had to explain the concept of "store" to Edmund, who only knew the word as a verb: *to store,* as in, to store grain for winter.

"We do visit the *costermonger* instead of the *store,*" Edmund explained. "London has those who will sell you apples or nuts in season, from a cart or stall, and shops of every kind, besides."

Despite London's wealth of offerings, Edmund was dumbstruck by the inside of Vons. He stared in open-mouthed amazement at everything from the seafood display to the wine selection to the brightly packaged loaves of bread. Halley had to grab his sleeve to tug him away from the cartons of identical white eggs.

"I stand amazed," he murmured over and over.

"Frozen foods this way," she said, guiding him to the selection of gourmet pints of ice cream.

She asked if he wanted to try mint chocolate chip, but he didn't answer.

Halley looked up from "Phish Food" and "Cherry Garcia" to see what had captured Edmund's attention. He'd thrust a hand inside the freezer case and was holding it there, in stunned silence.

"How is it that the chill of winter is contained within this box?" he asked.

"Electricity," murmured Halley. "And if you're not going to help me pick a flavor, we're getting Dulce de Leche." She reached for the carton and then gently pulled Edmund's hand back out of the freezer, shutting the door.

He was still marveling at his cold hand while Halley paid for the ice cream. "Do you have plastic spoons?" she asked the cashier.

The cashier handed her two. "Breakfast of champions," he said, winking as he bagged the ice cream.

Back in the truck, Edmund was as fascinated by the icy frost forming on the container as he had been by the freezer case. He was like a toddler playing with the wrapping paper instead of the gift. She eased the truck onto Coast Village Road, turning right for the beach.

"Careful," she said as they jolted along the uneven

pavement toward the Biltmore. "If you leave your hand on the container like that, you'll get frostbite."

Edmund looked up, smiled bashfully, and replaced the ice cream carton in the bag. "I did things equally foolish when I was a boy."

"If this foolishness involved something frozen and your tongue, I don't want to know."

Edmund laughed at this and vowed she should not, in that case, hear any more of his youthful folly.

The ocean came into view, the sun glancing off the water in a repeating pattern of diamonds that seemed to stretch all the way to the Channel Islands. Halley parked and the two scampered down a set of crumbling stairs.

"This way," said Halley, turning right and away from the Biltmore's manicured beach. She suspected the stairs on that end of the beach were *not* crumbling into ruin, but she preferred the golden sandstone cliffs to the cement-reinforced walls of the hotel's beach.

Edmund paused, stooping to retrieve a blue-grey rock from the beach. It was pocked with holes.

Halley crouched beside him.

"I have never seen the like," he said, turning the stone in his hands.

"It looks like someone took a miniature melon-baller to it, huh?" asked Halley before remembering he wouldn't know what a melon-baller was. "You should take it home with you. To remember."

Something flickered in Edmund's eyes as he met hers.

Swallowing, Halley stood and strode down to the water, allowing it to lap her feet. The pure cold of the ocean drove the drowsy warmth of Edmund's gaze away.

Silently, Edmund joined her, having slipped off his shoes.

They stood for a long while like that, the two staring out at the bright water.

"I dream of the sea," he said at last.

Halley turned to him. His face held a fierceness she hadn't seen before.

"You do?" she asked, fishing for more.

Edmund bent to pick up another rock, small and rounded and ordinary. He hurled it far, far out to sea. And then he spoke again.

"I dreamed of following Martin Frobisher and John White to seek the glories of the New World. But that was long ago."

The fierceness on his face had been replaced with something more like regret. It made Halley want to take his hand. Tentatively, she reached for it. Edmund held on tightly and did not let go.

## 33

## · *KHAN* ·

Dr. Jules Khan drove uphill towards Nieman's art gallery at precisely twelve miles per hour over the posted limit, desperately hoping Halley Mikkelsen and her "boyfriend" hadn't left yet. What he meant to say or do, he wasn't sure. Finding them came first. Khan had bluffed his way through any number of threatening situations as a temporal rift traveler, and in Latin, too. Surely he could manage a teenage girl barely out of high school.

Khan drove through a four-way stop without stopping and inched his speed up to fifteen miles over the speed limit. And then, just at the next curve, he saw an ugly blue pickup truck driving toward him in the opposite lane. Its driver did not make eye contact, being apparently too distracted by her passenger.

Slamming on his brakes, the professor reversed into a driveway and turned around to follow the pickup.

The pair made a stop at Vons, giving Khan time to consider what, exactly, he was hoping for out of an encounter. Licking his lips nervously, Khan decided *not* to follow them into the grocery store. It was too public. Too many people around who might overhear sensitive information. Instead, he remained in his car, its low profile mostly hidden by an enormous Hummer H2.

Within eight minutes, the pickup was on the move again. Khan kept what he hoped was a discreet distance and tried to will himself to stop worrying. Who, really, was more easily intimidated than an eighteen year old fresh out of high school? Khan had commanded the fear of hundreds of college freshman every year during his tenure as an instructor in the physics department. Though retired, he still purposefully referred to himself as a *professor* rather than as Dr. Khan. There might be more cachet in the honorific, but there was more intimidation in the job title.

The girl seemed to be heading for Channel Drive. Khan felt a sudden craving for one of Tonio's cayenne-sprinkled Mexican mochas. These exquisite drinks alone justified Khan's membership in the exclusive Coral Casino Beach and Cabana Club. He promised the mocha to himself as a reward for completing ... whatever was coming. Another cold chill ran along his neck. If the girl knew everything ... if she *told anything* ...

The blue pickup turned right, following Channel Drive along the cliffs above Butterfly Beach. The young couple were certainly taking the scenic route if their destination was their dilapidated apartment complex. Khan dropped back, slowing his speed, and watched as Halley Mikkelsen performed an awkward three-point turn, reversing her direction so she could parallel park her vehicle beside the stairs at the beach's less developed end.

Once the pair had exited their vehicle and gone down to the beach, Khan pulled his vehicle forward and past the truck, turning right onto Butterfly Lane which ran perpendicular to Channel Drive. He parked his car at the mouth of a private driveway with a sign reading "POSITIVELY NO TURNS."

And then he considered his next move.

# 34

## · HALLEY ·

Halley's eyes flickered over to Edmund's. He was still staring at the ocean, the mournful expression fading. He cleared his throat and spoke.

"When I was young, my father sought to discourage my love of the sea; my grandfather to turn my taste for adventure into a taste for life in Her Majesty's Navy. He sailed against the Spanish in 1588—ah, but I forget. You will not have heard of that battle."

"The Spanish Armada?"

Edmund looked curiously at her. "Aye."

Halley's eyes grew wide. "Everyone's heard of the Spanish Armada. I mean, I don't know details, but I know the English beat the crap out of the Spanish."

Edmund laughed heartily. "Aye, that we did."

"Wow. And your grandfather was there?"

"Aye. My father should have been as well, but he had broke his leg riding whilst he was drunken." He paused. "There are worse things, you see, than having no father at all." He turned his gaze to a chunky gold

196

ring worn on the index finger of his left hand. "It gives me no pleasure to say it, but I do not miss the ring I wore once to remember my father."

"Did you lose it?"

Edmund picked up another stone and threw it into the sea. "My brother Geoffrey contracted debts he was unable to pay. I sold the ring to satisfy his creditors."

"Oh." Halley, uncertain how to express her sympathy, said nothing, but she held his hand more tightly in hers.

"Yesterday, Geoffrey was given the means to purchase gifts for my grandfather's funeral."

"Wait, was this the brother you were trying to find when I met you at the theatre?"

"The same. Geoffrey cannot be trusted with wealth in his purse. He will lay it out against ale or a game of chance." Edmund twisted his remaining ring. "He is as like to what my father was as is possible."

"I'm sorry," murmured Halley.

"It cannot be helped."

Edmund was staring out at the sea again.

"You love the sea," she murmured.

"Aye. To feel the salt spray, to journey and see what none before have seen, to go where none have gone—" He broke off with a look of such longing that it made her own throat tighten. She knew what it was to yearn for things you couldn't have.

"Can't you, I don't know, be an earl *and* be an … adventurer or whatever it's called?" she asked.

"Were we of greater means, mayhap. But as things stand, I shall have to work all the days of my life to pay debts contracted by my grandfather."

"I see." She didn't. Not exactly. She could see that it wasn't fair. That Edmund shouldn't be punished and ... *held back* because his family members were idiots or spendthrifts. She might have a terrible mother, but at least Halley couldn't end up in a position where she had to spend her life paying back her mom's credit card bills. She hoped.

"C'mon," said Halley. "Let's sit and eat ice cream before it melts."

They found a spot back against the cliffs where someone had dragged a eucalyptus log. Together they sat, leaning against the log, digging toes into sand and spoons into ice cream.

"I stand amazed," Edmund said, upon tasting his first ice cream.

Halley snorted and then said, "You're *sitting*."

He ignored her. "It is like unto an egg custard the cook doth prepare in springtime, but sweeter." He shoveled another spoonful into his mouth. And then another. "And cold—as cold as winter itself."

Halley laughed. "Don't eat it all!"

Chastised, Edmund withdrew his spoon.

"You know what?" said Halley. "Forget I said anything. I can get ice cream anytime. Have at it."

Edmund's face seemed to draw tight as she said this, but like so many of the emotions that played over his angular face, this one was gone in an instant.

"Are you ... Are you *sorry* you'll have to go back home?" She passed him the ice cream tub.

He didn't answer right away. This time Halley could tell he was restraining himself from letting anything show on his face.

"In truth, I would stay longer, were it in my

choice to do so."

*He wanted to stay.*

For a count of three, Halley was happy. But then reality imposed itself, and her happiness cooled, withdrawing like waves from the shore.

"Come on," she said. "We should get back to my apartment and start researching how to disable security alarms for when you have to return."

The two rose, heading back up the crumbling stairs to face what couldn't be avoided.

# 35

## · *KHAN* ·

Khan, who had been sitting in his Tesla fantasizing about caffeine in all its varying forms for at least the past half hour, came to a sudden alertness. Halley and her boyfriend had just reappeared at the top of the stairs rising from Butterfly Beach. Khan's eyes followed them as they got back in the pickup. Should he race over to them right now? While they were trapped inside the truck, a captive audience? But what would he say? Would he bribe or threaten?

Thirty minutes hadn't been enough for him to make up his mind between bribery and threats, which were his only options when it came to keeping the girl silent. Well, there was always another, darker option.... Khan pressed his lips into a thin, tight line. That was the lack of sleep talking. He wasn't the sort of person to consider darker options. At least, not until all other options had failed.

Of course, if something did happen to the girl— an apartment fire or a violent undertow or a car accident.... Khan felt another chill running up his spine. What would he risk to be free of the fears clamoring for his attention? Or to put it another way, how was he supposed to keep his mind clear and focused on his work so long as the possibility of exposure lurked always in the background?

He remained frozen in his car. He hadn't even undone his seatbelt yet. He felt slightly ill at the ideas he was entertaining.

The girl placed her truck in reverse. Khan noted that her left side reverse light was out and that neither Halley nor the boy had put seatbelts on. They had all the confidence and folly of youth. Khan started his own vehicle, pulling farther back into the private driveway to remain undetected. What was the girl doing? Almost exactly perpendicular to him, she was now reversing into the part of Channel Drive where the cliff-side parking lane ended, becoming instead a dedicated bike lane. Her truck was dangerously close to the edge of the cliff at a spot where the safety railing was tilting ominously toward the sea.

Seeming to notice her peril, she swung slightly away from the edge, but this caused her back left tire—the one closest to Khan—to shiver up onto a concrete meridian holding a "Bicycles Only" sign. The truck shuddered, coming to an awkward rest with the front end still perilously close to the cliff edge. Was the girl a complete idiot? The cliffs here were notoriously unstable and her truck was *tipping*, thanks to that elevated back left tire. Khan watched as the girl held up her cell phone to snap a quick picture. Khan's stomach seemed to turn to ice; had she taken selfies in his lab, too? Just because she hadn't posted anything *yet* didn't mean she wasn't planning to later.

She smiled at something, completely oblivious to her hazardous parking job. It would only take some idiot barreling down Butterfly Lane to T-bone Halley's truck right off the cliff.

Khan licked his lips. Almost as if apart from his volition, he depressed the Tesla's park button to engage the emergency brake and then shifted his right foot from the brake to the accelerator.

# 36

## · EDMUND ·

Edmund, seated now in the cab of Halley's marvelous truck, glanced over to his fair companion, admiring the curve of her throat, the flash of her dark eye, the way her full lips thinned slightly as she pressed them together. He breathed her in, memorizing each detail. There was no future—only this: her face, sunlight glowing on her cheek. He wanted to draw her. He wanted to kiss her again. He wanted to stay.

She had said she wanted to "take" a picture from above the cliffs and was presently causing the truck to move in a reverse direction. He noted she had not required of either of them that they secure themselves with seatbelts. As he thought not well of the belts, he didn't remind her.

Once the truck was at rest, Halley gazed out to the ocean, clutching the pale green band she wore on a chain about her neck.

"Prithee," Edmund said, "What manner of jewel is it you wear?"

She dropped the ornament from her fingers.

"It's stupid," she muttered, tucking it back inside her shirt.

"It is fair to behold," he replied. "I have seen naught like it before. A fair jewel upon a fair maid."

Did she blush? Her eyes had dropped so that her lashes brushed her cheeks. The sides of her mouth turned slightly upward. Blushing or not, she had not taken the compliment amiss.

Halley pulled the ring back out, slipping it over the tip of a finger. "It's called jade. It's a stone. I think they mine it in China, but maybe other places, too."

"Jade? *Piedra de ijada?*" he asked.

Halley shrugged. "I've only heard it called jade. *Piedra* is Spanish for stone. *Ijada* sounds about right for 'jade.'"

"Aye, I read of this stone in translation—Spanish explorers recorded in 1565 its efficacy for the healing of loin and kidney ailments."

"Well, my kidneys work great, as far as I know."

Having said this, Halley slipped the chain from her neck, loosing a spiral of hair caught on the necklace. Edmund reached over to smooth her hair and felt her shiver beneath his touch. Her face flushing, she undid the clasp of the chain and slid the ring free.

"My dad gave it to me," said Halley, handing it to Edmund.

"It is passing fair." Edmund slid the ring onto his little finger and twisted it round, noticing slight variations in the color. It had been carved into a twisting pattern as of branches twined together.

"It remindeth me of a wattle fence," Edmund said.

"A what?"

"Have you no such fences?" He frowned. It was

true he had not noted any. "Wattle is made by weaving stripling branches. It is a poor man's fence, but in my family, we do esteem it. Some ancestor caused it to be put into our family's coat of arms. A raven on a wattle fence."

"Huh. *Wattle*. Well, I call it a "braid" pattern. You know, like how girls do their hair in braids."

"Ah, yes. The carving twisteth very like a braid. I see that. And yet, it much resembleth wattle. Or so any of my family would say." He paused, smiling, and passed the ring back to her. "It must be of great worth."

"To me it is, but rings like this are pretty cheap. In my world, anyway. DaVinci told me she saw a store with a bowl full of them down on State Street for like ten bucks each."

Edmund nodded. Halley had paid for the ice cream with something she called "five bucks."

"I don't know anyone who wears it for the, uh, medicinal values," added Halley.

"Mistress Halley," began Edmund, "The pattern upon your ring is so like a wattle fence that I believe such rings would honor my grandfather greatly. Think you I could barter mine own golden ring for … *bucks* sufficient to purchase six or seven of these braid rings?"

"Why do you want so many?"

"For my grandfather's mourners," said Edmund. Seeing her frown, he added, "I perceive it is not the custom in your world to provide gifts for mourners?"

"Uh, no."

"It is customary in mine to present the principal mourners at a funeral with rich gifts. Not to do so

205

would be dishonorable, both to my family and to my grandfather's memory."

"Oh, right," said Halley. "Mourning rings. I just didn't know they were … such a big deal. Okay. So your gold ring would have to be worth eighty bucks if you want to buy seven jade rings, with tax."

She shifted her attention to her purse, withdrawing five silver coins. "Five quarters supposedly weigh an ounce," she said, balancing them on one outstretched palm. "Give me your ring."

Receiving it, she hefted the "quarters" in one hand and the ring in the other. Then she passed both to him, asking if he thought they were of an equal weight.

He repeated her action. "Aye," he replied after a moment. "They seem to me to weigh equally. Mayhap my ring is the heavier."

At this, Halley laughed. "Dude, you're wearing, like, an ounce of gold on your finger."

She pulled out the device with which she communicated through air, stroking its surface several times. With wide eyes, she looked up at Edmund.

"An ounce of gold is worth around fifteen hundred dollars. So, yeah, you could buy a bunch of jade rings. More like, a hundred fifty jade rings."

"An *hundred and fifty*?" A smile of wonder grew upon Edmund's face. In his own world, the value of so many jade rings would far outweigh the value of his gold ring. With so many to sell, he might use the income to pay down the estate's debts.

"This news is most welcome," said Edmund. "Can you convey me unto the gold monger?"

"Gold … *monger*?" asked Halley. "I don't know

that word."

"It meaneth one who sells. Are there in your world those that do trade in gold and silver rings?"

"Oh. Yeah. I guess," said Halley. "Let's see what I can find." Pulling out her cell, she touched the surface repeatedly.

"Good news," she said a minute later. "This says jewelers will pay cash for scrap gold. I mean," she said looking up, "Your ring might be worth more as a *ring* than as scrap gold. We could check a couple stores to find who makes the best offer."

"I should be greatly relieved to return without the expense of ordering rings for grandfather's mourners," said Edmund. "And to have that in hand which might lessen the estate's debts."

Great though the relief was, it was knitted to the thought of returning—returning without Halley. His relief over the one seemed a small, pale thing beside the greatness of his dread of the other.

"The stores are open now," said Halley, checking the time. "Shall we?"

*Shall we …?*

Edmund's mind supplied other questions in place of the one she asked:

*Shall we two not remain here, together?*

*Shall we never part?*

*Shall we?*

"Yes, Mistress," replied Edmund, wishing that *yes* was in answer to another question.

He swallowed the bitterness of the *no* belonging to his circumstance, the *no* that must soon part them.

# 37

## · *KHAN* ·

In the end, it was reason that prevented Khan from using his Tesla as a battering ram. He was basing all his fears upon the one (possibly misinterpreted) clue of the boy's having reached for a sword. What if the boy hadn't been reaching for a sword? What if he was just an ordinary twenty-first century young man? Khan still had no proof positive that Halley Mikkelsen had been inside the lab, much less that she had used his equipment to bring someone here from the sixteenth century.

And then there was the Law of Inertia. Irregardless of whether it was ascribed to Galileo or Newton, the Law of Inertia could well have toppled both the truck *and* the Tesla off the cliff's edge.

Khan needed an opportunity that imperiled only two out of three of the participants. And he needed additional proof Halley knew more than she should.

"I'll have grounds more positive than this," muttered Khan, misquoting Hamlet.

# 38

## · HALLEY ·

As they drove, Halley reminded Edmund about keeping silent in the stores. "You really sound … *strange* when you talk. No offense." She looked anxiously to see his reaction.

"I am not offended."

"I mean, I like the way you talk. It's … *you*. But I don't think it's a good idea to draw attention to yourself." She frowned. "Maybe I better say the ring is mine. You can just stand there silently looking … rugged."

"Rugged?"

Halley laughed. "Trust me: it's a compliment."

Half an hour later, they were waiting at their first fine jewelry counter for someone to locate the assistant manager. In three different stores, they received roughly the same response.

"We only offer in-store credit for gold. You should take this to someone who specializes in antiques."

Unfortunately, the recommended places were all closed on the weekends. All but one: The Channel Islands Estate Jewelry and Loan Company was open seven days a week.

"It's a pawn and loan on the side," said the clerk who gave them the address. "They know their stuff. If you pawn your ring, you'll get a good loan rate, and if you sell it, you'll probably do better there than you would here." That last was spoken in a quiet whisper with accompanying wink.

Halley thanked the clerk and exited with Edmund at her side. He had done an excellent job of looking silently rugged.

The Channel Islands Estate Jewelry and Loan Company looked ... fortified. The windows were barred, albeit tastefully with custom wrought iron, and a security guard paced behind a locked door. When they were buzzed inside, they were greeted by a gentleman in a suit.

"Good morning," said Mr. Hernandez, introducing himself. "Are we in search of something in particular?"

Halley pulled Edmund's ring from her middle finger, the only digit upon which it would stay put.

"Do you buy old rings?"

Mr. Hernandez smiled and examined the ring, hefting it and turning it round and round. "Would you mind following me to the back of the store? I can give you a better idea if we just ..." He was already walking, the sentence trailing unfinished behind him.

They followed Mr. Hernandez, who slipped behind a counter and began to examine the ring under a series of lenses.

"Interesting. *Interesting.* Yes. If you don't mind, I'll need to …" Once again, he turned without completing his sentence. After dragging the ring over a black testing stone, he left them, passing behind a door leading to a private area in back.

He was gone for long enough that Halley began to worry, but just as she was considering knocking on the door, Mr. Hernandez reappeared.

"This is my colleague, Mrs. Wu," said Mr. Hernandez. "She is the owner and will be happy to assist you from here."

Mrs. Wu was already scrutinizing the ring. "What do you know of its history?" she asked Halley.

Halley cleared her throat. "I'm told it was made in London, around the time of the Mayflower."

"Mm-hmm," intoned Mrs. Wu.

"Or a little before. Supposedly it was to commemorate a death in the family."

"A memorial ring," said Mrs. Wu. "Sometimes called a mourning ring."

"That sounds right."

"And it was left to you?" asked Mrs. Wu.

"I, um, had a goth phase. You know, skulls and crossbones and stuff."

"It's valuable," said Mrs. Wu. Her gaze was fixed on something *inside* the ring.

Halley glanced to Edmund. "I just want to know what I can get for it."

"Of course," said Mrs. Wu. "You might consider leaving it to secure a loan, instead." She reached from below the counter and produced a laminated flyer describing the process of pawning a treasured item to obtain ready cash.

"Um, okay," said Halley.

Mrs. Wu turned for her office. "If you will excuse me a minute, there is a reference I'd like to consult."

Once Mrs. Wu was out of hearing, Edmund asked, "Think you it bodes well that she taketh such care?"

Halley shrugged. "I've never done this before." She flipped the loan flyer over and examined the image of a satisfied customer shaking hands with Mrs. Wu. Alongside the photo was an example of a pawn ticket, which looked vaguely familiar.

At this point, Mrs. Wu returned from her office. "You have an interesting decision to make."

## 39

## · EDMUND ·

Edmund listened as Mrs. Wu explained what she had been able to ascertain as to the ring's probable origin and possible value.

"From what I can determine, your ring may have been crafted by the painter and miniaturist Nicholas Hilliard, who also worked as a goldsmith in London. See the maker's mark here? Hilliard used a mark like this."

Edmund had never been more aware of the pain of holding his tongue; the ring was indeed of Master Hilliard's manufacture.

"I have to emphasize I'm not an expert in this area," continued Mrs. Wu. "The ring could be of 19th century origin, passed off as a family heirloom from an earlier time. Or it could be genuine. I can't make that determination."

"So you don't know what it's worth?" asked Halley. "I mean, it's got to be worth something because it's gold, right?"

"It is gold. Close to 24 karat. The scrap value of

the gold is this," she said, sliding a small slip of paper over the counter.

Edmund's uncertainty as to the squiggles on the paper were cleared up by Halley.

"Eleven hundred thirty-four dollars," Halley said softly.

Edmund raised his brows. This was more than enough to purchase jade rings for his purposes.

"You can get that price from me or anyone else who buys gold," said Mrs. Wu. "However, I strongly advise against it."

Edmund was on the point of asking *wherefore*, but restrained himself.

Halley gave voice to his query. "Why?"

A thin smile graced Mrs. Wu's face. "You ought to have the ring professionally evaluated." She slid a small rectangular card across the counter. "This is the woman I would trust to provide an accurate valuation. I should warn you she is generally backed up six to eight weeks."

Edmund examined the card. The name SOTHEBY'S was writ in large print, along with a woman's name in small print and a length of numbers. He knew not what the curious cipher might signify.

"This is a Los Angeles number," said Halley. "Isn't there someone I could talk to here in Santa Barbara?"

Mrs. Wu hesitated. "Martin Nieman is local, and I'm sure he would buy the ring, but ..."

"But ... *what?*" asked Halley. "You don't trust him?"

Edmund, too, had noted Mrs. Wu's hesitation.

"I recommend Christine Smith-Westley." Mrs.

Wu tapped the card on which the name was imprinted.

"I'm sort of in a hurry," Halley said.

"I understand," said Mrs. Wu. "Many of our clients find themselves in your position, but allow me to impress upon you the … *potential* of your item. A piece such as this comes through my door once a year, if that. If the Hilliard mark is genuine, it could fetch anywhere from eight to twenty thousand, auctioned through the right house."

"Sotheby's," murmured Halley.

"Exactly. Christine can determine the provenance of your ring beyond any doubt. If it is genuinely a memorial poesy ring of the early 17th century made by Hilliard, you owe it to yourself to investigate all your options." Mrs. Wu hesitated and then added, "If the piece were mine, it's what I would do."

"And if I don't? How much will you give me for it?" asked Halley.

Mrs. Wu turned over the piece of paper upon which she'd written the value of the gold. Upon this she jotted down a new figure.

"Two thousand five hundred," murmured Halley. "But you're saying it could sell for a lot more at an auction?"

"It could," said Mrs. Wu. "When I first examined the ring, I assumed it was of later provenance than what you suggested because of the inscription. Inscriptions were common in the *late* seventeenth century, not the *early*. However, I found examples of inscribed memorial rings from 1520 and 1592. Now, if on the other hand, your ring is an imitation of a 16th century style, it most likely dates from the 19th century when there were repeated revivals of Elizabethan era design. In either case, its value is well above the weight of the gold."

Halley nodded thoughtfully.

"Why don't the two of you discuss this over the lunch hour?" suggested Mrs. Wu, checking her wristwatch. "I have another client coming in by appointment in a few minutes."

Halley examined the card with Mrs. Wu's purchase price. "But this offer stands?"

Mrs. Wu nodded once.

"Okay," said Halley. "I'll think it over. When will you be free again today?"

Mrs. Wu smiled and handed Halley another business card. "This is my personal line. But I must advise you, if the ring has been in your family for over four hundred years, you'll want to be certain before you take a step you can't undo."

# 40

## · *HALLEY* ·

Halley shook Mrs. Wu's hand and then turned to exit the store with Edmund.

Edmund, however, was bent over a case of women's rings.

"This craftsmanship is remarkably fine," murmured Edmund.

Halley drifted to his side, leaning in close to examine the rings. In the still air of the shop, she could smell the scent of lavender clinging to his skin. She wanted to breathe it in deeply, to hold the memory of it. Of him. God in heaven, but she wanted him to stay.

"Never have I before seen such bright gems," said Edmund.

Halley's eye caught on one ring, narrow-banded, with three tiny diamonds set flush into the band.

Halley gasped. She knew that ring. It was *her* ring. Two Christmas's ago, Jillian had given custom-made friendship rings to Halley and DaVinci. Halley had lost hers nine months earlier.

"That's *my* ring," she whispered to Edmund. "It's

one of a kind. It's been missing since New Year's."
She turned. "Mr. Hernandez?" she called. "Can I ask
you about a ring in your case?"

The gentleman approached, beaming genially.
"It's dangerous, coming here with your *querida*," he
said to Edmund. "Which one would you like to see?"

"I don't need to see it," said Halley. "I can see it
just fine. That ring—" She pointed, tapping the
glass—"It was stolen. It's *mine*. I can prove it. My
friend had three of them custom made for me, her,
and our other best friend."

"Ah," said Mr. Hernandez. "In the event of stolen
property, of course we would restore the piece. We
work closely with local law enforcement to avoid this
sort of thing. If you'll give me a moment, I'd like to
check how we acquired the ring."

Before he'd finished speaking, an idea had lodged
in Halley's mind, and she felt sure she knew how her
ring had ended up here and why the image of the
pawnshop ticket had looked so familiar.

Mr. Hernandez busied himself on a tablet
computer, keeping the screen hidden. "Ah—it was
used to secure a loan," he said. "And in this case, the
item was not paid for after the expiration of the loan,
which is how it came to be for sale in our case."

"Who brought it in?" demanded Halley.

"I'm afraid that's confidential until such time as
we can establish—"

"Was it Inga Mikkelsen?" she asked, interrupting
Mr. Hernandez.

The gentleman's eyes narrowed for a split-second.
Long enough for Halley to know she'd been correct.

"It *was* her," fumed Halley. "Inga Mikkelsen is my

mother. She had no right to sell my ring."

"To protect all the interested parties, we adhere to strict procedures. If you'd like to, er, make a claim to ownership, there will be paperwork," said Mr. Hernandez. He pulled a sheet of paper from one of the shelves below the counter.

Halley took the sheet with shaking hands. Too angry to look at it, she folded it in half and then in quarters.

Stiffly, she said to Edmund. "Come on. Let's get out of here."

# 41

## · HALLEY ·

Outside, the morning had grown warm. Banners snapped in the breeze as clouds scudded past. Faint strains of music drifted down State Street. Halley appreciated none of it. Her mind was spinning. She clenched her hands into tight fists.

"Mistress," Edmund said softly. "Are you *oak-ay*?"

"No!" snapped Halley. "I can't believe my mother."

She broke off. Her throat had grown suddenly tight and if she tried to speak another word, she'd be crying.

Edmund took her by the elbow, gently guiding them both back to the truck. Once they were inside the cab, Halley tried to speak again, but she was too angry. Too hurt. Too *everything*. Bitter tears spilled over her lower lids.

"I ... can't—" She broke off into an angry sob. "I ... can*not*—"

"Hush," said Edmund. And then he gathered her into his arms. "Hush, lady."

She cried for a solid five minutes, soaking Edmund's shirt. In all that time, he simply held her, pressing her close.

She took a final shuddering breath and then pulled out of his arms.

"She had no right," Halley whispered. "No right to pawn my ring. It was mine. *Mine.*"

Halley didn't know how to explain what she was feeling. Edmund had always had things of his own. Animals, servants, a great hall, a title … How would she explain how much this small ring with its tiny diamonds had meant to her? It had been new, and *hers.* Not a hand-me-down, not something retrieved from her mother's discards. It had been a gift. A promise. Best friends forever. And her mother had pawned it for a loan and then defaulted rather than explaining to Halley what had happened to it.

"It's so … *despicable,*" muttered Halley, now drawing her sleeve along her eyes and nose. "I know she's selfish, but I never would have expected this."

"Lady, I am sorely grieved for thy hurt," said Edmund. His amber-flecked eyes were pinched with pain. "If aught I can do might help thee, I would gladly undertake it."

Halley stared at his earnest expression for a moment before releasing a single laugh. "Oh, Edmund…." She shook her head. "Thank you. From the bottom of my heart, thank you. But this isn't something that's fixable."

She didn't want to talk about her mother. Didn't want to think about her. She shook her head. "Never mind."

Edmund nodded. "Mayhap I might buy it for

thee?" he asked. "Once I sell mine own ring?"

"No," said Halley, sharply. The harshness of her response surprised even her. But she didn't want Edmund paying off her mother's debts, not even to recover her ring. She would fill out the claim form. She would do everything properly, and her mother would pay for it, not Edmund. She glanced towards the Channel Islands Estate Jewelry and Loan. Besides, she didn't ever want to walk through those doors again.

She fished in her jeans pocket for the cards from Mrs. Wu and crumpled them, tossing them to the floor of the cab. It didn't fix anything, but it felt good.

After that, Halley dialed the phone number for one *Martin Nieman, dealer in antiquities.*

"I'd like you to evaluate a four hundred year old ring for me," she said to the answering machine. "Mrs. Wu at Channel Islands Estate Jewelry says it's from the workshop of ... um ..."

"Master Nicholas Hilliard," said Edmund.

"Hilliard," repeated Halley. "Nicholas Hilliard. And I want to sell it."

## 42

### · NIEMAN ·

Martin Nieman did not make a practice of working weekends, but the coincidence had been too extraordinary to ignore. Another piece of jewelry from the workshop of Nicholas Hilliard? What were the chances?

Unless Dr. Jules Khan had a niece or lover to whom he'd given the ring.... The voice on the message had sounded young. Inexperienced. Uncertain.

It was more out of a sense of loyalty to Khan than anything else that Nieman returned the girl's call. And curiosity, naturally. He so rarely had the opportunity to acquire pieces older than two hundred years. Not to mention, should the piece indeed prove to be sixteenth century, and from Hilliard's workshop, the girl would probably have very little idea of its worth.

It was simply too good of an opportunity to let slip.

The girl had answered immediately and agreed to meet at Martin's home; he really couldn't bear returning to work again today—he had a gallery opening over which to preside tomorrow. Fortunately, his best set of jeweler's eye loupes never left his jacket pocket, and he maintained a small assay lab at home.

Five minutes prior to the appointed hour, Martin heard what sounded like a UPS or mail truck rattling up his narrow drive, but upon looking out the window, he saw it was an old pickup. It looked vaguely familiar. For all he knew of young people and trends, it was possible all of Montecito's hip youth drove about in inexpensive pickup trucks.

Pasting his most genial smile on, Martin waited for the knock and then welcomed his guest.

Or, rather, *guests*.

The girl had brought a young man she identified as her Danish boyfriend, who spoke little English. So much for Martin's theory the girl had obtained the ring from the professor in exchange for … *favors*. Although who knew, with today's bohemian standards?

Martin repaired his smile.

"Come in—*do* come in. Thanks *awfully* for agreeing to meet here." He was laying on the accent rather thickly. "It's just through here …"

"Thanks for, um, seeing us," she said. "On the weekend. Here's the ring."

Martin observed the girl wore the ring on her middle finger, and that there was no sign of a tan line on that digit. She'd not had it for any length of time, he surmised. He accepted it with another smile, beginning the examination with his naked eye. The piece was in good condition. *Very* good condition if it were genuinely sixteenth century. Martin's heart began to beat faster. In contrast to necklaces, such as the professor had brought in earlier, rings tended to show more signs of wear, but this one was barely marked.

Looking up, Martin murmured, "Fascinating," to the girl and her companion, and then withdrew his loupe set.

The girl seemed nervous. Enough so that Martin was seized with a sudden suspicion. Had she *stolen* the ring from Dr. Khan? The thought, once it presented itself, was unfortunately difficult to dislodge. Not to mention, it made his present transaction less straightforward. If he acquired the piece below its value and sent it to auction, as he planned to do, Khan would eventually discover it had surfaced and would blame Martin for saying nothing.

"Hmm," sighed Martin, as he examined the inside of the band. It was engraved with Hilliard's mark. "To whom else did you say you've shown this?" he inquired softly.

"Mrs. Wu, over at Channel Islands," replied Halley. "She's the one who told us it was made by the goldsmith Nicholas Hilliard."

Martin smiled, and this time it was a patronizing smile. Only an individual devoid of education in art history would refer to Hilliard as a goldsmith rather than as a miniaturist. The girl was an ignoramus. Oh, it would be such a sweet thing to pluck the ring from her for pence on the pound! But ... he had a duty to contact Khan before making a purchase. It was the right thing to do. It was the only thing he could do without putting his future business relations with Khan at risk.

In short, he could not buy it.

He looked up, removing the loupe. "I'm not certain I can concur with Mrs. Wu's opinion as to the ring's provenance. It's understandable, of course. She's a bit out of her depth." Another smile, conciliatory.

The boyfriend looked as though he was about to speak, but at a sharp look from the girl, the young Dane held his tongue.

"I'm sorry I don't have better news for you," continued Martin Nieman, "But at first blush, this does not appear to me to have been produced in Hilliard's workshop."

If the girl looked disappointed, the boy looked … *angry*.

"I could, of course, run a few more tests, peruse references, and so forth," said Nieman. He glanced at the boy once more. And then did a double-take. "I say," he began, staring pointedly at the boy's left ear lobe. "That looks interesting."

The remark was uttered completely without calculation. The golden earring the boy wore *did* look interesting. The ear wire was decidedly Elizabethan. Possibly early Jacobean. What if the professor had acquired his pieces from these two rather than the other way round?

"Might I have a closer look at your earring?" Martin asked politely.

The girl repeated something to her boyfriend in what Martin assumed was Danish, and the boy removed his earring, passing it over.

Once more, Martin withdrew his loupe. There it was: the curvature of the miniature clasping mechanism, the uneven fineness of the wire meant to pass through the earlobe—this was no contemporary piece. Before Martin could formulate a question, the girl spoke.

"It's another family heirloom. Really old. Maybe, like, Vikings or something."

Martin restrained himself from comment. This was no Viking piece, but it was old. It might be Danish, from the time of a King Christian or Frederick—they were all Christians or Fredericks in the sixteenth and seventeenth centuries.

"Or maybe not," the girl added nervously.

The boy murmured something in her ear.

"Um, Edmund wants to know the cash value of his earring. If you're, you know, interested."

"Of course, of course. It's in good condition." He withdrew his black test stone, scraping the earring over it before placing a drop of 18K solution on it. He raised an eyebrow and reached for the 22K solution. After a moment he addressed the young couple.

"The gold is of a high quality alloy. Very soft— you can see where it's bent *here* and *here*—" Martin rather doubted the girl could see it, but professional pride was setting in and he rattled off a few more reasons he could declare with certainty the piece was *old*.

The boy was whispering to the girl again as Martin concluded with, "It's incredible, really, that the ear wire has remained attached for so long."

"We'd like to sell the earring instead of the ring," announced the girl.

Martin smiled. He made a show of carefully weighing it to distract them from asking its value as an antique and then offered them its value as scrap gold. There were, after all, only so many opportunities he could pass up.

# 43

## · *HALLEY* ·

Half an hour later, Halley was driving Edmund, now one hundred seventy-five dollars richer and down one earring, back from Martin Nieman's home in Summerland. Driving northbound towards Santa Barbara on the 101 on a Saturday afternoon was bound to be bad, but it was doubly bad today as visitors from Ventura and LA streamed north for Fiesta.

Halley's focus drifted from driving to Edmund's gold ring and how they *still* hadn't found a buyer. He seemed content, though, having made enough cash from the sale of his earring to afford at least fifteen jade rings. He said he would have eight or nine to sell in London, where he could turn a pretty penny on his investment. Halley supposed that if Edmund was content, she could be as well. She certainly didn't want to accompany him back to the Channel Islands Estate Jewelry and Loan—the store that had accepted her friendship ring. Never mind they couldn't have known it had been stolen.

A car passed her in the slow lane, cherry-red and bedecked in Fiesta finery. Halley had been so distracted she'd practically forgotten Fiesta. How was Edmund going to survive the Applegate's post-fiesta bash? She was going to have to hide him away. Or hide away with him....

Her cheeks flushed with the thought. She wouldn't mind skipping the party to spend more time alone with Edmund. If she was honest, Halley was finding it hard to think of anything as more interesting than Edmund. Even the hoped-for meeting with the great Ethyl Meier seemed less do-or-die, more optional. DaVinci had always encouraged Halley to avoid pinning all her hopes on the internship with Ms. Meier. Was she finally gaining perspective?

Sure, costume design still mattered, but it felt less ... *urgent* somehow. It wasn't costume history that sparked her imagination; it was one *particular* costume hiding under a beach blanket in her truck that she couldn't stop thinking about. Or rather, it was the *owner* of the costume that she couldn't stop thinking about.

Was this what it felt like to fall in love?

The possibility kept her silent as she and Edmund crept along on the 101. Outside, the day had grown warmer, but a slight breeze blowing off the ocean kept the air moving. It was perfect weather for driving. Halley had just spotted the first sign for her Montecito exit when her phone vibed with a text.

"Read that for me?" asked Halley.

Edmund picked up her cell phone and examined the screen. "It is most puzzling, lady, but I believe that betwixt my time and yours, certain letters have been exchanged within the *alphabetum*."

"Really? That's weird."

"The letters 'u' and 'v' are not formed as I expect."

"Okay, but can you still read what it says?"

"It is from your friend Mistress DaVinci, who desires you to know: *I found a reference to "J. Khan Detective Services, Specializing in the Recovery of Precious Jewelry and Antiques." The business was only open for six months, from February 2002 through July 2002.*"

"So I was right," said Halley. "He *does* use his time machine to bring things back from the past."

"It would seem he has advanced from doing this for others to doing it for his own gain," replied Edmund.

Halley scowled.

"Ah," said Edmund. "Mistress DaVinci sends another message: *Will you send me back to Paris, April 15, 1874?*"

"What?" asked Halley.

"She further writes: *I want to go to the opening of the first Impressionists Exhibition. Can you imagine what that would be like? Think about it....* Shall I respond?"

Halley's frown deepened. "Yeah. Tell her it's not my time machine. And it's dangerous. I barely understand how it works."

Edmund looked alarmed, probably at the prospect of typing so many words.

"Just type NO," said Halley.

Edmund did so, and DaVinci responded.

"She writes: *But you COULD, theoretically, right? Send me to Paris on April 15, 1874?*"

Halley rolled her eyes. "Did she miss the part

where it's not my time machine?"

"Shall I ask her?"

"No. Just tell her … tell her I can't do it. I didn't see an input for exact dates on the machine. Don't write all that. Just say, the scale resolution is set in years, not days."

As Edmund typed diligently beside her, Halley suddenly inhaled sharply. *The scale resolution was set in years.* Years. Not days. That meant … What did it mean?

When she'd imagined returning Edmund to the right place and time, she'd imagined she would pick a day, pick a time of day, pick a year, and pick the location. But the screen on the podium had not provided a line for "time of day" or "day of the year." It didn't calibrate that way. There had been a line for "year" and for "place." That was all.

Her pulse picked out a staccato rhythm.

If she could instruct the machine only to send Edmund back to a particular year, who *knew* what day it would be for him when he popped back to his century?

Halley signaled to exit the highway onto Olive Mill Road.

"Edmund," she asked, her heart racing, "What month and day was it for you when I pulled you out of your own time?"

"The fourth day of August, lady."

*The fourth.*

Today was August fifth.

Yesterday had been the fourth—*for both of them.*

The choice of date and time must be automated, tied somehow to "real" time. If they had to wait another nine days to send him back … For Edmund, a week and a half of his life in 1598 would simply *vanish*. His family wouldn't know what had happened to him. For ten long days, they would assume he'd run away or been murdered or something horrible.

Halley took the exit, and then took an immediate right onto Olive Mill.

She was going to have to tell him, and he was going to be devastated. How many times had he brought up the necessity of finding his brother and preventing him from running up more debts? How much debt, exactly, could his brother run up in just ten days? Her stomach twisted.

Just as she was about to tell Edmund the bad news, her phone rang.

"The display readeth, *Jules Khan*," said Edmund.

"Jules Khan?" said Halley. "The professor?"

The phone continued to ring. Halley swore and pulled her truck to the side of the road.

# 44

## · *KHAN* ·

Half an hour earlier, the professor had been glaring at his cell phone, which had been turned face down and was ringing. It was an unwelcome interruption. As it rang a second time, a third time, he returned to ignoring it. But somewhere between the fourth and fifth rings, he decided he was ready for a break from his laborious calculations.

"Jules Khan," he said.

"Oh, I'm so glad I caught you. I was preparing to leave a message."

Man's voice. Trace accent. English. Oh. It was—

"Sorry, sorry. This is Martin. Nieman."

Yes. Khan smiled to himself. Nieman wanted the valuable sixteenth century carcanet after all. Nieman had doubtless spent the morning fretting over the piece he had *not* purchased, feeling upset with himself for not having snatched it up when he had the chance, before Khan had decided to up the going price.

And he would up the going price. He smiled more broadly.

"What can I do for you, Martin?"

"Yes. I—it's just … I'm sorry. Let me start over. I was prepared to leave a message, you know, only now you've answered—"

"Is this about the ruby and sapphire collar?"

"Ah. No. Actually I'm terribly sorry, but I must stand my ground on—"

"Then what?" snapped Khan, now able to feel properly irritated by the interruption.

"Yes. Well, it's about the items I acquired this morning, in a manner of speaking."

"A sale is a sale, Mr. Nieman."

"Quite. Yes. No, this isn't buyer's remorse." Nieman laughed nervously. "Quite the opposite, don't you know. It's just, I've only now finished the most extraordinary consultation, and I thought … well, I decided it would be remiss of me not to mention it to you."

"Mention what to me, Mr. Nieman?" Khan knew his impatience read clearly in his tone.

"Right. A young couple, surname of *Smith*, came to see me shortly after lunch at my residence—most unusual, but then I wasn't planning to go back in to work, not on the weekend—"

"Martin!"

"The thing is, this couple offered for sale a gold ring with a maker's mark I'm absolutely certain belonged to Nicholas Hilliard."

Khan stood suddenly. "A ring from Hilliard's workshop? Are you certain?"

"Ah, well, now, there's no need to call in question my ability—"

"Right. Of course you're certain."

He'd offended Nieman. If the antiques dealer was able to identify the workmanship of the pieces he, Khan, had brought in, naturally he would have been equally well able to detect the provenance of another piece from the same workshop.

"Quite," replied Martin Nieman. "And I thought I'd best pass the information along, in the unlikely event you had recently found yourself, er, deprived of anything valuable from your collection."

"I see," said Khan. He was pacing rapidly. Not usually a violent man, he nonetheless wanted very badly to break something. "I see," he repeated. "As I have not recently been deprived of any of my personal property, I imagine this must be merely one of life's odd … coincidences."

"Yes. A coincidence. Right-oh. So very glad to hear it. I'll just ring off then—"

"Just one more thing—could you provide a description of the young man and woman?"

Martin Nieman was more than happy to do this, going into more than enough detail to confirm their identities.

Khan's hands were shaking as he tapped the screen to end his call. This was no coincidence. This was the proof he'd been after.

"Surname of 'Smith,' my ass," he muttered, pacing before his desk. They'd assumed false identities. Which meant they knew they had something to hide. They knew they were in trouble. And they were. In deep trouble. Because the girl had been here—*here* in his inviolable sanctuary—and she had used the singularity machine.

In a swift motion, he swept a dozen photographs

off his desk.

He stared at the mess. He didn't like messes. It hadn't made him feel any better, either. He liked neatness. Order. Tidiness.

Carefully, he stooped and gathered the scattered pictures, muttering, "Coincidence, my ass."

Khan didn't believe in coincidences. He believed in tidying up, however.

Picking up his phone, he dialed Halley Mikkelsen's number.

## 45

### · *HALLEY* ·

Halley answered the call after the fourth ring.

"This is Halley."

"Dr. Khan here. Jules Khan. I wanted to thank you again for taking such good care of my property yesterday."

Yesterday? Had that been *yesterday*? It felt like an entire year had passed since she'd watched Khan's estate. It felt like the work had been done by a different person. Khan was waiting for a response.

"Sure," she said. "I mean, you're welcome."

"I wondered if you'd be interested in a longer term assignment?"

"Assignment?"

"House-sitting this weekend."

Halley grimaced. House-sitting was her mom's thing. Not hers. Never hers.

"I don't house-sit."

Another chuckle. "Some might beg to differ—"

"No, I really don't. Not professionally. Yesterday was a one-time thing."

She could feel a knot forming in her stomach. A memory returned. She'd been nine or ten and had created business cards, carefully copying one of her mother's cards in tiny, precise print, replacing "Inga Mikkelsen" with "Mikkelsen and Daughter." Her mother had scowled and thrown it away when Halley had presented it to her, but it wasn't this memory alone that was tying her stomach into a knot.

It was … *repulsion*. Halley's mind was racing ahead, telling her how easily she could end up trapped in her mother's life, with no friends, alone, until one day she woke up a bitter, demanding, selfish old woman.

"I'm sorry I can't help," she said.

"Wait—just hear me out."

She clenched her fists. She wasn't her mother. She had plans. She had friends. She had a life. She didn't have to hear the professor out.

The professor continued, oblivious. "I'm in a tight spot for this coming week. I can make it worth your while."

This coming week? Halley's gaze shifted to Edmund.

"How does a hundred fifty a day plus food sound?" When Halley didn't answer, Khan said, "I can go as high as two-fifty."

"Um, you said this week?" If it were possible to get Edmund back to his family sooner …

"Starting tomorrow evening."

*Tomorrow?* Halley's heart thudded in her chest. Tomorrow was too soon. She couldn't say goodbye tomorrow. She wasn't ready.

"Of course, if you're really not interested …" Khan allowed the thought to trail. "I suppose I can work down my list. I really can't afford to miss this opportunity."

*Boom. Boom. Boom.* It felt as if there wasn't enough air in the truck. Her hand scrabbled for the window crank. She needed air. Edmund, seeing her trying to get the window down, reached across her and smoothly turned the crank. Warm air and mariachi music from a passing vehicle floated into the cab.

"Tell you what," said the professor. "I'll throw in driving privileges for the Tesla."

"Can I call you back in a minute?" Her voice rasped as she asked the question. She tried to swallow, but her mouth had gone completely dry. She felt like she might be sick.

"Of course. I'll be right here."

The call ended.

The invitation to house-sit starting tomorrow solved a huge problem. It put her—and Edmund—eight days ahead of schedule, which was a godsend in light of what she had just figured out about the time machine's limitations. It was the right thing to do.

But how was she supposed to say goodbye to Edmund tomorrow?

She couldn't breathe.

"Lady—*Halley!* Thy lips are pallid. Rest thy head at a lower incline."

Head between her knees. Right. Good plan. Except, the steering wheel was in the way. Fumbling, she opened the door, swung her feet around, and leaned forward.

"Calm thyself," Edmund said, his voice gentle.

How could she? There was no calming this ... this ... *this.*

She had to say goodbye to Edmund *tomorrow*. She felt like she should be sobbing, wailing, keening, but her eyes were dry. Her mouth was dry. She was numb, because really, the decision was already made. This wasn't something she needed to take a moment for; it wasn't a decision that required deliberation. For Edmund's sake, she had to say yes to the professor. And as soon as she could start up that time machine, she had to send Edmund home. Tomorrow. There was no other possible choice.

"Lady?"

Somehow, without Halley having heard his movement, Edmund had exited his side of the truck and walked around so that he was now squatting beside her just outside the driver's side door. He placed gentle hands on her knees.

She opened her eyes. How could there be mariachi music? And sunshine? And a gentle breeze? How could there be color and light in the world when she had to let Edmund go?

She wrapped her arms around him. She had twenty-four hours. Maybe thirty. That was all, and it would have to be enough.

After breathing in the lavender scent of him, deeply, deeply, she told him about the phone call.

"Professor Khan needs a house-sitter starting tomorrow night, and my mother's busy. You can … you can go home sooner."

Edmund pulled free of her arms. Stood. Took her hands. Looked into her eyes, dazed at first, but then … something else. Pained. There was no mistaking the pain in Edmund's eyes. It took him a full minute to respond verbally.

240

"I understand," he said at last. His voice, grave, was a knife to her heart.

Halley exhaled heavily. "Come back inside. Sit with me."

Edmund circled the front of the truck, returning to the passenger side. Halley shut her door. The sound of it, metallic and solid, was the sound of things ending.

"There's an important reason for us to take this opportunity," she said. Her voice was steady. She could do this. "We have to, really."

"Mistress, I must ask, think you it is safe, this offer?"

Halley sighed. "Khan wouldn't invite me to house-sit if he had any suspicions about my trustworthiness."

Briefly, she outlined what she had just figured out about how the time machine worked, how she could return him to his right year, but only on the current calendar day.

When she had finished, Edmund didn't speak right away. A silent minute passed. Edmund shifted on the bench seat so that he was facing Halley. He took her face in his hands and their heads fell softly forward until their foreheads met.

"Ah, lady," said Edmund, his voice ragged with emotion.

Halley wanted a machine that would halt time, give them a way to remain here, inside this moment, with nothing changing or progressing or withering— only this: their two faces inches apart, foreheads tipped together, breaths mingled.

"Then I must go," he said at last.

"I know," she replied. Because she did know. He had to go. "I wish …"

Halley didn't finish the sentence. She wished and she wished and she wished, but she was one person and Edmund was responsible for a hundred.

"I wish things were other than they are, lady."

Softly, she kissed him. Once. Gently. And then she pulled out her phone.

When her call went straight to the professor's voice mail, she said dully, "I'll do it. Sunday night. I'll be there."

# 46

## · HALLEY ·

As she drove Edmund to buy the jade rings with his earring sale income, the initial jolt of his departure, earthquake-like, slowly receded. In place of shock she felt ... emptiness. A kind of aftershock of the heart. A yawning stretch of lonely years.

They found the store with the jade rings, purchased fifteen of them, and then took the clogged roads back towards Halley's apartment.

Edmund's departure was all Halley could think about. He was returning *to* something, to an entire household awaiting him, a hundred people praying for his return. She was staying. She would remain here, stuck with her mother, when Jillian and DaVinci moved away to college in a month. At the moment, even the thought of yesterday's fifteen thousand dollar sale offered no comfort. Club 33 might not accept her. She would be alone, friendless, gradually accepting house-sitting jobs, gradually turning into her mother.

"Mistress Halley?"

Edmund's voice rumbled over her thoughts,

mercifully drowning them.

She looked aside from the winding road, briefly meeting his eyes before another curve demanded her attention.

"Your distress is great, lady, and I am sorry for it."

Tears stung the corners of her eyes.

"Me too," she murmured after a moment.

She took a familiar curve a few miles per hour over the speed limit, and the small stack of mail collected earlier in the morning slid across the floor.

Edmund bent forward, retrieving the various pieces of mail. One of them seemed to capture his interest.

"What is it?" she asked.

"The name of the ... *club* into which you desire admittance," he began. "What was it?"

"Club 33."

"Lady, unless I mistake—upon this enclosure is writ 'Club 33.'"

For the second time in the past hour, Halley pulled the truck to the side of the road.

# 47

## · *EDMUND* ·

Edmund passed the missive into Halley's eager grasp, observing as she tore the sleeve-paper that she held her breath. She uttered no words, but having read the message, she gasped and then held her breath again. Eyes wide, she turned her gaze to his.

"They want me." Her voice was soft like that of a child, her gaze full of wonder.

Edmund could not be surprised that the company desired her admission to their number, but he saw plainly that *she* was surprised.

"Breathe, mistress."

She placed the flat of her palm over her chest and then secured it with her other hand, both hands pressed over her heart.

"Read it to me," Halley murmured. "So I know it's real."

He took the letter from where it lay upon her lap and read it aloud. The language was uncouth and the spelling strange, but the meaning was unmistakable: *admittance was hers*, should she deign to accept and immediately forward a named sum of money. The sum was interrupted by periods and commas in a fashion Edmund found unreadable. Not trusting himself to specify the amount, he left off reading aloud and instead, handing the letter back, pointed to the sum.

Halley, too, seemed baffled by the numeric representation.

"Canst thou puzzle out the meaning?" he asked, indicating the written sum.

"Yeah," she murmured. "Yeah. But … this can't be right." She turned the letter over, revealing further sums arranged in a schedule, such as Edmund had seen the bailiff present unto his grandfather.

Halley's brow furrowed in strong emotion. Edmund could not tell if it was anger or confusion or some other thing altogether, but he felt sure she was distressed as she gripped the letter in one hand. His eyes fell to her other hand, lying forlorn on the seat, palm up. He placed his hand upon hers.

She looked over, set the letter down, and exhaled heavily.

"Lady? If there be aught I can do for thee—"

Her voice flat as a calmed sea, she spoke. "They want more money than I was expecting."

"Canst thou not contest the amount?"

She shook her head. "No." She fluttered the paper. "I have to pay annual dues on top of the initiation fee. Up front. When I accept my nomination. And I don't have money set aside for dues."

"I see," Edmund said gravely. "And thou must find—forgive me, lady—*you* must find this sum or all is forfeit?"

"Yes."

"How great is the sum?"

She pointed to one of the figures, speaking it aloud. "Eleven thousand five hundred dollars in dues, plus the *Platinum Petite for Under-Thirties* initiation fee of fifteen thousand. I need twenty-six thousand five hundred dollars by the twentieth of August."

Edmund frowned, recalling the various "auction" values suggested for the gold ring he wore in memory of his father. Even half the greatest possible sum would see Mistress Halley out of her difficulties.

It was clear what he must do.

He removed the gold ring from his hand.

"You must take and sell my ring."

# 48

## · HALLEY ·

Halley was silent for a slow count of ten after Edmund made the offer. She could feel her heart hammering in her chest. This was the solution. This would solve everything.

Her breath caught on the word "everything." No. This would not solve everything. But it might make it possible for her to bear losing Edmund. Taking a deep breath, she reached for her golden memory, reached for her father laughing at her side. She needed this membership. She needed to belong. She needed something to keep her moving forward, to keep her moving away from the lonely future she saw so clearly.

She looked at the ring in Edmund's hand, but as she considered taking it, something inside her refused. Something deep. Something visceral and non-verbal. Something she didn't understand but had to obey.

Slowly, she shook her head *no*. Murmured an answer.

"I can't."

Her eyes blurred with tears. She blinked them

back.

"I need it not, lady. I have secured rich gifts for those who mourn my grandfather." He laughed softly. "Of the fifteen rings, I shall sell eight when I am returned home. Their worth in my world will be far above that of the ring I offer you."

He extended the hand that held the gold ring.

"It's not that," said Halley. She hadn't even considered the fact he was offering her something of considerable value not just in *her* world, but also in his. "I just ... I can't take it."

Halley avoided Edmund's eye. She could feel him staring at her.

"Wherefore will you not?" he asked softly.

Why not? Halley wasn't sure. She didn't know how to explain what she was feeling. She didn't know if she *could* explain her response. It felt ... *personal.* Deeply personal. Her response wasn't a thing she could *speak*, with words; it was a thing she *felt*, a thing with no words. It was an ugly taste in her mouth: bitter, metallic. It was familiar; it was tied to her mother. Tied to the way her mother took and took and took and *took*.

It was the same thing that stopped Halley from keeping the clothes Jillian loaned her, even when Jillian said she should take them. It was the same thing that kept her from emptying the professor's pantry when her mother had as good as ordered her to. Halley had grown up alongside someone who took and took, and she didn't want to be a taker.

But she wasn't sure she could explain this to Edmund. She'd tried to explain her feelings about *taking* to Jillian, and Jillian hadn't understood. Jillian just kept insisting it wasn't the same thing. Halley hadn't been able to explain it, even to her best friend, the reticence that made her say *no* and not *yes*. And if she couldn't explain it to Jillian, there was no way she could explain it to Edmund. How could he possibly understand? He didn't have a crazy person for a mother. He didn't have to wake up every morning afraid he was becoming more and more like her. Edmund wouldn't understand. She glanced over to meet his solemn eyes.

He sat waiting, still holding out his ring. Probably still waiting for an explanation she couldn't give. Her throat tightened.

"I just can't," she murmured.

"I understand thee not. Why wouldst thou give up thy dream?"

Her hands clenched into tight fists. "I'm not giving it up. I'll get the money. Just ... not from taking a ring that doesn't belong to me. I can't. That's just the way it is."

"How then will you obtain the money?"

Her heart sank. How indeed? She was close. Unbearably close. But even if she sold her truck, she wouldn't have enough. Sure, by next year, she would have time to earn enough to pay her annual dues. But this year? This week?

A heaviness descended on her, pushing her down, down, down. She was going to fail. She'd gotten this close only to fail. If only she'd sold two paintings instead of one. If only she'd stayed in the booth yesterday. If only ...

And then, suddenly she saw her way forward. Of course. It was so obvious. So perfect. She had a way to get the money on her own terms, by herself, with no ugly reminders of a past she wanted to leave behind.

She turned to Edmund.

"I'm going to set up the art show booth again tomorrow."

It didn't seem impossible. It wasn't impossible. She wouldn't let it be impossible. She had the booth back at the apartment. She could put it right back in her truck, along with the credit card processor and the paintings. She had the reserved space, just waiting for her. She had a way forward and it was pure. It was untainted.

Hope spilled out of her in a tangle of sentences. "I'll sell another painting. I only need to sell one. There will be a whole new crowd of customers all wanting something to remember Fiesta Week by. I already know there are people there who can pay my prices. If I sold a painting yesterday, I can do it again tomorrow."

It was the first step toward breaking free of her mother. Toward meeting the father her mother had kept from her. She remembered it as if it had just happened. How the seventh birthday with her father had been granted conditionally: *If she met with him this one time, Halley must* promise *never to bother her mother about him again.* By the time she turned twelve, Halley had broken that promise, demanding an email, a phone number, an address, something—things she hadn't known to ask for as a seven year old. Her mother had flown into a rage: *You don't need a father. You have me. And I have no idea how to reach him. He's gone! Gone! Gone!*

Halley had never asked again. Never heard from

him again. But this was her chance. Sell a painting. Join Club 33. Meet her father. She needed this like she needed a heartbeat.

Edmund interrupted her thoughts, bringing her back to the present.

"Did you not vow to attend your friends tomorrow at the gallery?"

Halley felt her heart sinking. DaVinci's show opened tomorrow. How could she have forgotten? How could she miss that? DaVinci would never forgive her. Or Jillian. Tears blurred her vision. It wasn't fair. She needed this. She would find a way to explain, a way to apologize, a way to make her friends understand what this meant to her. They would have to understand. And if they didn't … She wouldn't let herself consider that possibility.

Edmund spoke again. "You promised to attend Mistress Jillian and Mistress DaVinci. I am certain you gave your word."

She hesitated before responding. "Circumstances have changed."

It was *Edmund* who had changed them. Knowing she was about to lose *him* had shown her just how alone she was in this world.

Halley grabbed the letter from Club 33 and began folding it to place it back inside the envelope. Edmund should understand. Edmund who had kissed her half an hour ago as if his heart was breaking.

"You must not do this, Mistress Halley."

"DaVinci will understand," said Halley.

"It is not a question of understanding," replied Edmund. "It is a question of honorable conduct, mistress."

Halley felt her face heating. "Stop calling me that. It's Halley. Just *Halley*."

"Halley, I beg you to reconsider. Can you not place your wares for sale upon another date?"

She took a slow breath. She owed Edmund an explanation.

"I would love to sell on another date, but I can't. There aren't any other dates when I can exhibit at the Arts and Crafts Show. Artists try to get in that show for years, Edmund. We applied through a special process for VADA students—that's our school—but it was for Fiesta weekend only. I need the money *now*, not six months from now or five years from now or however long it would take me to get juried into the Arts and Craft Show. I need cash *now*, Edmund, and tomorrow is the last day I can exhibit."

"Would not the sale of my ring provide what you need?"

Halley breathed out heavily. He was trying to help. Trying to be kind. She wished she could make him understand.

He spoke. "Mistress Wu declared—"

"I'm not going back to that place," murmured Halley, remembering her ring inside the glass case.

"Then let us unto Master Nieman's—"

"No. I'm not taking money from the sale of something that doesn't belong to me. I can't. I have to do this for myself. I have to do it my way."

"I understand you not," Edmund said after a long pause.

For a minute, they sat in silence. Then Halley inhaled deeply.

"If I took your ring, it would be exactly like—"

The words stuck in her throat. This was hopeless. If she tried to make him understand, she would only fail, just like she had time and again with Jillian.

"Never mind," she whispered, blinking back hot tears.

Halley started the engine, put the truck in gear, and headed for her apartment.

## 49

### · *EDMUND* ·

Oftentimes, Edmund found it difficult to understand Halley's words, but her silence was even harder to understand. Rather than accepting the gift he offered, she was choosing to attend once more the faire, whereby she hoped—*hoped only*—to make up the difference between her holdings and what the 33rd Club required.

It was folly. Folly and stubbornness. And ... something else.

*If I take your ring, it would be exactly like—*

Like what?

Edmund considered this question as they drove back alongside the ocean, passing the swaying poletrees that lined the beach, passing a small lake and grassy fields, finally returning to the rented rooms wherein Halley dwelt. By the time their travel had concluded, he thought he understood.

As soon as she stilled the mighty engine, he addressed her.

"Mistress, forgive me for touching again upon the

subject, but I must speak. Your refusal to accept my gift, is it because you believe you would be repeating your mother's transgression? When she stole away the jewel bestowed on you by Mistress Jillian?"

Halley's gaze darkened. She undid her buckle, climbed out of the truck, and slammed the door. Edmund followed, chasing her up the narrow stairs and inside the apartment. Only once the door was closed behind them did Halley respond to Edmund's question.

"I refuse to act like my mother."

"The two actions are dissimilar, lady. Your mother took your ring without permission. I offer you this ring freely, as a gift."

Surely she saw the difference. She must accept that he was right. But instead of indicating her acceptance, she shook her head.

"It might not look the same to you, but it *feels* the same to me," she said. "I've already had this conversation with Jillian about the same issue. I'm no good at explaining it."

"I am not Mistress Jillian. Might not I understand where she could not?"

Halley seemed to consider his question. She sank onto a low couch. After a minute had passed, she spoke again, her voice calmer than before.

"Here's the thing," she said. "There must have been a moment, once, when my mother said *yes* to something that was offered to her, just like you're offering your ring to me. Mom must have said yes. And that yes led to another yes and another and another until she couldn't tell the difference between when she was accepting things and when she was demanding them, and now that's all she does—she demands things. She expects things. She takes and takes and takes and if I say yes to you now—" She broke off, wiping her eyes. "What if this is the action that sends me down the same path? I won't risk that."

There were tears running down her face. Edmund reached to wipe them away, but she turned, preventing him.

He spoke softly. "It is not this act which would liken you to her—"

Halley looked weary as she turned back to meet his eyes. "You don't know that."

"Lady—"

Halley cut him off again. "You don't know what it's like living with my mother."

Ah, but he knew what it was like living with Geoffrey. What it had been like living with his father. Why could Halley not see she was nothing like any of them?

He tried again, using a different tack.

"Lady, we can none of us alter the circumstances of our birth. Can an apple sprung from an apple tree declare it would be a ... a *strawberry* from hence forward? Nay, and yet ..." He paused to consider the remainder of his argument, but before he could speak, sharp words flew from her mouth.

"I refuse to believe that. If I believed that, I might as well give up. I might as well—"

She turned away from him, her dark hair tossing as a mare might shake its mane before battle. Oh, but she was glorious in anger.

How ever would he bear to leave her?

# 50

## · HALLEY ·

Halley took a slow, shaky breath. She needed to pull back from Edmund. Even though everything in her said: *yes, this: him*, it was time to get out of the pool and towel off, not take a jump off the high dive.

"I need to ..." She needed to what? She needed to stop thinking about him? She needed to get him out of her head? She needed to walk away?

"I need to ... take a walk," she murmured. She needed to clear her head. To polish the surface of her memory until the reflection of her amber-eyed earl was erased.

She crossed to the door and shut it behind her, not waiting for a response.

She thought about taking her truck, but she needed to move. She was full of adrenaline, angry, aching, restless. She walked all the way to Butterfly Beach and then turned west, walking along the south-facing shore.

At first, she thought only of how angry Edmund had made her, calling her just another apple from the apple tree, but gradually she admitted it wasn't Edmund she was mad at, not really. It was ... *everything*. It was the fact of him and the loss of him. It was the unexpected acceptance into Club 33 and the even less-expected annual dues, hitting her like a slap in the face. It was the discovery her mom had taken and sold the ring from Jillian. It was *everything*. It was all of the things which were given to her only to be snatched away.

She looked at the ocean. The tide was out now. Suddenly her life felt like a battle against a hungry, ever-receding sea which pulled from her all that she valued, all that she desired.

The low tide allowed her to skirt the cliffs below the cemetery at the far end of Butterfly Beach, so she continued walking, first to the long expanse of East Beach and then on to Leadbetter Beach.

Why did everything she wanted have to be taken from her? Why couldn't the tide of her life turn, bringing hope within reach, spilling treasures at her feet so that she could comb through them, gathering them at will? She kicked a dried clump of sea kelp from her path, stirring up a contingency of flies. The beach stank of decay.

She thought again about Edmund's ring. About how easy it should have been to say *yes* instead of no. About how impossible it was to say yes instead of no. About how, despite what Edmund said to the contrary, it would be just like what her mom did. Like Jillian, he'd argued there were differences, and like Jillian, he couldn't see that the *differences* didn't matter. It was the *similarities* that mattered, that would matter for years to come. The *taking* would be the same, and the *selling* would be the same, and if Halley paid for Club 33 with the money from Edmund's ring, she'd be reminded of her mother's selfish, careless cruelties every day of her life. Every time Halley ascended the stairs to the elegant Club, she would remember seeing her ring in the pawn shop. She would remember the ache of her mother's betrayal. She would shudder, wondering if the genes in her were turning her into the same person. And those remembrances, that fear, would poison her club membership, they would intrude every time she searched the faces at the bar, hoping to see one face that looked familiar....

Halley's feet had begun dragging sometime after she'd passed Stearn's Wharf. Shoreline Park stretched ahead and it was almost dark. She needed to get home. She needed to sleep. Tomorrow, she had to get up early and set the booth up by herself. Turning, she began walking east, joining the sidewalk because it was easier to walk on than the sand.

Finding herself back on the Art Show sidewalk, she experienced a minute of self-doubt. Was she doing the wrong thing?

She lifted her eyes and continued walking. She might not be doing the right thing, but she was doing the only thing she could do. Edmund was leaving. Her friends would move away next month. Club 33 offered hope, and Halley didn't think she could bear to go on living without hope.

She was tired. So tired. It had been stupid to walk so far away. But she'd needed the time to sort out everything she was feeling.

She called an Uber and was back to her apartment twenty-one minutes later, a few dollars farther away from being able to pay the Club's annual dues. The lights were all out in the apartment, and when she entered, she found Edmund asleep on the sagging couch wedged between the oven and refrigerator. He'd managed to open the apartment's one working window, so that the small space was redolent with the scent of the eucalyptus lining one side of the parking lot.

Halley stood in the dark apartment. She was hungry. She was exhausted. She was terrified of what tomorrow might—or might *not*—bring to her. She stared at Edmund, watching his right shoulder rise and fall in the rhythm of sound sleep. He'd draped his scarf over his torso so that it looked like a toddler-sized blanket. Sighing, Halley went into the room she shared with her mother and grabbed an afghan off her mother's queen sized bed. After draping it softly over Edmund's sleeping form, Halley returned to the bedroom where she threw herself on her own twin-sized bed and curled into a tight ball, eventually crying herself to sleep.

# 51

## · *HALLEY* ·

Halley woke early the next morning to the sound of her cell phone alarm. Rising, she moved in virtual silence. Edmund was still asleep in the combined kitchen and family room. She didn't want to wake him. She didn't want his smile drawing her in any deeper. She had to learn how to live without it.

Outside and downstairs, she unlocked the storage closet where her booth and paintings waited and loaded them into her truck. When she passed a window on her last trip to the truck, she saw a lonely girl looking back. She turned away.

At the foot of the stairs, she debated whether or not to return to the apartment for a bag of stale potato chips she'd seen in the bedroom.

Her hunger won out. When she opened the door, Edmund was still asleep on his side, with one arm draped over his exposed ear. He looked so peaceful. So beautiful.

Suddenly, she wanted to beg him to come and stay with her in the booth today, their last day together.

But wouldn't that make it even harder to say goodbye?

She needed to let him go.

After leaving him a note to say she'd be back at 6:40 and that Jillian would be coming by to pick him up at 10:00 for the Gallery Opening, she slipped out the front door.

She felt a pang of regret—for Edmund, for the opening—but what choice did she have? The booth space was a one-shot deal. Tomorrow, when Edmund was gone, it would be too late to make the money she needed.

She was doing the right thing. She was doing the only thing.

Steeling herself, she walked back down the stairs and checked the back of the pickup to make sure she hadn't forgotten anything. Change box? Check. Stool? Check. Receipt book, booth, sign … Everything was there. Except her bag of potato chips. She'd forgotten them *again*, distracted by Edmund.

A part of her leapt at the chance to look at him one more time.

She started the truck engine and drove away.

Without help from Jillian and DaVinci, it took Halley nearly two hours to set up the booth. She arranged Jillian's fruit sculptures prominently in the front of the booth. If she sold her friends' pieces, it might soften the blow of her absence. But even as she thought this, she knew the truth: nothing would make up for not being at the gallery. Certainly not dollar bills.

A seagull swooped down, attempting to make off with a sculpted strawberry. Halley shooed the bird away, and it screamed at her, accusing.

She was making a terrible mistake. She should tear the booth down, pack up, and race over to the gallery right now. She had just enough time…. But then she remembered the creamy vellum of the invitation to join Club 33. For eleven years, she'd waited for this opportunity. For more than half her life. She was too close to turn her back on her dream, annual dues or no. Another sale today would get her the rest of the way there.

If there had been any possible way for her to be there for DaVinci, she would have. It came down to this: Halley had no other way to get the money she needed. She didn't have wealthy parents, like Jillian. She didn't have generous parents, like DaVinci. This was what she had. This was all she had. It was the only way.

Halley pasted on a smile for a customer who crossed inside the booth to examine the asparagus painting. She took a deep breath when the customer gestured for a man to come take a closer look at the painting. Held that breath when the woman, immaculately dressed and wearing a diamond sparkly enough to power a small city, turned and addressed Halley.

"Our daughter paints, too."

"That's … great," said Halley. It meant the couple already understood that artists had a living to make. Her heart began to beat faster. If she made her first sale right away, there might still be time to race up to the gallery.

"This piece is really lovely. Are you the artist?"

Halley smiled and nodded. "It's been a real favorite this weekend." Was that what Jillian would have said? Or was that just stupid humble-bragging?

"You've got a great eye for color," said the woman. Then she turned to her husband. "Chip, I know exactly what I'm going to ask Muffy to paint for us for our anniversary!" The woman smiled, oblivious to the hopes she had raised and dashed.

Halley's face heated with anger, but she just smiled and wished the woman and her Sperry-shoed, argyle-sweatered husband a good morning.

The same painting continued to garner praise throughout the increasingly hot morning. There was no breeze, and Halley realized she'd forgotten to pack a water bottle. Occasional beads of sweat tickled down her spine, but she kept smiling, kept wishing people a great day, kept thinking: *this is the one!* every time someone stepped into the booth to admire the three green stripes on the charcoal background.

Several stepped close enough to examine the price. Half a dozen said maybe they'd come back later. Two asked if there was some wiggle-room in the pricing. One laughed at the price. *Forty-five thousand dollars.* What had she been thinking? She should scratch one of those zeroes off right now. But if she did, it wouldn't quite cover the gap between what she had and what she needed. As the day wore on, she began to answer that, yes, there was room for negotiating on price.

At two o'clock, when she still hadn't sold a single painting, Halley found a piece of paper and wrote BUY ONE PAINTING, GET ONE FREE on it, pinning the paper to the front of the booth. By three o'clock, she was worried the sign made her look desperate and she pulled it down. At half past three, an earlier admirer of the asparagus painting returned with her son. Both were dressed in the sort of casual elegance that spelled old money in Santa Barbara. Halley let slip that she had lived in Montecito all her life. Then immediately regretted it. Her own apparel—vintage St. Vinnie's—gave her away as a *poseur.*

The mother and son smiled politely and drifted out of the booth without having made any overtures to purchase. By 4:30, Halley was fighting back tears. And then, at 5:00, her mother appeared, exiting a taxi from across Cabrillo Boulevard and heading straight for Halley's booth.

## 52

### · *HALLEY* ·

Halley was in no mood to talk to her mother, but seeing her at least had the effect of completely quenching the tears. She wasn't letting her mom see her cry.

"Halley!" Her mother bee-lined for the booth, waving wildly, apparently on the off chance Halley hadn't noticed her. Her loud cries, in concert with her loud billowing silks and loud red sunhat made it unlikely anyone within a quarter mile failed to notice her.

Halley, accustomed to her mother's noisy entrances, felt only the barest twinge of embarrassment and even this was swiftly drowned in a swell of anger as she remembered her discovery in the pawn shop yesterday. How could her mother pawn her ring from Jillian? And say nothing about it—even when Halley had asked if she'd seen it?

Halley forced herself to take a slow breath. This was not the time to confront her mother about the ring. This was her place of business and she had only one more hour to sell a painting.

Her mother waited until she entered the booth before she spoke.

"I just heard you sold a painting for over ten thousand dollars two days ago." The accusation rang sharply in the tiny booth. "I had to hear this from DaVinci's mom. When were you planning to tell me?"

Halley felt her own accusation welling up inside, but reminded herself why she was here, stuck in a booth on East Beach. She closed her eyes and took a calming breath.

"It's been busy—"

"Obviously. You're too busy to let your own mother into your life."

"Mom," began Halley. But then she stopped.

She had nothing more to say. There was no, *Mom, I'm sorry,* or *Mom, I meant to tell you,* or *Mom, isn't it exciting?*

The woman in her booth was a stranger. Someone she'd shared living space with, but nothing more. The thought was freeing, and Halley felt her lungs expanding with the new revelation. But just as quickly, she felt the pressing devastation of it. She was motherless. She was alone.

Her mother didn't wait for Halley to continue.

"I just want to be clear that after this … *stunt*, you can buy your own tires. And our refrigerator needs replacing. Since you're in the apartment more than I am, I think we can agree you should be the one to replace it."

Halley's eyes grew wide. She wasn't hearing this.

Her mother plucked one of Jillian's sculptures off a display table.

"Put that down," snapped Halley.

"It's not like you're even contributing to the rent," continued her mother, snorting at the price of Jillian's sculpture.

"I said, put that down!"

The bowl of painted apricots *clunked* onto the display table.

"You're almost eighteen. It's high time you contributed to this family," murmured her mother.

High time she contributed to the family? To the "family"? What *family*? Where was this "family"? She sure as hell hadn't seen it anytime in the last decade.

Halley threw her shoulders back. "*We* are not a family. DaVinci has a family. Jillian has a family—"

"We are too a family!"

"No, Mom—"

"There's no 'Dad' in our lives? Is that your problem? I thought you'd gotten over that childish obsession."

Something solidified inside Halley. Something cold, icy, metallic. "The lack of a father is not what keeps us from being a family. We're not a family because you treat me like a ... like a ... a *roommate* instead of a daughter."

Her mother's refined nostrils flared. "Well, excuse me if my European style of parenting doesn't suit your American ideal of family."

"European style of parenting?" Halley coughed out a single laugh. Her mom had no "parenting style," Danish, American, or otherwise.

"Becoming a parent was the stupidest thing I ever did," muttered her mother.

There it was: the simple truth, battery-acid-caustic.

Corrosive. Honest.

Angry tears burned behind Halley's eyes. She blinked hard. Tried to focus on where she was. On what she had to do. Taking in a shaky breath, she spoke.

"I'm going to have to ask you to leave. This is my place of business. I am working right now."

"I paid twenty dollars to take a taxi here to speak to my daughter—"

Halley opened the cash box. Held out a twenty. "Which you did. Go. Now."

Her mother stared at the extended bill. Snatched it. Glared at Halley. Turned to go. Turned back.

"We are not done with this conversation, Halley."

But they were done. They'd been done for years. Maybe for always. Halley just hadn't noticed it until now.

"I'll move my stuff out tonight," Halley said flatly.

Her mother's face turned pale, and then reddened.

"Fine. If that's what you want, then … *fine*. But don't expect you can just come crawling back the next time you need something."

"I don't want anything from you," Halley said softly. But as soon as she'd said it, she realized it wasn't true. There was something she wanted from her mother. Something she needed desperately—as much as she needed that membership at Club 33.

Her mother was turning to leave.

"Wait!" said Halley. "There is something I want. You owe me this. I want a name. My father's name. I didn't even get his name the one time we met."

Turning back around, her mother stared at her blankly. "The time you met? What are you talking

270

about? You've never met your father."

Halley felt a swell of anger rising, but she kept her outward calm. "I met him once when he took me to Anaheim."

"Anaheim?" Her mother looked genuinely baffled. "You've never been to Anaheim with your father. You couldn't have been."

Halley felt as though her throat was swelling shut. Had she somehow imagined that memory? Created it out of the deep need she had to know her father? No. *No.* She knew the truth.

"My father took me to Disneyland when I turned seven. For my birthday. I know it happened. It was real."

Her mother's expression shifted from confusion to something else. "Oh, that."

*Yes, that*, thought Halley. She swallowed.

"You knew how to get in touch ten years ago. I want his name and I want that contact information. I don't care how old it is." It was better than nothing.

"Halley, that was an actor."

"What?" Halley heard her pulse swooshing in her ears.

"An *actor*. You wouldn't shut up about wanting a father, so I traded cat-sitting with an actor who took you to Disneyland to play the part of your father. I think he's in a psychiatric hospital now—"

"My father is in a hospital?"

"No, Halley. Try and keep up. " Her mother's tone dripped sarcasm. "The actor who pretended to be your father so you would stop pestering me is in the hospital. I have no idea who your father is. I went to a donor bank to get impregnated."

"You—I—*What?*" The ground seemed to shift under Halley's feet. "That's not possible...."

Her face twisted with pain. It had never occurred to her that the man who called himself her dad ... *wasn't.* Her broken dreams, her mother's un-kept promises, all of these swarmed her, a rush of noisy wings beating the air. They pressed against her, crushing her lungs: the thousand small ways her mother had made her feel unloved, uncared for, unwanted.

Halley couldn't breathe. She paused and placed her hands on her thighs, leaning forward to catch her breath. Her eyes were brimming. Her chest ached. She forced herself to breathe. To speak.

"How *could* you? What kind of person lets her child think ... *Who are you?*"

Her mother made a *harrumph* sound. And then she turned and left, her silk wrap billowing out behind her like a storm cloud.

Halley stood still for a count of ten. And then retreated to the stool in the back corner of the booth. And started to cry.

Five minutes later, Edmund found her with her back to the sidewalk, heaving with broken sobs.

# 53

## · EDMUND ·

"Lady?" Edmund said, alarmed.

Halley looked up, her eyes reddened as if from prolonged sorrow.

"Art thou injured?" He examined her face and clothing, looking for signs of hurt.

She shook her head and opened her mouth to speak, but the attempt only produced audible sobs and not words.

"Thy suffering is great," murmured Edmund, kneeling beside her. "Might I ... might I assist thee?"

Halley, her chest heaving convulsively, threw her arms around his neck and held him like a drowning soul clinging to preservation.

He remained there, on the summer-dry grass at her feet, holding her, supporting her weight, allowing her to cry out the dreadful grief inside of her. On either side of Halley's booth, purveyors were taking down their temporary structures, their work days completed. At last her sobs quieted, and Edmund released her, reaching for his handkercher only to realize he had none upon him. Nor did the lady, it seemed. He unwound the soft scarf from his neck— her tears had already soaked one side of it. "Here, lady. Dry thine eyes."

Her voice rasping, she spoke her first words since his arrival. "Why are you here?"

"I thought to aid thee at day's end," he said.

"You ... *walked* all the way here from the apartment? To help me tear down my booth?"

He smiled softly. "For what reason else should I be here?"

At this, fresh tears streamed down her cheeks.

Edmund's heart seized. "Forgive me. I meant not to increase your distress."

Halley shook her head. "You haven't. It's just ... I was horrible to you last night. I owe you an apology. You were right. I shouldn't have abandoned my ... my ... *friends.*"

At this final word, her voice cracked, and he opened his mouth to offer comfort, but she kept talking.

"DaVinci has wanted her own gallery show since we were six years old. I didn't even text her to tell her I wouldn't be there. I was too scared because I knew it was wrong, but I did it anyway. I abandoned her. I abandoned them both. What I did was unforgivable."

Edmund didn't know how to answer. Though her friends had been unwilling to speak to him of it, he had observed the provocation aroused by Halley's absence.

"Might they not forgive thee if asked?" he said at last.

"I don't deserve it."

"Few of us deserve all the good or ill we receive," said Edmund.

Halley sighed heavily and reached for him. He held her long, tightly, until at last he felt her pulling away. Her eyes were dry now and Edmund thought she looked calmer. And glad to see him again, in spite of her grief, in spite of the fact he was leaving tonight, in spite of everything. She even attempted a smile. It was a thin, wan thing, gone almost at once, but it made his pulse race.

"Is there aught I can do to relieve thee?" he asked.

Her brows drew slightly together. "You're speaking in *thee's* again."

Edmund felt his cheeks warming. "You will forgive me, pray."

He had done well the whole day, using only the formal "you" with DaVinci or Jillian, and keeping silent around others. But to see Halley in such pain and to speak to her in the cold, formal address of "you"? He had switched to the intimate form of "thee" without thought.

"Will you allow me to aid you in the dismantling of this structure?" he asked.

Halley nodded and dabbed at her eyes with his scarf.

"Rest," he said. "I will do all."

"No. I'm good. I can help," she said. "Well ... give me a minute. I need to call DaVinci and Jillian."

Nodding, Edmund turned to the booth and began to pull the paintings down, stacking them carefully one inside another and eventually resting them upon a clever wheeled device Halley pointed him to, behind the booth. Before he had begun to disassemble the booth itself, Halley had finished her calls.

"They didn't pick up," she said. "I left apologies."

When all the parts of the booth had been loaded onto what Halley called the "hand truck," they walked together to Halley's pickup. Edmund had been considering how to ask Halley about her earlier grief, which he suspected indicated a failure to sell her wares. He had concluded there was no gentle way to do it.

"Mistress," he asked as they re-set the tailgate, "I would not increase your grief, but I would know whether or no you earned the remaining payment for your club."

Halley sighed heavily. Tears filled her eyes but she did not allow them to spill.

"That," she said as they settled in the cab, side by side, "Is a complicated question to answer."

## 54

### · HALLEY ·

Halley started the truck and pulled into Fiesta weekend traffic. She didn't answer Edmund's question right away. She wasn't sure she *could* without completely falling apart, and she still had big things to get through before the day ended. She had an apartment to clear out of. She had Edmund to say goodbye to.

*Edmund.*

Her heart ached.

She cared for him. She might even love him. Not his beauty, not his sixteenth century quirks, but *him*. But whether it was care or love or something in between, she had to let him go. The only way to care for him, *truly* care for him, was to accept that he had needs and responsibilities and a life to return to.

So how was she supposed to answer his question about Club 33?

She couldn't bear the thought of Edmund spending the rest of his life believing she'd lost her own life's dream. She didn't want him sad or pitying when he remembered her. She wanted him to remember their laughter. Walking up State Street ... Branson's pizza ... their kiss.

Sighing, Halley pulled herself back to this moment. She'd made it all the way back to the apartment, and she still hadn't answered Edmund's question. She killed the engine but didn't get out. What could she say in answer to him? She didn't want to lie. You didn't lie to the people you cared for—the recent contact with her mother had driven this home. A partial truth then. The truth told *slant*.

Swallowing hard, she undid her seatbelt. And then, turning to face Edmund, she spoke.

"Something came to my attention today that made me realize ... I realized I don't want to join Club 33 after all," she said. She took a deep breath. "I'm going to use the money I made to get my own place, instead. I'd love your help grabbing all my things from the apartment, if you don't mind, before we head to the professor's."

His brow furrowed with worry, but then he seemed to accept what she'd said. Nodding deferentially, he replied. "As you wish, lady. I should be honored to assist you in any manner."

It was polite. It was kind. It also felt ... *distant*.

But perhaps this was best; she had to accept they were parting. Distance was a given.

But then he exhaled heavily and spoke again. "Forgive me, mistress, but are you certain all is well? I found you in great distress only a little while since. I would do anything, nay, I would hazard all to see you happy." He dropped his voice. "Surely you must know this."

Halley's chest tightened.

He cared.

Or loved.

Or something in between.

He would do anything...

Would he stay for her?

She saw the answer in his eyes. He would stay. For her. She couldn't breathe.

And he couldn't stay.

She couldn't let him abandon the family and people relying on him.

She took a shaky breath. "Just hold me."

And he did. He held her like she used to wish her mom would hold her when she scraped her knees. He held her like her friends held her when she got bad news. He held her like a lover with a broken heart.

And she breathed it in. She memorized the feel of his arms around her, of his face pressed to her hair, of his pulse keeping time with hers. This was real. This was true. This was something no one could take away from her. For all she knew she would face tomorrow friendless as well as homeless, but right now she had Edmund. And tomorrow when this moment belonged to the past and not the present, there would still be one thing no one could take from her: the knowledge she had mattered.

It gave her the strength to pull away from him.

"Come on. Let's get this over with."

## 55

### · HALLEY ·

Halley swept through the apartment like the hot Santa Ana winds that gusted over the Santa Ynez Mountains. She was thorough and she was swift. Anything that might be considered to belong to "both" herself and her mother, she left behind. Many of her personal things—earrings, eau de toilette, tweezers, nail files— had ended up on her mother's small vanity table.

Halley combed the vanity left to right, careful not to knock over the dozen miniature picture frames resting on it. Only one picture was of Halley. At three years old, she'd posed with Oprah Winfrey inside Pierre Lafond's. Halley's mother was still in hopes to get a call someday to dog-sit for Oprah. The rest of the pictures were of Inga Mikkelsen smiling with various celebrities. Halley left the Oprah picture behind.

The only thing Halley hesitated over was a pair of Ugg slippers. She'd been twelve dollars short when she'd bought them. Her mother had spotted her the money, later insisting the hundred dollar slippers were "twelve percent hers." In the end, Halley left the slippers behind because she didn't want to deal with the phone calls and texts from her mother, irately demanding the return of her "twelve percent."

It was at this point that Halley's fifteen thousand dollars offered a small measure of consolation. If she absolutely couldn't live without Uggs, she could buy new ones. She'd been thinking a lot about her money and how far it would get her living on her own. The answer was: *not very far*. She needed a job. A couple of times this summer Halley had insisted she was getting a job, but her mother had always vetoed the idea, saying she needed to know she could count on Halley to help out in a pinch: *I get migraines, Halley: migraines!*

Halley rolled her eyes. She'd let this go on for *way* too long. But when she stood by the front door for the last time, when she removed the apartment key from her key ring and set it on the kitchen counter, Halley felt tears threatening. Edmund noticed at once and placed a gentle hand between her shoulder blades.

"It's nothing," said Halley. It *was* nothing, but she hesitated, still clutching the apartment key: the last vestige of what she'd called *home*. "We should head over to the professor's."

"Lady, I should like to gaze upon the Pacificum one last time."

*One last time.*

The request made it clear what she was really saying goodbye to today. It gave her the strength to drop the key on the counter, walk outside, and shut the apartment door forever.

She felt lighter as they descended the stairs.

"Perhaps we might visit the beach of the

butterflies," said Edmund.

Halley smiled. "It's Butterfly Beach. And yes. Absolutely yes."

In less than ten minutes, they were leaning on the eucalyptus log backed up against Butterfly Beach's golden sandstone cliffs. The sun hung over the silvered ocean, an orange orb. The sand had been in shade long enough that it felt cool beneath their toes.

It was Edmund's last night in the "New World." These were the last hours she would spend with him, but Halley couldn't settle and enjoy these stolen minutes. Her mind was back in the apartment again: spinning, racing, consumed by all the physical reminders of her mother's self absorption. Halley wanted to leave it behind, to padlock it and forget the combination. But what if she couldn't? What if the genes in her body were already at work, slowly turning her into her mother? Was her destiny already decided?

Wasn't she, after all, an apple from an apple tree?

Halley felt her throat swelling. "Do you really think I'll end up like my mother?"

Edmund removed his gaze from the sea. His eyes narrowed, their golden-brown irises catching the sun's last light.

"Like what you said yesterday," she murmured, dropping her eyes. "That I have to be an apple because she was an apple."

"Ah, mistress ..." Edmund sighed heavily and took one of her hands in his. "I must beg your forgiveness. It was ill spoke."

Halley felt the warmth of his palm as it pressed against hers.

"But did you mean it? Do you think it's true?"

He paused before responding. "Know you of the four humors?"

Halley frowned, feeling vaguely as if she'd heard the phrase.

"Learned men of medicine do blame our humors for faults of disposition," said Edmund. "We say of a melancholic humor that it makes a man sad and given to thought, whereas one who is sanguine interesteth himself in others. The phlegmatic man is at rest within himself and seeks the betterment of others while the choleric are aggressive and accomplish much."

This did *not* answer her question.

"Those who do practice physick say we are born thus," Edmund continued. "And yet, it seemeth to me—pardon, it *seems* to me—that there is more at play than that with which we are born."

Halley watched the sun. In twenty minutes it would be lost into the sea. For some reason, the thought made tears gather on her lower lids.

"Halley, it seems to me that there are people in this world who have not much to give unto others."

As he said it, she felt her shoulders tense. "Yeah. Do you think I'll end up like that?"

Edmund turned to face her, taking her other hand in his. "Lady, I believe you have been shown how to live in such a manner. But that you do ask the question? Methinks this speaks to a difference in your temperament."

"I was selfish today. I chose to do the booth even when you tried to talk me out of it."

Edmund was silent for a moment before responding.

"You seem to me to care deeply for others. If you

do not always behave in the best way, it is perhaps that you have had bad example."

"Maybe," murmured Halley. "But I'm so afraid I'm going to end up just like her—"

"Nay, lady. Can you not see that your very fear is the proof you will not? Would your mother fear to be as she is?"

Her mother would justify the hell out of it, thought Halley. Slowly, she shook her head. "She sees no problem being the way she is."

"There is your answer."

Halley drew her knees toward her chest. She dug her fingers into the cool sand, then lifted her fingers, allowing the sand to fall away. Then, on a whim, she placed a handful of sand in her pocket. She could carry it home and store it in a tiny jar, a small way to hold this moment forever.

"Mistress …"

Halley looked up.

"Was it for this you were weeping when I found you at the faire?"

He still didn't know what she'd been crying about. Halley felt her shoulders tensing. She could say *yes* and leave it at that. It would be simpler than explaining the truth: that she'd wept for the loss of the man she'd thought was her father, that she'd cried for her mother's careless indifference, for the years of small and great injustices. For finding herself alone in the world.

"You need not give answer. I have no claim upon the secret spaces of your soul."

But … he did. He *did*. He had lodged there, in the secret spaces of her soul. She'd given him a piece of the truth. A slant version of the truth. But now Halley felt suddenly weary of slant-truth. She wanted to tell someone the whole truth, just for once. She wanted to tell *Edmund* the whole truth. To be known. To be heard. To be real.

Just for once.

So she told him the whole truth.

# 56

## · *EDMUND* ·

Edmund had never been so aggrieved as he was hearing Halley tell her tale. Her pain was of a sort he had never imagined. For a time he was too distraught to speak and could only hold her. But gradually anger replaced the deep-seated sorrow. How had Halley's mother dared to commit so great a fraud upon an innocent child? To perpetuate it as she had done by keeping silence. It was unthinkable. Monstrous.

And it meant ... it meant Halley had lost her compass-star—the "club" upon which she'd set her sights. She was as rudderless as the tiny barks he and Robert had once launched onto the mill pond. He could not bear to think of her thus without purpose, without aim.

Before thinking of what he was asking, he said, "Come away with me."

Halley's arched brows rose.

"To Hensley Manor."

"To 1598?"

Edmund could hardly hear for the hammering of

his pulse in his ears.

"Be mistress of all I call mine. I cannot promise you will want for nothing, but I swear you will never want for love."

Halley's brow contracted. "Edmund ... I—" She broke off, shaking her head. "I don't know what to say."

*Say yes.* He wanted to shout it aloud, to outroar the very ocean. *Say yes.*

But she said nothing, only continued the running of sand through her fingers.

"Do you not care for me a little?"

"How can you ask? Of course I care. A lot. But you're asking the impossible, Edmund. The kind of thing you're suggesting is fine in the movies, because it's always happily ever after and fade-to-black. But I don't know the first thing about being a ... a *housewife* in the sixteenth century. And I know nothing about being an earl's wife, either."

"Thou canst learn, surely."

"*Canst* I? I don't even know how to talk right in your time. I'll make a thousand errors a day, just like I've seen you do here. But here, the worst thing that can happen is people think you're eccentric. Harmlessly crazy. What would happen if I didn't go to church with you on Sundays? Or if I did? Without knowing what to say or do, when to kneel or rise or cross myself—"

"We are not papists, madam."

Halley shook her head. "That's exactly my point. I'm not even sure what a papist is. I don't know if it's dangerous to cross myself or not cross myself in your world. And if I start behaving strangely in church or the marketplace or the kitchen, what will that look like in your time?"

Edmund frowned. He saw to where her argument tended. "Thou mightst be questioned by the parson for lack of conformity."

"I might be burned at the stake."

"I would never let that happen!"

"Edmund, seriously? Have you ever seen witches burned at the stake?"

"Aye—"

"And was there a single thing you could have done to stop it?"

He frowned darkly. At length he replied. "Nay. But it might never come to that."

"Do you think I would risk putting you through that? Allow you to live day to day in fear of what crazy thing I'm going to say or do next?"

He did not respond. His eyes were fixed on the horizon, on the setting sun, glowing like fire about to be quenched by the sea.

"I wish I could say yes, Edmund. But I've seen how hard it is for you to fit in here. It would be impossible for me to fit in there, with you. I want you free from that kind of fear. I want you to have a long, happy life—"

Halley broke off. She was staring blankly into the distance.

"What is it?"

Without speaking, she rose.

## 57

### · HALLEY ·

Halley's breath caught in her throat. What if she *was* a part of that long and happy life? Could she have been? Could she be? There was a simple way to find out: *Wikipedia.*

"I'll be back in a minute," she said before tromping around the sandstone outcropping that had been providing a sort of privacy wall for the two of them. On the other side of the outcropping, she typed EDMUND ALDWYCH, EARL OF SHAFTESBURY into her phone. And waited.

And found him. There was a portrait—those were his eyes. And there was the year of his birth ... and the year of his death. A shiver ran along her spine. This was wrong. She shouldn't know this. She wanted to un-know it. But she needed to know one more thing. What if the name of his wife was *her name?* Her heart hammering, she scanned through the paragraph describing Edmund, the second earl of Shaftesbury.

Where was it? *Where was it?*

Her heart in her throat, Halley's eyes landed on a

name.

It wasn't her name.

Edmund's wife was listed as *Maria Hallcote of Lavenham*, a wealthy widow two years his senior.

So.

Edmund would marry.

But he wouldn't marry Halley Mikkelsen of Montecito.

Her heart cracking, she read on, unable to stop herself. He would have ten children, six of whom would survive to adulthood. His wife's dowry would pay debts contracted during the first earl's lifetime—

Halley tapped the page shut.

She felt ill. She couldn't breathe. She shouldn't know these things. Edmund couldn't know these things.

She took a slow breath. In. Out. She'd found the truth: Edmund would return to his own time, without her. Again, it felt like all the air was being sucked out of her lungs.

"Mistress Halley?"

She snapped back to the present, hiding her phone guiltily even though there was no chance Edmund had heard of Wikipedia. She took a shaky breath. Things were clear now. Horribly, incontrovertibly clear. She had no choice but to stay here and let him go. History had already been written, and it was a good history, for Edmund. For his legacy. For his household. Feeling as though her feet were weighted with lead, Halley turned back to rejoin Edmund.

She sank into the cold sand beside him. His eyes fixed on hers, then dropped to her lips. When he met her eyes again, his pupils were dark and large. His hand gripped hers as though he was afraid she'd vanish. As though he wouldn't let her.

The inches closed between them until their foreheads touched. She felt a tremor run through him and his grip on her hand tightened.

"Halley," he murmured. "Lady."

And then words became unnecessary.

## 58

### · *EDMUND* ·

After kissing her, Edmund lifted a hand to her cheek. Touched the pad of his thumb to her ear, slid it down along her jaw line. And then once again, his mouth found hers and he kissed her across four hundred years, across a continent, across seas of time and space that conspired to separate their souls. He kissed her as if by kissing her he could bend time to his will, reforming what might have been into what could be. And in that kiss, he saw a future *here* and *now:* a parcel of land where they tilled the soil together, churned butter from their goodly cow, picked apples from a small orchard. He saw a future where he learned the art of brewing root beer and brought Halley root beer floats by the ewer-ful. She would teach him to speak aright in this time and he would teach her to judge soils, whether better for corn or for pasture. He saw all this, and then he saw it swept away by duty and obligation.

Shivering, he pulled back from the kiss.

"Ah, lady," he said, sighing. And again, "Ah,

lady." There were tears in his eyes.

"Kiss me again," she murmured.

So he did. And this time he felt only his loss, his hunger, the ache that would fill the rest of the life he must return to. Her lips warmed beneath his and he took her in his arms, tumbling her back against the cradling sand. He wanted to breathe her in until he knew no other scent. To memorize the beat of her pulse until he heard nothing but the way her heart raced beside his.

But then she pulled away, out of the kiss.

"You have to go back." Her voice was soft and flat.

"Nay, lady—"

"Yes. You do. Now. You have people who depend on you. Do you know what it's like to have no one you can depend on? I do. I wouldn't wish that on anyone."

"I cannot leave thee."

"You can't stay."

Edmund's head fell forward, cradled in his hands.

He sat like that, inwardly weeping. A minute passed. And another. Five. Ten. He cared not. All the while Halley remained beside him, her head resting on his shoulder, her small hand in his, his sole comfort. At last, he raised his head and nodded.

"It is time."

## 59

### · *HALLEY* ·

They pulled into the professor's estate just as the first stars began to shine in the purple-black sky. Halley sighed. DaVinci would know what to call such a color: DaVinci, who might never speak to her again.

"Mistress Halley?"

"Yes, Edmund?"

She pulled the truck past the guesthouse, parking it next to a side door of the main house. Overhead, the lean palms towered, their slender forms outlined in black against the night sky. Halley heard crickets and what might have been a lone frog. The scent of eucalyptus and roses was heavy in the night air.

Pulling hard, Edmund slid his memorial ring from his finger. Then he took Halley's hand, opened her palm, and dropped his heavy ring into it.

"I no longer ask of thee to sell it," he said, his voice raw with emotion. "I ask thee to keep it always, to remember me by, when I am gone."

Halley's eyes flicked up to consider his, but his gaze was fixed somewhere outside, on some one of the thousand things he would never see again after tonight.

She hefted the ring in her closed hand. Felt its weight. It no longer felt like a reminder of her mother's betrayal. It felt like Edmund's soft smiles, his deep laughter. The way he took offense at things he didn't understand. The way he'd walked all the way to East Beach today to offer help.

She clenched her hand more tightly around the ring as if by doing so she could keep Edmund here at her side.

She thought back to the first moment she'd seen him. The handsome face hovering over hers, checking to be certain she was alive. Only minutes later, offering to give her a lifetime of employment and support. *Canst thou bake or brew or mend?* He was already struggling to meet his debts, yet he'd offered to help her, a stranger.

Halley felt a lump forming in her throat. Her mom wouldn't so much as pay for a set of tires without something in exchange, but here was this stranger who had been willing to commit to feed, house, and clothe her for the rest of her life.

She pressed the ring into her palm, then slid it onto the middle finger of her right hand, the only finger it would stay put on.

"I would like that, Edmund Aldwych. I would like that very much."

# 60

## · KHAN ·

Jules Khan was not by nature or inclination a violent man. He'd never intentionally harmed anyone, unless you counted the incident with Dr. Littlewood, which Khan most energetically did not. And yet, given the correct set of circumstances, even the most mild-mannered must unsheathe his claws, or so Khan consoled himself. He wished no harm to the girl or her boyfriend; they were simply *in the way*. The professor had studied the situation carefully and concluded there was no way around, under, or over them. Like extraneous variables, they had to be eliminated.

And so, the stage had been set. The necessary items purchased. The tasers (two of them) charged and, at least as importantly, practiced with. Halley and her sixteenth century ... *boyfriend* were to arrive by 8:00, and although Khan had texted Halley to say he would be leaving at 4:00, that had been a lie.

Everything about the operation was regrettable, yet what blame could be lain at Khan's feet? He was not the person who had decided to sneak into someone else's private laboratory and play with the equipment willy-nilly. In all of this wretched business, he could hold himself blameless. He might not like it, but he had no choice. The boy and girl were uncontrolled variables; they must be eliminated.

Rather than focusing on the unpleasantness of the task at hand, Khan found it useful to focus on a hypothesis he'd been wanting to test. Until now he'd been without the means—without the requisite *volunteers*. Should his theories prove sound, he would be able to add a *second* law of temporal inertia to the one he'd already created and named after himself. (This wasn't hubris. There was no one else working in his field at a level to warrant naming it for them.) Tonight, then, he would find out if his hypothesis held water.

After all, unpleasant tasks aside, he was first and foremost a scientist.

# 61

## · HALLEY ·

Halley marched slowly from the guesthouse back to the main house where she had left Edmund to change into his Elizabethan garb. It was 8:25, nearly half an hour later than Halley had promised to arrive, but the professor had told her he would leave keys under the guesthouse mat.

They'd been there as promised: a set of keys for both buildings. There was even a hastily scrawled *Thank You* on the back of the envelope holding the keys. Halley had decided they would enter the main house using a side service door to decrease the possibility their entry would be detected by the professor upon his eventual return in three days time.

"This is the easy part," Halley said to Edmund, unlocking the door. "We still have to figure out how to get into the basement *without* keys."

A few minutes later, they were at the base of the stairs where Halley's adventure had begun little more than forty-eight hours ago. This time, however, the door was not ajar.

The two of them stared at the closed door.

"Any ideas?" asked Halley.

"You do not happen to have upon your person a lock-pick set?"

Halley looked at Edmund in surprise. "How do you even know what a lock-pick set is?"

Edmund smiled softly. "DaVinci introduced me to the delights of movie binge-viewing. After her gallery opening, I listened to three of the *Jason Bourne* movies."

"Listened?"

"Aye."

"Don't you mean, you *watched* them?"

Edmund frowned. "In my world, we do say that we 'hear' a play, but, aye, I did *observe* them as well. I learned much new speech of your world. Although, many of the strong oaths have not altered with time."

Halley shook her head. "Well, to answer your question, I don't have a lock-pick set. That would have been a good idea. I guess we could try brute force."

"What doth 'brute force' signify?"

"Smashing something." She would do it and suffer the inevitable questions and suspicion if she had to, but she was hoping for a better idea. She glanced at Edmund.

Edmund had changed back into his Elizabethan clothes while Halley had gone to retrieve the house keys. He was once again wearing a sword. Could it whack the door handle loose? Before she had a chance to ask him, Edmund stepped forward and tried the handle, which turned out to be unlocked.

"Why didn't I think of that?" asked Halley.

"Perhaps you, too, should engage in binge-viewing of Jason Bourne."

Halley smiled. Humor was good. Keeping things light was good. She didn't think she could handle another emotionally drawn out scene with Edmund.

"After you, lady," said Edmund, holding the door wide.

Halley stepped inside. "That's odd," she said, peering into the dark.

"What, prithee?"

"Last time the lights came on automatically as soon as I stepped into the room."

"You are in need of a switch of lights," said Edmund.

Halley grunted out a small laugh and grabbed her phone, intending to use it as a flashlight, but then she heard a sound she couldn't place, electrical, maybe, followed by a sound she *could* place.

The sound she recognized was that of a body hitting the floor.

Edmond had been struck down.

# 62

## · KHAN ·

Khan's first taser shot struck perfectly. As he'd hoped, the young man's body fell forward as 50,000 volts racked his body, leaving Khan free to secure his hands behind his back. First, though, he had to incapacitate the girl. Before Halley could so much as emit a gasp of horrified shock, Khan fired his second taser. The professor might have lacked a natural taste for violence, but he made up for it by planning each of tonight's steps with a choreographer's precision.

The moment the girl was down—on her side, which was less than ideal—Khan slipped plasticuffs on the boy's wrists, binding them behind his back.

Twenty-one seconds down. Khan had only another nine seconds before the volts shooting through Halley's system completed their cycle. He nudged her onto her belly and tied her wrists together as well, completing the task more swiftly the second time.

By the time Khan had secured the girl's wrists, the young man was mumbling, albeit incoherently. Next came a tricky bit. After expending two precious seconds to turn on the overhead lights, Khan then used his foot to roll the young man onto a throw rug, enabling him to slide the boy to the far side of the room beside the singularity device. Then, snaking an extra long cable tie through the boy's plasticuffs, Khan secured his victim to a heavy equipment rack, which he reasoned would prevent the boy from running.

By the time the professor had run back to retrieve Halley, she was groaning and trying to roll onto her side again, possibly with the intention of rising and running herself. Khan reached her in time to prevent this. She was small enough that he didn't need the assistance of a smooth-gliding rug underneath her. Grasping her feet, Khan dragged her back beside the boy and secured another tie through her wrists to the same rack.

They weren't going anywhere, which was fortunate as Khan felt as though he'd just run a marathon. A consummate planner, he had even anticipated his present need for water and grasped a bottle that was waiting for him on the podium.

After assuaging his thirst, the professor stepped onto the podium's transport platform and began to prepare the singularity device for use. By the time he'd begun that task, the two detainees were whispering to one another. Khan didn't bother *shushing* them—they were helpless and talking wasn't going to change that. In some ways, this wasn't so different from proctoring an exam.

He was on a schedule, however, so he interrupted them as soon as he had completed preparing the machine.

"I have a few questions," he said.

Aware of the adrenaline coursing through his veins, Khan was surprised by how calm his voice sounded, as though he were only discussing an experiment with a pair of grad students.

"Let's start with the most important question. Edmund Aldwyssen, in what year were you born?"

# 63

## · HALLEY ·

Before Halley could caution him, Edmund answered the professor, who gave a nervous nod and thanked him.

"Your candor makes things much more straightforward," added Khan. "Now then, Edmund, since joining this century, have you experienced any physical irregularities? Headaches, nausea, loss of consciousness? Anything out of the ordinary?"

"I have not," Edmund replied, his brow dark and murderous.

"What do you want from us?" asked Halley.

She watched as the professor tapped a pen to his lips. Once, twice. He seemed to have developed a twitch in one of his eyes. Was he ... *anxious*? Why would *he* be anxious? He wasn't the one cable-tied to a massive metal shelving unit. How could she have been so stupid? So trusting? Of course Khan had been onto them. She'd been such an *idiot!*

"Ideally, I would run diagnostic testing on you, Master Aldwyssen—"

"It's Aldwych," said Halley. "And he's an earl. He's important." This might be an exaggeration, but Khan didn't need to know that.

"Hmm. Yes. I wasn't able to find the surname *Aldwyssen* in any lists of Danish family names. Thank you."

Was that sarcasm? Halley couldn't tell. It had seemed genuine. Or maybe just automatic.

The professor returned his attention to Edmund. "Unfortunately I will not be running any diagnostics on you. There isn't time. Not to mention, with the shock your nervous system has just sustained, results would be highly inaccurate."

"What do you want from us?" Halley repeated.

"Just a few answers," said the professor. "I'm afraid you have nothing else to offer me, other than the tangible evidence provided by Edmund that it is possible to survive a journey such as his."

"Let us go," said Halley. "We're not going to tell anyone about your … experiments."

"I have a few questions for you, Halley," said the professor, avoiding her gaze and her request. "Plainly, you tampered with my equipment. Could you tell me everything you remember from the moment you broke into my lab?"

Halley was tempted to say nothing unless he released them. If she was any judge, the professor was very uncomfortable with what he was doing. She might as well see how far cooperation got her, for now. She glanced to see what Edmund thought, but he had grown inattentive and withdrawn.

Turning back to the professor, Halley told him everything that had happened, from the open basement door to Edmund's accidental journey into the twenty-first century. The professor took copious notes, nodding and prompting on occasion. When Halley had finished her narrative, he asked for clarification.

"You are certain your length of stay in 1598 was not more than fifteen minutes?"

"Pretty certain. I mean, my cell wasn't working, obviously—"

"Quite. But you weren't there for, say, thirty-five minutes, were you?"

"Definitely not," said Halley.

He murmured to himself, staring at his notes. At last he looked up with something of a triumphant expression.

"What?" asked Halley. "Why do you looked so pleased with yourself?"

He gave a small shrug and answered. "I have posited that the singularity device might be capable of managing separate, distinctly programmed journeys at the same time. Now I have proof. Despite your ... interference, the experimental program guiding *my* journey functioned properly. Well, always excepting the earthquake."

"The *earthquake*?" asked Halley, her eyes widening. "You don't mean ... Did you have something to do with the earthquake on Friday?"

Without looking up from his note-taking, he said, "Believe me, I find the earthquakes troubling." And then, as if to himself, he added, "But I don't see any alternative to extending the length of stay beyond the allotted pocket...."

"Allotted *pocket*?" asked Halley.

"Ah. Yes. The temporal singularity device—my *time machine*—is normally limited to opening what I call a 'temporal pocket' for only five hours divided by the square root of the total number of years traveled. Which makes travel to the Old Kingdom of ancient Egypt highly inconvenient. Unfortunately, when I have attempted to extend the allotted pocket ..." The professor shrugged.

"Earthquakes?" demanded Halley.

"Mmm," agreed Khan, his nose once again in his notes.

Halley felt her stomach twist at his calm demeanor. "Someone could have *died* from that!"

Khan looked up. "As we've already established, I find the earthquakes most troubling."

Halley, her mouth shrinking in disgust, looked away from the professor. Her gaze fell on one of the several Egyptian sarcophagi in the room. Although she didn't know her Old Kingdom from her New Kingdom, Halley couldn't help wondering if the professor had "extended the temporal pocket" to retrieve these items. Were his activities—his selfishness—responsible for the spate of earthquakes in the past six months?

The thought was sobering. Halley was pretty sure someone *had* died during last April's quake. People needed to know about this. She and Edmund had to get out of there.

"Have we answered all your questions?" Halley asked. At her side, Edmund remained silent and still. He seemed eerily focused on *something*, but she had no idea what.

"What was that?" asked the professor, looking up

from his notes.

"Have we answered all your questions?"

"Yes. Yes, I believe so."

"So let us go." Her heart was pounding as she spoke. "We won't tell anyone *any*thing." Could he tell she was lying? She felt the plastic bite into her wrists as she clenched her hands into fists.

"I'm afraid I can't take that risk," replied Khan. Eyes off his notes, he turned in her direction but did not meet her eye.

Her chest felt like it might explode. If he wasn't going to release them ... what was he going to do?

"Let us go," Halley said softly. "You don't want us on your conscience."

She couldn't say, "*you don't want to kill us*," but she noticed Khan flinching as if she had.

"Regrettably, I cannot allow you to go."

Which meant what? They weren't getting out of this alive? Or they weren't getting out of this in this century? Her gaze shifted to the machine, to the slight flickers of color reflected from the podium screen onto the professor's face.

"My work is too important to me," said the professor. "To me and to the world."

For several seconds after this, Halley was silent as despair threatened to choke her breathing. But then something inside her snapped.

"You're saying you're prepared to make us *disappear* for the sake of your work?" Halley spat the words out. "Your so-called *work* of stealing valuable artifacts from the past so you can live in a mansion?"

The professor's lips thinned as he pressed them together. "Not that I owe you an explanation, but I do *not* steal things from the past."

"Buy them. Whatever. It's still fraudulent. And what about the … the butterfly effect? You're playing God. You have no right—"

"I have *every* right," said Khan, his voice rising. "I have the right of the mind which seizes opportunity rather than shivering on the sidelines. I have risked more than you can imagine to achieve breakthroughs that will change the way humanity conceives of space-time."

Halley felt her stomach churn with revulsion. The professor was just like her mother—always prepared to justify whatever had been done "for the greater good," which in her mother's case meant "personal financial gain" and in the professor's case meant "scientific advancement." Halley looked to Edmund to demand some support, but he had slumped forward and his eyes were closed.

"Edmund?"

"He's praying," murmured the professor. "It is a marvelous thing, the human capacity for hope."

Halley examined Edmund, who *did* appear to be praying. His lips were moving slightly. So were his hands. Halley felt a wave of pity: Edmund, who clearly didn't understand the first thing about plastic cable ties, was trying to free his hands. But then she realized he was doing more than wriggling his hands.

Fortunately for Halley, her hair fell forward at that moment, shielding her shocked expression from the professor's view. Edmund had a knife. At some point in the confusion of being tasered and confined, the professor had taken Edmund's sword, but he hadn't remembered to search for Edmund's small folding knife, and now Edmund was using it to slice his hands free. The angle at which Edmund was forced to grip the knife was awkward and the plastic wasn't giving up easily, but Halley could tell Edmund would cut himself free within a few minutes, as long as he didn't drop his knife first.

She had to be ready.

And she had to keep talking—to keep Khan's focus on her and off of Edmund.

"You can talk about the advancement of science all you want," said Halley, "But if that's all you cared about, you wouldn't be driving a fancy car."

The professor's eyes narrowed.

"Not to mention maintaining that private collection upstairs. You're nothing more than a thief."

Khan stood, but instead of shouting at her, Halley thought she detected a tiny smile. He clasped his hands behind his back and began pacing back and forth beside his desk. He *was* smiling.

"Am I entertaining you?" she asked dryly.

He looked up, an amused expression on his face. "Hmm… Yes, I suppose you are. You see Miss Mikkelsen, I am in possession of information of which you are ignorant. Would you like to know one of the universe's little secrets?"

Halley shrugged. The universe could keep its dirty little secrets for all she cared. All she wanted was to keep Khan talking so Edmund could cut himself loose. She was dying to risk a glance at Edmund.

"Think of it this way," began the professor. "The temporal continuum resists change, much like a large mass—a train, say—resists a change in motion. As it turns out, temporal inertia is far greater than has been thus far proposed—proposed prior to my work, that is. In fact, I may have proven that permanent changes to past timelines are impossible. I call this *Khan's First Law of Temporal Inertia.*"

"Of course you do," Halley muttered under her breath. The professor was too caught up in his explanation to overhear her.

"Inertia, of course, is resistance to change, with 'temporal inertia' describing space-time's resistance to change. Thus far, I have only been able to rupture the temporal continuum in small 'pockets' for an allotted, specified period. When the temporal pocket closes and I return to my own time, all objects that were there in that other time necessarily *remain* in that time due to temporal inertia. However, all objects within my temporal pocket—including a sort of envelope surrounding me and what touches my skin—necessarily *return* to my own time; once again, temporal inertia is at work preventing the rupture of space-time. This results in what you might call a 'duplication' of objects. This duplication is the necessary result of space-time healing itself."

Halley sat dumbfounded. When she spoke at last, she said, "You're kidding."

The professor's smile disappeared. "I never joke about my work."

Frowning, Halley tried to remember something from her Physics for Poets class. "Isn't there some law of conservation of mass or energy or ... something?"

"America's public education at work," the professor commented dryly. Then, seeming to gather himself, he continued, "The Law of Conservation of Mass and Energy expresses what is true in an isolated space-time region. This law of conservation has proved inadequate to describe the space-time continuum, hence my Law of Temporal Inertia, which describes what I have observed through the use of the singularity device."

"So the machine is like a ... photocopier?"

The professor frowned. "The crudeness of your explanation is appalling, but if we make allowances for your limited knowledge and comprehension, then *yes*, we might say the singularity device causes space-time to function in a manner similar to a 'photocopier.'"

"You're saying you could steal the crown jewels from the Tower of London, but the crown jewels would still ... be there? In history?"

"And in the present, yes. They are conserved in their original position, but because I hold them as I journey through space-time, they are conserved with me as well."

Halley shook her head. "Unbelievable."

"As I said, I am no thief."

Halley glowered at him. "But you have no problem poking space-time with a stick to see if it can fix itself."

Khan's face remained unperturbed.

Halley thought of something else. "Are things, er, *duplicate things*, left behind, too? In the past?"

"No," said the professor, with the air of someone speaking to an ignoramus. "As I've already indicated, anything that travels within the protected temporal pocket created by the singularity device is duly returned where it belongs."

The computer on the podium made three shrill pips.

"Ah," said the professor. "It is, as they say, show time at last."

He reached for one of his tasers and loaded a new cartridge.

"What are you doing?" Halley asked with rising panic.

"I'm tidying up the mess you made," murmured the professor. He seemed to be having trouble loading the taser cartridge. Crossing to his desk, he picked up a sheet of instructions, examining them carefully. Then, with an audible, "Ah," he turned the cartridge upside down and reloaded it.

Swallowing, she noted there were another half dozen cartridges stacked neatly on the professor's desk. "Are you planning to kill us with the tasers?"

Khan pursed his lips in distaste. "No."

But when Halley prodded him for more, he ignored her, suddenly preoccupied with the time machine.

This preoccupation provided Edmund, who had opened his eyes and was looking earnestly at Halley, with the opportunity to do two things. First, Edmund passed her his knife, indicating with a glance she should start cutting herself free. Then, weaponless, he rose and charged the professor.

## 64

### · *EDMUND* ·

Edmund delivered a solid blow to Khan's mid-section, smiling to himself when he heard Khan struggling to draw breath. Next, Edmund had to reach the pistol-like weapons. The professor was in no position to pursue him, and he dashed to the far side of Khan's desk, sweeping the boxes of additional weaponry away.

Next, Edmund grasped the pistol itself and attempted to understand the controls. The professor was still having difficulty breathing. Edmund did not consider this likely to be feigned, considering the strength of the blow he had delivered to Khan's belly.

Unfortunately Edmund had cause to regret this appraisal when Khan hurled himself forward, holding a writing instrument in his hand.

Edmund felt a moment's confusion, wondering just what his assailant meant to accomplish with the small pen, but his confusion came to an unhappy end when the professor succeeded in driving the pointed end of the instrument into the base of Edmund's neck. Now gasping in pain himself, Edmund raised the professor's pistol-like weapon, to use it as a bludgeon if nothing else, but the professor brutally tugged the writing instrument from Edmund's neck before raising his hand as if to strike again.

Edmund saw Halley's eyes fly wide, heard her cry out a warning, but it was too late. The expected second blow with the pen never came—it had been a feint. The professor turned the pistol in Edmund's grasp and fired a shot.

Edmund fell to the ground, shaking once more, unable to think or see or speak.

# 65

## · HALLEY ·

Halley screamed.

The professor was already dragging Edmund's inert and bleeding body toward the machine and then up onto its platform.

"Stop!" she cried, pulling against her bonds. "Where are you sending him?"

She clung to the belief that Edmund would survive this. He had to. She'd seen it on his Wikipedia page.

The machine began to whine.

"Send me, too!" she screamed over the noise of the machine. Furiously, she began sawing at her plasticuffs again.

Ignoring her, the professor tapped the podium screen once and then leapt backward and off the platform. Almost at once the giant coils came to life as electricity snaked back and forth between them.

"No!" screamed Halley. "Edmund—"

But it was too late. The blue lights flashed and Edmund was gone.

Gone—but where? Had the professor returned Edmund to his own time? Had he dropped him in the middle of some frozen ocean a thousand years ago? Her words catching in her throat, she choked out, "Please. Where is he?"

Khan, recovering from Edmund's attack, was still breathing heavily. He didn't seem inclined to answer, and Halley had nothing to force him to answer. No leverage. Nothing.

She would never see Edmund again. There had been no last kiss. No words of love. Nothing. Just this: a fallen body, bleeding and shot through with 50,000 volts, sent backwards through time. She clutched at the bare facts from Wikipedia.

*Happily married to Maria of Lavenham.*

*Ten children, six surviving.*

*Debts paid off with his wife's dowry.*

Halley told herself to breathe. Just breathe. This wasn't the time to feel. She couldn't look at her loss right now. Right now, she had to free herself. Taking a shallow breath, she started cutting her bonds again. The cuffs dug into her flesh each time she drew the knife against the plastic. She forced herself to focus on Edmund. She had to do everything in her power to make certain Edmund was okay. And if he wasn't, she had to figure out how to undo whatever Khan had done.

*Think*, she told herself. *How can you get the information you need?*

She had to get Khan talking again. Start him talking and he wouldn't shut up about himself, his achievements, his time machine. She could trick him into revealing something.

317

She swallowed. Cleared her throat. Took a slow, calming breath. And spoke.

"You just told me Khan's First Law of Temporal Inertia states permanent changes to past timelines are impossible. That means Edmund survives. It has to mean that. Right?" Her hand faltered as she cut. More softly, she pleaded, "Right?"

Khan looked up.

"Your imprecise use of language is truly appalling. To begin with, I said Khan's Law *may* have proven changes to past timelines are impossible—"

"So you admit you can't kill Edmund. You admit he survives."

The professor frowned, his eyes now averted.

"Are you this bad at paying attention in school?" he muttered.

She sawed harder with the knife. Her wrist screamed, the skin torn and raw. "That's not an answer—"

"So figure it out yourself," he shot back.

Figure it out herself? Dread lodged in her belly, slowing her knife hand. What was she supposed to figure out? What had Khan said so far? She made a list.

*He might have proven he couldn't change past timelines ...*

*Time was "self-healing," which resulted in a photocopy effect ...*

That was it. Just those two things. She couldn't remember him making any other claims.

And then her brain seemed to catch fire. The photocopy effect—it happened only once a return was made. Did it, then, extend to *human beings*? Did it extend to Edmund? Was that why Khan was so interested in Edmund's state of health? Were there ...

two Edmunds? But if there were two of him, and if one had never left Elizabethan England, then the second Edmund—*her* Edmund—was in deadly peril. For him, there were no guarantees of a long and prosperous life, a wife and six children.

Halley felt her stomach heaving.

"There are two of him," she whispered, horrified. "The historical Edmund and the Edmund I know."

The Edmund she loved.

The Edmund she had lost.

She raised her eyes, brimming, pleading.

"Yes," said the professor.

## 66

### · *HALLEY* ·

Halley's heart stuttered. She sucked in a shallow breath. Exhaled. There were two Edmunds. There were two, but the one she loved had just been sent away.

*But where?*

*And when?*

Professor Khan had stepped back onto the platform and was now tapping new orders into the time machine.

Her head was spinning. Her heart was breaking. *Breathe*, she told herself. *For him. Breathe. Think. Keep Khan talking. Fix this.*

"What are you doing?" she managed to whisper.

"I'm disengaging the singularity device," Khan replied. "Which will allow me the opportunity to test a hypothesis I've resisted testing to date, for obvious reasons."

She had to be strong. She had to stay alive. She had to finish cutting her bonds. And she had to get information from Khan.

"Tell me ... tell me about this hypothesis. About

what you've done," she said, her voice stronger this time.

"I'm not sure you really want to know," said the professor.

"I do," Halley said huskily.

"Hmm." Khan had fixed his gaze on a spot somewhere across the room, but Halley felt certain he wasn't seeing whatever he was looking at. He was lost in his own thoughts.

At last Khan made a sort of *harrumph* sound. And then, for the first time since he'd sent Edmund away, the professor met Halley's gaze.

"Very well. I owe you—that is, I believe that I'm indebted to you," he said. "It seems likely you saved my life on Friday."

"I *did*?" Halley frowned.

The professor nodded. "You reported that you rebooted the singularity device—that it awaited a Y/N response. This was new information to me." He paused. "Until you explained your actions, I assumed the failsafe protocols had rebooted the system apart from ... human intervention. I will need to make alterations so that they do, in the future.

"Unfortunately for you, when you pressed 'Y,' you didn't step off the platform. If the machine senses a body, it will engage transport. I must look into altering that protocol as well. But in any case, because you rebooted the program, I returned with the singularity device's assistance. If my hypothesis—the one about which you inquired—holds water, I survived my return journey because of what you did. I like to repay my debts, so ... I'll answer your question about the nature of my hypothesis." He took a deep breath, tapped the podium twice, and continued.

"The singularity machine focuses the passage through ruptured space-time, rendering it possible to travel swiftly to a particular time and place in the historical past. However, as Khan's First Law of Temporal Inertia states, space-time abhors such a rupture and will not allow a person or an object sent back to *remain* in the historical past.

"With or without the focus the singularity device provides, the space-time continuum will itself expel what does not belong. So long as the machine provides a focus for this ... *expulsion*, a traveler returns swiftly and without injury—"

"But you just turned it off," Halley blurted out. "What happens without the focus being ... focused? What happens without the machine?"

"We will know with certainty in—" Khan glanced at his watch—"In less than six minutes."

"Why six minutes?" Halley's pulse, already throbbing against the bite of her cuffs, began to race.

"It's another of the space-time continuum's peculiarities. The pocket of time, once ruptured, will remain open for five hours divided by the square root of the number of years the traveler has traveled back. The return journey will be accomplished with or without the machine's assistance. Space-time *will* repair itself. The machine simply focuses the journey, speeding it up from the perspective of the traveler, as it were, and providing considerable safety."

Halley looked at him blankly.

"Edmund—*your* Edmund—will begin his return journey in six, no—four and one half minutes, from our perspective." The professor grew quiet for a moment. "For us, his return will appear to be instantaneous, much the same as if he traveled with the machine's aid. For him however, apart from the temporal focus the device provides, the journey forward will last over four hundred years."

Halley gasped in horror. "He's going to be stuck time-traveling for *four hundred years*? Because you turned off the machine?" She shook her head. "*How could you?*"

"It's not as horrible as it sounds. In two minutes or so, he should expire from asphyxiation. I theorize the bacteria he carries with him will live for a significantly longer time. In short, I believe that when he returns, it will be in a state much like the human remains within my sarcophagi." He gestured to two Egyptian mummy cases. "That is, in a very desiccated state."

Halley's jaw dropped.

"At least," added Khan, "The orchid I sent recently returned thus."

"You're … *despicable!*" As soon as the words were out, Halley felt the cable tie she'd been cutting give way.

"I have been as kind as was possible, given the circumstances," said the professor. "I sent him, however briefly, back to his own time. Let us hope his relief at seeing London once more will calm him before his … final journey."

For a terrible handful of seconds, Halley's hands seemed to remain stuck, and she thought she'd cut the wrong cable tie, but then her hands burst free, and knife in hand, she sprang toward Khan.

## 67

## · *HALLEY* ·

Halley held Edmund's knife extended in her left hand, leaving her right free to work the machine's touch-screen. As she'd hoped, Khan backed away long enough for her to punch *RESUME* on the screen. She hoped that was the right decision.

"Step away from there *at once*," shouted Khan. "You have no idea what you're doing—"

"I'm saving Edmund's life," she shouted back. "You'll have to get past me if you want to do anything about it."

Khan rushed her, trying to reach the podium screen, but she thrust her knife at his upper arm. Crimson blossomed through his sleeve and he emitted a sharp cry. Just as swiftly, he pinned her knife-hand with his good hand. Halley formed a fist and struck him, aiming Edmund's golden ring on her third finger right at Khan's nose. Unfortunately, just before the blow landed, Khan wrenched the knife from her grasp.

Khan, cursing and blinking from the blow to his face, nonetheless managed to hold the knife steady, threatening.

"Back away," he grunted.

"Make me." Halley, now caught dangerously between the machine's twin coils, heard two things in rapid succession. The first was a gentle sound—sand spilling onto the platform from where she'd pocketed it away a lifetime ago on the beach with Edmund. The second sound Halley registered was the thunderous groaning of the machine. Instinctively, she grabbed the sand from her pocket and threw it upwards, right into the professor's face.

It struck him squarely in the eyes. Roaring with pain, Khan stumbled toward her, knife raised, half-blind, and then, just as he lurched onto the platform to reach her, she jumped off of it. The Tesla coils fired to life and the professor, knife in hand, was frozen in their grasp. In less than three seconds, Khan disappeared, but as he vanished, a powerful arc of electricity discharged from the point of his upheld knife, blasting up and into the ceiling.

And then Halley was alone, listening to the whine of the engines as blackened bits of ceiling rained down around her.

# 68

## · *KHAN* ·

Jules Khan, veteran of dozens of journeys into the past, felt the familiar sensations of heat and noise and then the extended fall that meant arrival. He landed, bleeding from Halley's knife wound, in the empty Curtain Theatre in the year 1598. It was twilight.

Before he had the chance to do more than curse the girl, he realized he wasn't alone. Edmund Aldwych stood on the opposite side of the stage, dressing his puncture wound with his shirt, now removed and torn.

The two, seeing one another, froze momentarily. And then Edmund charged.

The professor raised the small knife to defend himself, but Edmund was not caught off guard this time, and Khan was injured and without his taser. Edmund disarmed Khan with a single swift kick to the elbow.

Before Khan crumpled to the ground, he realized the snapping sound he heard was the breaking of his ulna.

He shrieked in pain, clutching his arm to his chest,

and then he screamed again, releasing his too-tight grip.

Edmund shifted his focus to the dropped knife, spinning lopsidedly toward the edge of the stage. With a tremendous leap, Edmund managed to retrieve the knife just before it fell off the front of the stage. Then he turned to face the professor.

"Where is Mistress Halley?" he asked, his voice low and dangerous.

And then the young man froze in place and vanished from the year 1598.

# 69

## · HALLEY ·

Shaking, Halley approached the podium keeping well away from the platform. On the screen, she saw a timer counting down.

Fifty-four and eight-tenths of a second remained.

Fifty-three seconds.

Fifty. She looked up and saw tiny flames licking the charred edges of the hole Khan had blasted in the ceiling.

Forty. She knew she should be concerned about the fire, but her heart clung to one thought alone: *Edmund.*

Thirty. Burning debris fell from above. Halley stamped out the flames.

Twenty. *Edmund.*

Ten. Nine. Eight. Seven. Six. Five. Four. Three. Two. *One.*

*Edmund.*

Halley backed away from the mighty Tesla coils as arcs of whitish-blue electricity shot between them, lighting the chamber like an exploding firework.

A moment later, she saw him. He was bleeding. He was sinking to the ground. But he was also alive and reaching for Halley's outstretched hand just as the ceiling overhead burst into brilliant orange flame.

## 70

### · EDMUND ·

"Fire!" Edmund cried, rising. He held Halley to himself as though she was the boat mast in a tempest.

"The stairs," she said. "Now!"

Together they crossed the room, Edmund feeling his strength returning moment by moment. He was alive. His lady was well. They were together and Edmund vowed never again to part from her.

They had not quite reached the stairs when a terrible wailing noise began.

"That's the fire alarm," said Halley.

"We must attempt to douse the conflagration." Edmund looked about for buckets or basins.

"No, we've got to get out of here," said Halley. "The professor wants to kill us and he'll be back any minute. Well, in ten minutes or so. Or maybe less—I'm not sure."

They had reached the top of the stairs. Alarms were sounding throughout the manor house.

"Mistress, it is not right we should stand by idle whilst the building is encompassed in flame."

Halley swore. Edmund was right. They couldn't just let Khan burn to death when he returned. She thought quickly, remembering things her mother had told her about the estate. "This building is hard-wired so that the fire station gets a message as soon as alarms go off," Halley said, "But we could get a garden hose or something…."

"Let us hurry!" Edmund cried.

"I should call 9-1-1, just in case," she said. "Oh, no—my phone! It's gone!"

"The professor did remove it from you," said Edmund, "After you were first fallen."

Edmund looked back at the stairs. A curl of dark smoke wisped its way up from the basement.

"We've got to get that hose *now*," said Halley.

Edmund was on her heels, about to reply in the affirmative when rain began to fall upon them from the ceiling. He looked up, bewildered.

"How is it that rain falleth through the ceiling?"

"It's sprinklers," said Halley. "That will slow the fire down, at least."

They dashed for the entrance of the manor, slipping on the wet surface of the marble floor. Before they had reached the door, there was a loud noise as of a firearm discharging and then the manor was plunged into darkness.

# 71

## · *HALLEY* ·

As they ran out the front door, Halley saw sparks flying in the air. She looked up; a small box was exploding on top of a power pole.

"I think that was the transformer for the estate," she said to Edmund. "Oh, no...."

"What is it, lady?"

"The time machine," she said. "It's powered by electricity. Oh no..."

"Mistress?"

"It's the professor. Without electricity, the machine will stop working. When the temporal rupture, or whatever the hell it's called, tries to pull the professor back, it will take him four hundred years to get here, without the machine's help."

"Mean'st thou we are vouchsafed never to see him again?"

Halley nodded in horror as fire truck sirens sounded, wailing in the night.

# 72

## · HALLEY ·

The fire trucks rolled in. Forty-six minutes later, they had misidentified the professor as just one more mummy among the sarcophagi. Halley had promptly been sick when she heard about the misidentification. Edmund had discreetly loaned her his "handkercher" to mop her brow.

After Halley had answered questions and filled out forms, after the fire trucks had rolled away, after the stars had melted from the graying sky, she told Edmund everything the professor had revealed. She told Edmund that his other self had made good on the debts of his family's estate and passed the family name on to a new generation. And then, with a shaking voice, she explained to him that he could never go home again.

"At least, not for more than fifteen minutes at a time," she concluded. She willed him to meet her eyes, but for a handful of seconds, he stared into the heavens, lost deep in his thoughts.

When he turned back to her, his expression was

somber.

"Lady, it is my dearest wish to remain evermore with thee, and thou wilt have it so."

Halley cupped a hand around his face. "I will have it so," she replied. And then she laughed and placed her other hand at Edmund's waist, pulling him closer, closer, closer as if to keep even the dawn from coming between them.

# 73

## · HALLEY ·

Halley walked towards one of the empty tables in the back of *¡DULCE!*, DaVinci's favorite bakery. DaVinci was nowhere to be seen. Jillian smiled apologetically from where she sat, like a bird on a perch.

"DaVinci said she'd be here," murmured Jillian, looking uncomfortable.

The two didn't hug. Halley felt the winter's chill between them and for the thousandth time regretted her decision to set up the booth. It had all become so clear when she was tied to a piece of lab equipment in the professor's basement: her friends were her *family*. Cousins and sisters and aunties all rolled into one. Halley had been a fool crying for the moon when she had the sunshine of her friends' love right in front of her.

Or, rather, she *had* had it. Now she wasn't sure. Edmund had advised Halley to meet her friends alone, and Halley had agreed, but now she wished he were here at her side, a warm hand in hers to counter Jillian's coolness.

"I'm so sorry," began Halley.

"There she is," said Jillian, speaking over Halley. She stood to catch DaVinci's attention.

DaVinci didn't look cool or aloof. She looked angry.

"I'm so sorry," Halley said again, this time to both of them. "I'm not asking you to forgive me, but I needed to tell you I know what I did was ... horrible." Her throat swelled.

"Edmund said it was something to do with seeing your father," DaVinci said. Her tone was grudging.

"It doesn't matter why I did it," said Halley. "It was wrong and I—"

"It matters to me," said DaVinci, her tone still angry. "So you'd better explain what was so important that you ditched me on the most important day of my life."

Halley blinked rapidly and then, while she shredded a paper napkin with *¡DULCE!* embossed on both sides, Halley explained everything. Her secrets. Her dreams. Her mother's revelation. Moving out. Everything.

"And then last night," Halley said, concluding, "When I thought I was going to die, the worst part was thinking I'd never get a chance to apologize."

Jillian's brows flew up.

"Last night when you *what?*" demanded DaVinci.

"Oh." Halley chewed on her lower lip. "So ... Right. A few things happened last night when Edmund and I went to professor Khan's."

Long before she'd finished explaining the near-death experience, Jillian was crying and holding Halley's hand while DaVinci growled (at Khan) and

336

hugged Halley from the other side. Halley tried to dry her eyes using the shredded *¡DULCE!* napkin until Jillian pulled tissues from her new Irina Tran purse.

"Can we please still be friends?" whispered Halley, drying her eyes. "I don't know what I'd do without you both."

DaVinci hugged her even more tightly. "Of course," she said. "Of course."

Jillian murmured her agreement.

Then DaVinci grunted out a deep belly laugh. "Almost getting murdered or mummified or whatever totally gets you a pass, you know, for pretty much any stupid choices."

Halley winced and was about to apologize again, but DaVinci held up her hand.

"I said you had a pass. Now, can we please talk about something nice for a change? Your hot earl maybe? When is he going to model for me?"

Jillian ordered a lavish assortment of pan dulce and donuts, accompanied by a steaming French press of dark coffee, and the three gradually slipped back inside their decade-long friendship, closer for the knowledge of what could have been lost.

~ ~ ~

The Applegate's Post-Fiesta Bash that afternoon started at 4:00, which gave Halley and Edmund enough time to sunburn on Butterfly Beach for several hours after Halley left her friends.

Halley's phone, which had been returned to her by one of the firemen, woke Edmund and Halley with an alarm set for 3:15.

"Uh-oh," said Halley, rolling over on the beach blanket.

"What is't?" asked Edmund.

Halley was frowning at a patch of bright pink skin. After they'd left ¡DULCE!, she'd spent an astonishing eighty dollars on a new bikini top, which Jillian had talked her into it and even tried to pay for, but Halley said *no*. The new bikini top, unfortunately, had exposed new skin to the sun.

"That's gonna hurt later," Halley said, tapping her chest. "In fact," she said, "I'm not wearing this at the pool party after all. How's that for irony?"

Edmund stared at her blankly.

"It's silly," she said, "But three days ago I thought getting a new swim top for Jillian's pool party was a pretty big deal." She laughed, and Edmund joined in, even though he clearly had no idea what she was laughing about.

Half an hour later, the two were dressed and driving in Halley's truck to the Applegate's. Halley had rummaged through her two duffel bags of clothes and found a strapless black beach coverup that could pull double duty as a strapless black dress in a pinch. Edmund was outfitted in sandals, below-knee shorts, and an ivy-green button down shirt with the sleeves rolled up. Jillian had picked and paid for the outfit at the same exclusive Coast Village Road boutique where she'd tried to pay for Halley's bikini top.

Halley had to agree the color of Edmund's shirt did something amazing for his already amazing eyes. Everyone at the party was going to want to get close to him, and Halley was very glad Edmund had agreed to whisper *laryngitis* to strangers who tried to engage him in conversation.

After they pulled through the Applegate's

entrance and stopped by the cluster of valets, Edmund cleared his throat. "Lady?"

"Hmm?" asked Halley, handing her truck keys to a smiling valet.

Edmund waited until they were both out of the truck.

"Your ... *cell phone* was not the only thing recovered from the basement last night." He looked troubled. "It would seem ... That is ..." He shook his head and reached inside his shorts pocket, removing what looked like several strands of pearls. Then, as if he'd made up his mind to something, he took Halley's hand in his and strode rapidly to a small stone bench in front of an enormous cluster of bird-of-paradise.

"What is that?" Halley asked.

"This carcanet was my mother's."

He held the strands apart so that Halley could see it. It was an exquisite Elizabethan necklace, hung with a jeweled pendant.

"My mother gave the pendant to my brother the selfsame morning thou and I met. He was to sell it and buy rings," said Edmund. "It would appear my brother parted with it at any rate. Or perhaps the professor stole it."

"How did you—where did you find it?"

"After the mage—that is, the *professor*—attacked us, I saw it on a table. I retrieved it late last night, after the firemen departed."

"It's beautiful."

In the center of the pendant there was a ruby, cut square, surrounded by gold work and hexagonal blue stones. A narrow row of small pearls bordered the pendant, which hung from the twin strands of larger pearls forming the necklace. It was lovely. Lovely and vaguely ... *familiar.*

And then Halley's eyes grew wide. She knew where she'd seen this necklace before. When she'd looked up Edmund's Wikipedia page, Edmund's ... *wife*, Maria Lavenham, had been wearing this very necklace in her portrait.

Halley exhaled slowly. Somehow, even though Khan had bought (or stolen) the pendant from Edmund's brother, it had been recovered to the family. It had remained there, in 1598.

Before she changed her mind, Halley blurted out several things she'd been dying to tell Edmund.

"I promise I'm not going to go all soothsayer on you every time you bring up your past," she said, "But you should know a few things. Your estate recovers from debt. Your brother becomes a Puritan. Your mom lives a long life with, uh, the other *you*, and she's adored by all the kids from your, well, your *wife*, who wears this pendant in a portrait. I've seen the portrait with my own eyes in a ... historical record."

"Indeed?" Edmund looked puzzled. He said nothing for several minutes. At last he turned to Halley. "I am much relieved to hear of the history of ... my second self." Then, his amber-colored eyes softening, he added, "Whatever its odd history, wouldst thou consider wearing the pendant for my sake this day?"

Halley touched her chest self-consciously. She'd taken off the chain with the jade ring. She hadn't gotten rid of the ring, just in case she felt differently someday, but she'd decided she didn't want to wear it for now.

But how did she feel about wearing a necklace that Edmund had (apparently) given to his wife in the past? It gave her pause. She turned slightly away. And then, she smiled. She smiled because she was being ridiculous. *Her* Edmund hadn't given this to his wife. *Her* Edmund hadn't offered this necklace to anyone—except her.

"I should be much honored," added Edmund, holding the necklace out.

"Edmund," she said, meeting his eyes, "I'm the one who would be much honored."

~ ~ ~

Much later that evening, after Halley had despaired of meeting Ethyl Meier, the great woman herself strode over to where Halley was sitting in a quiet corner with Edmund, DaVinci, and Jillian.

"That piece is *stunning*," said Ms. Meier, pointing to Halley's necklace. She then held out her hand. "Ethyl," said Ms. Meier.

Halley shook hands. "Halley," she said. "It's a family heirloom from the late Elizabethan period. And I know who you are. I applied for an internship in your costume shop—"

Ms. Meier held her hand up. "Internship's already been assigned for the fall."

"Oh," said Halley. "Oh." Her heart sank.

"But I'm hiring hand stitchers. Do you hand sew or embroider?"

"Yes." Halley felt a giggle rising in her throat. *And bake and brew, too,* she wanted to say. Corralling her runaway thoughts she added, "I can do several kinds of hem stitches, tent-stitch and other embroidery, and I can sew on a hook and eye so tight it will *never* come

341

loose."

"Pad-stitching?" asked Ms. Meier. "Black work? Keyhole style buttonholes?"

Halley was silent. She didn't know what any of these things were.

"I can learn," she asserted, her heart pounding against her ribs.

Ms. Meier reached inside an elaborately beaded purse. "Here's my card. Come by the costume shop tomorrow. If Josefina approves your needlework, you're hired." She stared at the necklace again. "Lovely. Truly lovely. Would you mind?" Ms. Meier held up her phone, indicating she wanted a picture of the necklace.

"Go right ahead," said Halley. By the time her eyes recovered from the bright flash, Ms. Meier was gone. "Um, guys? I think I just got a job!"

"Yay, you!" said Jillian, clapping her hands together.

Edmund was beaming at Halley. She wanted to kiss him very badly.

DaVinci, who'd been sketching Edmund all evening, suddenly asked, "So you say you've got a brother?"

"I have a brother," replied Edmund, turning to DaVinci.

"Don't go there," Halley said to DaVinci. "Besides, his brother grows up to argue against Art as a worldly vanity."

DaVinci frowned disapprovingly. "That's just wrong," she said. "Although, it's a lot more wrong you've got an Edmund and I don't." She pouted.

"The time machine's still in working order," said Jillian, repeating something Halley had told them earlier.

"Huh-uh," said DaVinci, shaking her head vehemently. "I don't want some creepy photocopied boyfriend."

"Never say never," said Jillian, smiling.

DaVinci, rolling her eyes, grabbed Jillian's arm. "Come on. Let's go get some of that insane apple pie. Maybe the caterer will give you the recipe. Or just sell you the bakery."

"I want to frost the cakes, not own the bakery," replied Jillian.

"And right now," DaVinci said with a pointed look, "You want to give these two some privacy."

After the two girls had gone, Edmund looked puzzled.

"Wherefore should they desire to give us privacy?"

"So I can do this," said Halley, pulling him closer. Just before their lips met, Halley whispered, "I'm no soothsayer, but I see a lot of this in your future."

And they kissed, across the table, across the continents, across four hundred years.

### THE END

For information on all releases by Cidney Swanson:
cidneyswanson.com

# A Thief in Time

## Acknowledgements

Writing A THIEF IN TIME has been a stretch for me. I've left the familiar worlds of invisibility genes and Mars colonies for ... *research*! While I've always loved reading time travel adventures, I was frankly terrified about the research that would be involved in writing one of my own. I owe a debt of gratitude to some writer friends who have said, through the years, that the research is the *fun* part. Really? They must have said it often enough, because they managed to convince me to give it a whirl. Monique Martin and Sarah Woodbury: hats off to you both!

Beyond convincing me to try it, I am further indebted to Sarah and Monique as well as to Melissa F. Miller for beta reading. Each of you made the story stronger by telling me what you liked and what ... *wasn't quite working*. Thank you! Next, there's my longsuffering husband, who patiently explained the theory of special relativity *and* the theory of general relativity and also gave me the math to explain that in my world, the farther back in history you travel, the more quickly you get shoved back home again. Thank you, Dr. Science. Lastly, to my readers, you are a terrific reason to get up and write every single day, and I am grateful for you *every single day*!

CPSIA information can be obtained
at www.ICGtesting.com
Printed in the USA
BVHW081340011219
565291BV00002B/210/P